For: You, Nani,
and Carmen &
Grandmothers everywhere.

What will come will be.
No doubt you will think of me as you read.
Trust, I have only given you this from curiosity.

There is a wave in each of us
bent on quelling
the very flame we need to live.

somethingmeanthenovel@gmail.com

More from the Author:
Please visit

Www.mindbodyexchange.org

IG: Mind_Body_Exchange

@MindBodyX

Something Mean

A novel by
Tiffany L. Fuentes

Part 1
Chapter 1

Fire under Water

What we've got here is failure to communicate. Some men you just

can't reach, so you get what we had here last week,

which is the way he wants it. Well, he gets it.

I don't like it, any more than you do, men.

– "Cool Hand Luke"

Song #1 Lost in Translation, Nordlight

Adam wiped a water droplet from Mina's forearm. The East river misted their bench in the breeze. It was July 6, 2006. Cars riding the FDR hummed above them. Yesterday's downpour left the river high and had washed away most of the gun powder party junk from Independence Day. Explosive scraps of what used to be colorful fireworks were saturated and stuck to plastic containers and other random garbage. Stuff spilled out of the city's rusty metal bins to join the current that raced for sewers but in a city like New York, puddles stretch across intersections before they make it underground. Mina slipped her foot out of her sandal to move it closer to Adam. She was always doing things like this; his side of the bed, couch, it didn't matter.

Her leg reached for Serpico, Adam's dog, named after Adam's man-crush, and look-alike according to him. Serpico collapsed onto his back to offer his spotted belly. There were two Al Pacino posters in Adam's apartment: one in the bathroom and another in the living room, along with an almost complete DVD collection.

"Are you gonna be back tomorrow night?" She rotated Serpico's chest with the ball of her foot. Normal weekends for Adam consisted of Shabbos dinners in Long Island followed by a usual return to the city sometime Saturday night.

"Don't know yet, why?"

"You know why." She tucked her chin into her shoulder and gave him an unblinking stare. She pressed her body into his, and asked without words if she was going to sleep in his bed, but something was off. This wasn't a question that needed asking. She was reluctant to let him go, but why? She was anxious. He seemed uninviting. The more she thought about it, the less present she was to the conversation. She struggled to find charm and wit, not even her reliable warmth could be felt. How could she turn things around and why did she feel like she had to? How did she get into a position where being herself was suddenly something she had to try for?

Mina wasn't Adam's *girlfriend*. She couldn't even say that word or other related words without smirking. It was a stupid title, for both genders, and a futile attempt to be any guy's girlfriend. She and Adam were on an unofficial 'don't ask, don't tell basis,' but he did mention how he wasn't looking for *anything serious* within their first week of dating. They had a common ground that kept them familiar: family, humor, and love of restaurants and wild nights in their city, yet they also had their differences. Mina was third generation from Naples, raised on 12 years of Catholic school, somewhat obsessed with grades in high school, and lived for art. Her time with Adam started from a genuine interest and amusement in his secret life. He was a part-time-Jew, and while she never saw him go full Jew, the little treasures of traditional Orthodox garb found in his apartment were delightful. He wasn't Hassidic. Most people hear Orthodox and think, big hat, Jew curls, and strange outfits walking in the street, even Mina had been guilty of this. *Little hats* were what she called his collection of very decorative yarmulkes. He only wore them when working and because she had never seen one on, they quickly spawned a game she coined *Rabbi*, as in, 'Let's play Rabbi.' The first time she found one she put it on and chanted with her eyes closed. He snatched it from her head removing her smile as well, using the silent glare an adult uses with children.

In this game, he had to wear his Rabbi glasses too, again that was what Mina called them. They were thick black plastic-framed glasses kept in the top drawer of his nightstand, next the Torah and condoms. He read from the Golden Calf from the book of Deuteronomy.

"*You made yourselves into a golden calf. You turned aside quickly from the way that the LORD had commanded you. So I took hold of the two tablets, and threw them out of my two hands, and broke them before your eyes. Then I neither ate bread nor drank water, because of all the sin that you had committed, in doing what was evil in the sight of the LORD to provoke him to anger.*" The first couple of times they played, Mina screamed with laughter sweating from an extreme blush. She answered him with rebuttals like,

"I didn't do anything," or "You're crazy," but it wasn't long before *Rabbi* became a way for her to surrender to him as part of role-play. He reprimanded her with authority continuing with the passage, sometimes smacking her hard on her backside.

"*I took the sinful thing, the calf that you had made.*" Smack!

"What are you talking about?" It was usually at this point when he put her on all fours, pulling off what little clothing was left on her body, burying her with his weight and tossing the book to the floor.

"*And I burned it with fire,* he pinned her hands above her head. "*...And crushed it,*" he leaned heavily on her, and brought his head to hers. "*...Grinding it very small,*" he danced his hips along hers, lifting his left and dipping his right. "*..Until it was as fine as dust.*

He always stopped at dust, and it was then that she felt tiny. As if she had transformed under his hands into something like sand, slipping through to everywhere and he was larger than anything she had ever known, so large that in order to be with her he had to sacrifice her.

Song# 2 Pissing in a River, Patti Smith

Mina sat speechless on the bench while phrases and thoughts shared between them marked her like tattoos. She replayed what happened on the night of July 4th over in her head, and like ink up an arm, she didn't know which way to turn her head. Each angle produced a different ending and imagination was picking up where her memory failed. Her desire and adoration for Adam was certain. She wanted her name listed in a category titled: *For the Future.* She assumed he set aside such a category for her, and that this is what people did. The potentiality of that being a farce, even though they hadn't discussed it flooded her with emotions. Like earthworms post rainfall, she had to show herself, unveil her feelings, and state what she wanted.

"I might come back Sunday instead, my sister just got back from Isreal." Mina and Adam didn't typically have Sunday sleepovers.

"Which one?"

"Yael."

"How long has she been gone?"

"Oh, I don't know, three weeks or so?"

"And what about her husband?"

"Ishmael? He'll be there and sure to make things interesting."

"Why?" She already knew the type of person Ishmael was and Adam's feelings on him, but if she was going to start this *feeling* conversation, she needed more time.

"Ugh, my sister's nuts. She complains about everything and he lets her." Mina laughed at him.

"What do you suggest he do?"

"Tell her to stop. I don't know. He put his hands up and then let them fall onto his lap. "Maybe he doesn't hear her, maybe he tunes her out, but all she does is complain. Then, when we tell her she's complaining, he gets defensive and starts fighting with my father right in the middle of Shabbos dinner."

"He's very protective of her?"

"Of course he is, as he should be, but at the same time there's no talking to him. Once he gets started, he's off, and the way he speaks to us is so strange. It's as if he harbors all the negativity she has ever felt towards her family. I mean it's great that he loves her that much, but it's just not logical."

"Oh, if only we could all be as logical as you Adam," she rolled her eyes. "What was the last fight about?"

"I can't even remember."

"Yes, you can."

"It's not important."

"Of course it is." Mina pleaded for him to go on. He scratched his bottom lip with his teeth.

"It had something to do with her body. She was reading some bullshit celebrity magazine and talking about spending time at the gym, I really don't remember, complaining about how hard she works only to come here and ruin her diet. Whatever it was, it made my father very upset. He immediately started blessing the food even though we weren't ready to eat, pontificating about how lucky we all are to have this bread, to have this wine. Please. It went on all night. Thank god the Rabbi wasn't there."

"Your Rabbi comes to your house?"

"Occasionally."

"And wait, your dad's rebuttal was that the food is holy?"

"Yes. But Mina you don't get it. You don't understand how religious my family is. He was basically saying that she's an ingrate. I mean Jews don't actually consider a meal a meal unless there's bread, and everything has to be blessed with its own special blessing. Our food is very sacred."

"I can understand that, I'm Italian ya know?"

"Mina, of course, you understand, because you're Italian!" He looked around but no one was near them. But my dear, this isn't about spaghetti and meatballs," he laughed.

"Oh. Right. It's about Matzah balls." He put his arm around her and squeezed tightly.

"I want to tell you something, okay?" He said softly rubbing his lips on the edge of her ear. "My family doesn't eat Matzah balls on Shabbos."

"Yes you do. Liar." She pulled away bringing her shoulder to her cheek, wincing from the tickle of his whisper.

"Come here." He continued to pull on her arms bringing her ear and neck closer to his mouth so he could talk in a provocative manner. "We light candles for our food." He licked his lips "...and pray for it before we eat it." She pulled away but was still smiling.

"Okay. It's a little weird, but not insane. Don't you light candles for everything?" She joked. "My family's meals have bread in it too ya know and we say grace." She trailed off into a silent pause between thoughts. "And we eat bread with everything too: the sauce on Sunday, with pasta, with soup, and salad. And there are certain things that are blessed even if it doesn't come with a prayer and lighting of a candle. Like my parent's neighbor Candy asks for 2 jars of sauce every Sunday because it's that good. And my sister eats most of the Pecorino Romano cheese before it makes it to the table and the worst is finally, when it's all done and we're starving, my mother searches for the brownest meatball in the pot to serve my father before the rest of us can eat."

He adored her cadence, the lists she created, her volume, her fingers peeling other fingers to count the ways she was right. He loved the fire inside of her, and thought of her as his hot-blooded Italian. He bit his lip for a minute just looking at her. Mina had olive skin, with brown curly hair and the tiniest freckles on both sides of her nose. They disappeared after her first sunning, but were prominent until then. The most beautiful part of her face was undeniably her eyes. They were long-lashed and reddish brown with bright green centers. She was the only grandchild with her Mamaw's eyes and as life would have it, she was her grandmother's favorite.

Chapter 2
Taboo

Mina worked across town from that shady bench at the Museum of Natural History. It granted her intellectual freedom and the right to say anything liberal. She knew a ton about art, making it, dissecting it, and the names of people who spent their lives worshipping it. She fancied architecture and the Grecian way of life. Mina loved saying those two things, and when asked what was best about her year abroad, she would say, *nothing was like reading and studying the Duomo, and then using it everyday as a place to meet friends.* Walking through the installations of stuffed field mice, painted mannequins and hanging birds hardly fulfilled her passion for art, but it was a start. She lived on 35th street in a small three-story building. Adam lived just three blocks up but still off of first Ave. The main difference was his building had fifty floors, a pool, hot tub, tennis courts, and a remarkable view. Although this wasn't where they first met, it was easy for them to run-in to one another now that they knew they were neighbors.

They were charismatic articulate adults, dog people; people who made storeowners, bartenders and doormen, even bouncers smile. Adam was a busy man with suits and ties hung neatly next to one another just like his appointments. He played with money and it's what he thought about. The minor convenience of her proximity guided their seamless friendship in the way a drop becomes a drip.

Just the night before their conversation on the bench they slept at his place as they had for the past two days due to the holiday. They were on a mini stay-cation. She packed a bag like she didn't live close by and used the puffy white towels to and from his pool and Jacuzzi on the 12th floor. Her body was curled away from him. The hour was late and of course Adam fell asleep first. She nestled deeper into the mattress matching the ebb and flow of his inhalations, but even with the calming rhythm of sleep next to her she was insecure. It wasn't that she was thinking about her feelings for him, but she hated the thought that what happened the day before, could prevent him from loving her. It was bad enough that she wasn't Jewish, and what they were doing was—this was the heart of the matter, and what kept her awake—the secrecy, intangibility, the unanswered, unasked question of what— just what were they doing?

She took in the smell of Freon coming from his humidifier. It was a nostalgic scent that brought the vision of her Great Aunt Mariella's attic. The door leading the way, opened with a skeleton key permanently poking out of the knob. There was a beautiful dollhouse that lived in that attic, had been her Aunt's when she was a little girl and was all Mina could now think about. She traveled her open palm over Adam's taut bed-sheet. The texture ran one ribbed line against the silky weavings of another smooth line. The lines raced away from her to the foot of the bed as she listened to city static twenty floors beneath them. She drifted to sleep from that spot next to him in his bed, breathing that familiar smell in the muffled sounds of summer, feeling small and perfect like a doll in a dollhouse.

~~~

Song #3 Merry Happy, Kate Nash

Back on the bench Mina was making things more complicated than they needed to be. Despite her paranoia, they were perfectly content, now and the night before. The day was beautiful and with the river so high, even the air smelled great.

"What?" she asked about his squint and tempting lick of his bottom lip.

"Nothing."

"You used to always tell me I bit my lip, but now you do it?" He dug teeth harder into skin.

Adam had a list of women that he liked to be seen with. They were long legged beauties with expensive hair and designer shoes. They fit him and the regal cleft in his chin. His slicked back salt and pepper hair accentuated the bowing ribbons of grey in his navy eyes. He could make any face, and often contorted to flip between characters when telling stories. Three things that did not change were his extraordinary height of six-foot for a Jewish guy and a washboard stomach with little to no butt. He had ample hair, and not just on his scalp. His chest, back and shoulders were shaded with a thick curly protection. He went for a full body waxing once a month. Mina knew this about him, made fun of him for it, yet still felt insecure whenever she dressed to meet him out somewhere. She was short, graced with a wide set of hips. She liked to get dressed up but it wasn't a must.

"You have great feet you know that, you don't wear heels that often do you?" he asked.

"No. I wear them sometimes," she said shyly.

"Your feet don't look like bird feet." She lifted her leg so they could both examine her petite foot and even smaller orange painted toes.

"What's a bird foot Adam?"

He put his hand onto her thigh, right above her knee and thought about the smoothness of her skin, especially on the small of her back. This is where he usually kept his hands when he was on top of her. The thought of being in bed with her took him to his apartment and he remembered smelling her the other day when she wasn't around. It wasn't perfume. It was something else, and it was all over her: her face, neck, arms, and hands. It came out of her pores and stayed with him after they parted. It had been a few months that they regularly shared each other's company and still, he didn't know what it was about her that smelled so good.

"A bird foot, my dear, is like a dinosaur foot with mangled toes that make one big claw-like toe," he said making a C shape with his finger.

"You're insane," she laughed.

"About your family, you should eat that much bread, that's what Italians do, Meen. Us Jews, on the other hand, we bless our food based on how it grows. There's blessings for produce, one for that which grows in stalks, another for food grown on trees, a blessing for what we drink, other than wine, and of course the wine's special blessing." He took a pause. "Interesting man your father is though that he likes his meat a little brown, huh." Adam had secretly visited tanning salons, but each time sub-par sanitary conditions forced him to retire from trying to match Mina's golden hue.

"Mina," he said wrapping his arm around her to bring her in close. "We bless the bread Friday night, so that while we bless the rest of the food on Saturday, it doesn't feel left out. Can you imagine how crazy it is to consider the feelings of bread?" They sat close for a while as objects of the summer's affection. The dogs mouthed each other and it was a sublime Thursday afternoon. Mina's dog was a mixed breed from the shelter that she named Rags, as in rags to riches. Rags was black and white, with both colors split evenly down her nose.

"Do your parents know that you took the elevator last weekend? Mina referred to the laws of Shabbos. A specific law that prohibited the use of electricity from sundown on Friday to sundown on Saturday."

"No." He lit a cigarette.

"They didn't call and ask, seeing as you didn't go to Long Island?"

"My dad mentioned it during the week. He asked me what I did with the dog."

"Wait, would that be considered using electricity, like pressing the button, or is it breaking the other law of not riding or driving a vehicle? Or is it a double whammy? What happens when you commit a double whammy?"

"Shut-up," he said with a smile.

"So what'd you tell him? That you raced down the stairs with Serpico for a good workout?"

"Exactly, you little shit. How'd you know?"

"I know you. Don't you think that's weird though, it's like your dad knows that you don't follow everything completely."

"No. He just asks questions. Isn't that what parents do?" Adam asked. Mina got a sudden wave of confidence. She was sure from Adam's comment that he was a reasonable man and the conversation she wanted to have was easy, and one they were sure to feel similarly about.

"I know I joke a lot about your double life, to Jew or not to Jew," she held up air quotes. "And it's funny. I just want you to know I don't mean to diminish the weight you carry living this way. I know it's not easy, or at least I don't know how it could be."

"No it isn't. But, it's what I have to do," he answered quickly.

"I don't get that. They love you. Why wouldn't they understand that you have the right, and will to choose a life that makes you happy?"

"Yea man. Free love. Free life. Power to the people." He mocked her with a peace sign moving his head like Stevie Wonder, except she was nearly positive he didn't know Stevie. "It doesn't work that way Mina, you sound like the cat lady in your building."

"What cat lady?"

"The crazy lady with all the cats! She was holding that poster for peace, just came back from her anti-Bush rally when we passed her on the stairs. Hello? Are you feeling alright?"

"When were we at my apartment?"

"Oh stop it!" he said with a nasal whine for effect. "Mina you are something else. I ask if we should go to your place, but you always want to come to mine," he smiled. "Look, it would be nice. But we can't all be like you. The bottom line is that my parents would be devastated. They won't respect it is as a decision I am making, but a mistake. A mistake that goes against all of their hard work and money invested in my future."

"But it isn't going to waste," she begged. "Can't you just tell them that you don't want to live according to some religious prescription? It's not like you're denouncing everything about the religion. You can still hold onto the faith."

"You don't know what you're talking about. That isn't how the world works." he interrupted her.

"Maybe." Mina was embarrassed. He took a drag of his Newport, and she didn't know what else to say. She asked herself what the world had to do with this.

"What you're suggesting will ruin my relationships with my family, my friends, my neighbors, my clients, my bosses, everyone. Everyone that I have grown up with, have known since I was a kid, that watched me grow, supported me, taught me, parented the kids that I went to school with, that are now in businesses that I can work with. You're acting like its no big deal to just go on without any of these things. My world will be ruined if I consider your suggestion."

"Okay. Okay. I'm sorry." A long silence started.

Chapter 3
Independence Party

Song#4 Que Bueno Biala Usted, Benny More

The empty city was delightful. Many residents were away for the holiday and the city slowly re-populated in waves as it does every summer. She could have spent the rest of the day testing benches with him. He often said he wasn't romantic and he rarely if ever kissed her in public, but he absolutely loved to take her, especially when she was wearing a dress, and throw her onto the ground. He didn't actually throw her onto the ground, but it looked that way to those that watched their fake fights. She would get on top of him and fight back as best she could, after having been taken by surprise, as well as being a whole foot smaller than him. At the finish, she stood completely disheveled, with hair in her mouth and sweat on her forehead. Men loved watching these games. She never knew when it was coming either. He was spontaneous with everything that he did, which is why it was so hard for her to talk about what happened on July 4th.

While she and Adam were as open as a stadium, she still felt like a boundary had been crossed that night. She knew it was wrong to slap his friend Uri on the ass and dance with him, not when she did it of course, because she was nearly blackout drunk. However, she currently had enough sober guilt to know that clearing her name was the only option, yet due to the nature of their involvement didn't know if it was worth mentioning. She was most confused about what to own up to though: slapping Uri, getting wasted, or that she couldn't remember the night if she tried. She had no idea what Adam was thinking or how to apologize, also was unsure if she should see this as an opportunity to reveal what she wanted from their *future*.

Adam's jealousy, real or perceived, excited her but this was going to be a sobering conversation, essentially their first fight, and she didn't want it to quell the forbidden and inexhaustible heat between them. Uri was Adam's friend from kindergarten and Mina gathered from the occasional story that there was an annoying competition between them. Uri was the kid with the Jew fro sitting next to Adam in the 1st grade photo Mina examined in the very beginning of the night.

She was already dressed to go to dinner, as was Uri, who had just arrived to the apartment. Neither Mina nor Uri had seen each other before. They were both standing in the kitchen when Uri phoned the restaurant.

"I called to push back the reservation! Don't rush or anything Adam! Uri yelled so Adam could hear him from the bathroom."

"You drink wine Mina?" Uri opened the fridge, bending to scan for a bottle. He didn't wait for an answer and closed the doors fruitless in his searches. He turned to notice Mina holding a bottle of Riesling.

"It was thawing in the sink." Adam found it in the freezer this morning.

"Who's better than you?" he asked her.

"Adam. It's his bottle. I'm surprised it didn't burst."

"Good job Adam! Hey pretty boy, you keep your wine in the freezer!" he yelled into the wall. Mina propped herself up on the counter to watch Uri work his way around a kitchen he didn't know well.

"Do you deal with his tardiness all the time?" Uri poured two glasses.

"I suppose," Mina shrugged her shoulders. "It takes him a long time to get out of the bathroom, but once he's out, he's good to go."

"Tell me something Mina." He stared into her eyes and she didn't know what to make of him. His pupils were like black holes deeply set in the crystalline blue he knew for eyes. He had thick curly black hair and his conversation was mostly inconsequential, however this meeting was Adam's first attempt to introduce Mina to his world of friends and family. She caught Uri fiddling with his curls to frame his face just right. There was nothing religious about him and yet he was Adam's closest friend. They moved into the foyer so Uri could look at the mirror. His body was well sculpted, and Mina thought it was safe to say that he was preoccupied with aesthetics.

"What do you do?" he asked her, finishing his manscaping.

"I work at the Museum of Natural History."

"Oh right. I remember now. That's where you guys met. Very cool." He finished half of his wine in one sip as Adam exited the bathroom.

"Thanks, I'd love a glass," Adam said. "What the hell were you guys yelling about?"

"Your pretty ass. Did you finish your make-up Adam?" Uri looked at Mina for praise in the form of laughter but got none. What Uri didn't know was that all this talk about make-up reminded her of the eyelash curler she found in Adam's bathroom just a few hours earlier.

Song #5 Exilo, Thievery Corporation

Her and Adam had spent that day together and had shared the freedom to move in and out of each other's space, including the bathroom. If he was brushing his teeth while getting ready, it was perfectly normal for her to come in and talk to him. This was a quick progression for both of them and just that morning, she found something unexpected. Adam was watching a news program when it happened. He was one of those that became engrossed in market analysts of every kind, as in he kept an open mouth and was incapable of maintaining conversation whenever the TV was on. Mina used this time to do things alone like pluck her eyebrows, but first she opened the mirror to look for moisturizer. He let her use it once before and gave her permission to take what she needed without question, however instead of face cream her search stumbled upon a Revlon eyelash curler. It rested on the top shelf, and as she reached for it on tippy-toes she imagined the long legs that placed it there for safekeeping. She knew they weren't monogamous, but the find still bothered her. She just held it, shocked. She opened and closed it in her hands a few times as she talked to herself. *Who leaves an eyelash curler?* When she was done perfecting the arch of her brows and feeling as beautiful, if not more, than the imagined Revlon model without her trusty silver curler, she reopened the cabinet and fearlessly carried the instrument with her to the living room.

"Hey..." she prolonged the sound of the y addressing Adam playfully. She waited patiently for him to look at her.

"I wasn't searching. I was just grabbing some lotion, but I have to ask, why do you have an eyelash curler?" She stood in the entranceway to the living room, holding the tool behind her and leaning on the wall.

"What are you talking about?" Adam asked without turning his head.

"Why do *you* have an eye-lash curler?" She smiled and brought it out in plain sight.

"Come show me what you're talking about." He patted the seat next to him on the couch, and turned his eyes back to the television. Maury Povich was on and a fight had just ended. Adam could flip back from garbage like this and news all day.

"This?" He grabbed the instrument, opened and closed it a few times, then gave it back to her. "This is mine, but you can borrow it if you like."

"What! Don't lie to me. I can borrow it? You're ridiculous!"

"I'm not lying," he said without smiling.

"Put it back please. I am not ready for it. I use it when I get out of the shower." He wasn't alarmed by the implications of such a find. He resumed and Mina did as she was told. She didn't believe it was his, despite his feminine details, obsessive personality, and strange hygienic habits, but she respected his cool dismissal and didn't mention it again.

~ ~ ~

After the trio's Fourth of July dinner they waited for a water taxi to Spice, a rooftop club. Juice mixers on ice greeted their cozy corner sofa and bottle menu. Mina's drinks disappeared as she danced, mingling on their own as lost drinks tend to do at parties. There was one balding man on a couch in front of them in the middle of the club. A few white hairs were glistening against his scalp and the night sky shined over them. He and the six beautiful women that surrounded him were all everyone could gawk at. It may have been what started Uri's quest for some hot Fourth of July women, along with his very descriptive plans of what to do with them at Adam's apartment. Cocktail waitresses carrying trays of red white and blue shots circulated about and were the beginning of Mina's decline.

She seduced Adam mimicking the provocative moves of the old man's escorts. He sat with a sideways smile, looking at her hungrily but the public display also made him uncomfortable. Uri, inebriated as well, locked hands with Mina for a moment to grind in front of Adam. It was several moments before she pulled away. He continued to dance on his own, grabbing and thrusting his body onto the poles of the canopy. Mina found it difficult to follow, both because of the erratic nature of the movement and her temporary lack of coordination. Adam was too subdued to outwardly join in and in finding her rhythm; she danced her way over to Uri and slapped him on the butt a few times. He turned and danced with her, lifting her up by the waist and at the highest point positioned his arms around her bottom. She hit the tops of his shoulders to come down and that was the abrupt end of their dancing.

Uri naturally invited himself to Adam's apartment for a *freedom* joint with them. This is what he was calling it in light of the holiday and a mockery to the United States' movement to turn all things modified "French" in to *Freedom*. They sat in front of the bay window sharing half-witted conversation smelling rain that hadn't yet fallen. Al Pacino joined them with his signature Scarface tall-chaired photo from the movie. It read, *"Say hello to my little friend,"* and was positioned above a single Japanese White Pine bonsai. Despite its name, nothing about the tree was white.

Adam became hungry nearly seconds after the joint finished, and gorged himself on chicken liver, pickle, and potato chip sandwiches in the kitchen. These were tiny little sandwiches where chicken liver held a pickle like a seashell on sand to then be smashed between two greasy potato chips. Typically, he would carry on eating them with noises and faces of enjoyment to gross Mina out, but she was falling in and out of sleep on the recliner. Uri talked about a bartender named Crystal while admiring Mina's bare feet. Adam popped out of the kitchen, said something to him in Hebrew and disappeared. Uri turned on the TV and stopped browsing when he landed on soft porn. Mina could barely keep her eyes open, but upon looking up at the TV, she sat up.

She didn't want to deny Adam sex, especially with the lame excuse of being tired or drunk. She compared herself to the Revlon model again and peeled herself off leather to join him in the kitchen. Uri watched her every move. She dropped to her knees and pretended to need Adam's help to get up, but once he bent down she reversed the order and sat on his chest. She tried to be serious, but manhandling him in the ways he usually does her was hilarious and her body shook with laughter. Adam became aroused and reduced her efforts by lifting her entire body into his caresses. Uri ran over to join them but by the time he arrived the commotion was more intimate than a battle.

"Bro, what are you doing?" Adam asked with his hands still on Mina.

"What do you mean what am I doing?"

"It's not like that," Adam replied.

"Definitely not like that! Awkward," she laughed and stood to fix her dress. "Do you two normally swap swords?" Mina asked.

"No!" Adam said.

"Wow, you two are nothing but a bunch of sword swappers." She walked towards the bathroom using drunken hands to locate the zipper along her ribs. Uri followed her but Adam didn't.

"What's your problem with sword swappers?" Uri asked.

"Me? Why are you saying I have a problem? I just didn't know you two did that sort of thing."

"What if it wasn't two guys? Would you like it then?" She was too drunk to be offended but knew to close the bathroom door on him. She slid to her knees, with the side of her face on the door and gaze on the cabinets. They spoke in Hebrew and she closed her eyes to listen. Still unsuccessful at finding the seam, she pulled her dress over her head and laid under the shower's stream.

Chapter 4
Foreplay

Song #6 Lost in my Mind, The Head and the Heart

Rain dripped onto the black oak floor from the windowsill. The balcony windows were left open and humidity moistened their sleeping bodies. The smell of rain was palpable. Adam woke up first, closed all the windows and made coffee. He brought her the yellow mug she used every time she slept over and was inclined to have coffee in bed. Mina had a terrible headache, as did he, and they smothered the bed with dead weight and party-breath. Uri was nowhere to be found.

"Did you have fun last night?" Adam questioned.

"Yea, you?"

"I did. You and Uri danced a lot," he said.

That was all that was the last of it before they both drifted back to sleep. When they woke again a few hours later, the only thing on Adam's mind was food. He hopped out of the shower before her and continued to talk to her as he dried his body in the bathroom.

"You know you wanted to sleep in here last night," he said putting a toothbrush in his mouth.

"I did?"

"*Just leave me here, I'll be fine,*" he said mimicking her drunken stupor. She was mortified.

"Why was I in the shower?"

"You don't remember taking a shower?"

"Not at all," she said.

"Do you remember coming home and eating chicken liver with

me?"

"Oh my god! How did I get that drunk?"

"Nooo!" he said laughing. "I'm fucking with you. You didn't eat chicken liver, but you and Uri were gonna take a shower together, do you remember that?"

"You're crazy." She knew he was exaggerating but also couldn't be sure of anything. There was definitely some truth behind these playful jabs concerning Uri. "I can't believe I wanted to sleep in the shower. How did I get out?"

"I carried you my dear."

"Oh my god. How embarrassing?"

"What? Don't be embarrassed."

"I shouldn't have gotten like that."

"Mina, forget it. You were fine. Are you hungry? I want to get some food and make this omelet I had the other day."

The kitchen was a disaster from the night before. Also, it didn't get the same attention as other rooms in the apartment. He ordered the omelet at the Seaport Diner sometime last week and devoured it like an animal eats through skin. His strange relationship with food stemmed from years of restriction based on the rules of Kashrut. The traditional Orthodox consummation of dairy is never on the same plate with meat, even if it has been washed. Many Orthodox communities follow this exactly as it was written in Leviticus, a book written before 1400BC. These laws or Kashrut maintain every kosher household keep two sinks, two sets of china, and several hours between eating the two. Not having dairy and meat on the same plate prohibits almost all modern day food combinations, marking his ripe age of 29, not only a year of hypocrisy, but also the first time he can enjoy fancy omelets, or any dish, for that matter, combining meat and cheese.

Mina agreed to walk to D'Agostinos for ingredients despite the rain. A man wearing thick glasses and a blue poncho greeted them standing when they walked through the automated doors. His head was cocked up to the left as he read a coupon book held in his hand like a newspaper. His crooked smile and uneven glance reminded her of Red Cross Christmas bell-ringers, except instead of caroling and asking for donations, he repeated:

Buy a bag of chips get a free salsa. Pause. *Okay.*

Buy a bag of chips get a free salsa. Pause. *Okay.*

"Now there's a nice guy you can settle down with Meen. Go talk to him. The two of you could sleep in the bathtub every night if you want. *Just leave me here. I'll be fine. Okay.*" He continued to make fun of her for the night before using poncho man's intonation. He watched her blush and reach for a cart.

"You know how you can tell a crazy person?" she asked.

"How?"

"Their volume. So often a stranger looks totally normal, you say hello or ask them a question, and once they start speaking, you know they're nuts! They open their mouth too wide, talk too loudly, or have one of those unruly tongues. I mean sometimes you just know they're crazy before you speak to them, but you can't always tell, you know?" He turned the corner and parked the cart, as if he knew exactly where the cucumbers were going to be. He squeezed each before collecting them in a bag.

"Oh Man! Can you smell those bagels?" Mina lifted her nose to catch a better whiff of the sweet scent of bread coming from the bakery.

"Oh Right. I meant to tell you. Listen to this. The other day I was coming home, at like four in the morning, and I saw this bagel truck, Best Bagels, Hot Bagels, some bagel shop I've never heard of with an OU on it, picking up bagels from H & H!"

"What's an OU?"

"It's a kosher thing."

"Okay. So?"

"So?" he asked dramatically.

"What's your point? I bet a lot of bagel companies get their bagels from H&H, unless you're saying you don't know why, because then I'm with you, I don't think they're good either."

"My point is that this truck had an OU, on it. H & H isn't OU. They sell ham, salami, bacon, all that shit, with cream cheese right next to it," he said with a disgusted face.

"Adam what are you talking about?"

"Hi. Have we met?" He paused looking at her with pursed lips. "You know I'm Jewish right?"

"Yes," she laughed.

"Maybe you have heard? Us Jews, we eat this thing called kosher food? Israeli stamps are slicked with certified kosher glue. Kind of a big deal. You get it? Okay?"

"Yes. I know kosher pareve. Is that how you say food in Hebrew?"

"No! He rolled his eyes. Pareve literally means neutral, as in not dairy or meat. Anyway that's not even the hechsher I'm talking about. Oy Vey."

"The who?"

"The hechsher. The certification that guarantees the food my people eat is kosher. Just stay with me."

"Oh. Okay," she said peeling her eyelids back, to express interest.

"There are five major seals that guarantee kosher quality. It doesn't matter what seal they have at H & H. I know it's not an OU."

"Oh an Ohhh Uuuu?" She made fun of his severity.

"An OU is the Orthodox seal. All the other seals are basically signed by non-rabbi's that put their picture up guaranteeing the business there is under kosher supervision. It's bullshit!" He raised his volume. "How would they know? They've never even been there!"

"You know that I know little of what you are actually talking about and your volume is reaching that crazy level I was explaining before."

"It's all a scam, these seals and certificates are just another business. Bottom line: Jews are making money off Jews. He made his point and wrapped a bundle of asparagus in a green tinted plastic bag and tossed them in the cart."

"Okay," she nodded, glad his rage had concluded.

"What do you mean okay? It's mutiny!"

"Take it easy Adam, how do you know all this?"

"I went to see for myself." He picked up some tomatoes on the vine.

"You're totally insane." She watched him park his cart slowly and kneel down to examine blocks of cheese. A large trough filled with plastic wrapped animal milk, blended with herbs and peppers from different parts of the world lit up his face.

"Maybe you can tell a crazy person by what they notice or spend time theorizing about," she said watching him.

"I know but get this, these hechshers sometimes come from another city or state, and the poor schmuck buying a bagel from Hot Bagels thinks its OU, meanwhile its been sitting next to bacon all morning. Crazy? Eh?" He didn't need a response. He lifted a block of cheddar cheese to his nose. "Cheddar?"

"is mo' betta."

"Or Pepper Jack?" He threw down the block of extra sharp cheddar.

"That works."

"Oh man. Jalapeño Swiss, or Muenster. These all look good." It was impossible for him to choose as he brought each cut of cheese to his nose.

"Too hard to make a decision?" she asked commenting on his life.

"You ever have horseradish cheese?" he asked.

"Yep. So wait, you read kosher labels on everything you eat?"

"Hell no." He laughed. "I'm going to follow my Italian instinct, and get us Parmesan."

"An Italian instinct on a Jew might be awkward."

"No its not. You're on me all the time." She walked away from him rolling her eyes.

Song #7 Freedom Like a Shopping Cart, NOFX

Adam began driving the cart as if one of the wheels was possessed. He jerked it from left to right lifting one of the wheels for effect. One minute he was pushing it straight then he stopped it short and started fishtailing, shouting things like whooaa, like the cart had a mind of its own and was ready to flip over. He hadn't known Mina very long, and he wasn't usually this jokey but it was so easy, so incredibly corny and she enjoyed it. He cut her off without warning, nearly crushing her feet with the cart and every time he did something like this it reminded her of how awkward he had made their first kisses. Their very first time was normal, in the way lips connect to form a kiss, but after pulling away he pretended as if he didn't know how to find her mouth again. He pulled this trick regularly. He would close his eyes, move in extra slowly, and still miss her lips getting bits of her nose and eyebrow.

The cart's zigzagging stopped on freckled linoleum and he bumped out from the driver's position to survey egg cartons. He opened and closed lids to check shell condition and size.

"C'mon Adam, just grab em already. I'm starving now."

"Yesiree, we are ready. I hope you're hungry," he said pretending he didn't just hear her. "I bet you don't know how Jews use the express isle?"

"Nope. Tell me."

"No seriously, you can ask any Jew. We always use the Express aisle, because an item only counts once, no matter how many you have of it."

"Sounds Jewish to me."

"You got a lot of nerve you know that." He was full on acting now.

"Why?"

"You're more Jewish than me. How could you be an anti-Semite?" Mina began grabbing things from the cart with a smile on her face, but he quickly reprimanded her in an Irish accent.

"What in God's name do you think your doing? Ya keep on touching me groceries like that and I'm not buying em, not even one item."

"Jesus Mary and Joseph, I'm just putting them on the belt for God's sake," she came back at him in a brogue of her own.

"Ya don't even know how I like em." He arranged his items in size order, covering every part of the belt. He stacked them close to one another, and she watched him act out an idiosyncrasy that was dangerously close to the control issues present in his true personality.

She didn't help unload the cart after that and was distracted by a star-struck magazine. She hid her face in pictures of a sex scandal between three very well known celebrities, and turned herself on thinking of their sex. He walked closer to Mina by the front of the cart and grabbed the cheese from the child seat.

"Oh excuse me, is that your leg," he said as his hand wrapped around her inner thigh. She stepped back and turned away shaking her head. "Oh my, is that your ass? Wow! Sorry, oh I am so sorry, I thought it was mine." She turned to face him, frozen laughing and not sure where to go to avoid his ass grabbing. "I had no idea you were there, really, excuse me. I just wanted to get some gum. Fresh breath is important. Really sorry about before, I didn't even see you." He hooked one of his fingers in her belt loop and pulled her into him with great force, yet catching her by her breast before she fell into his chest. He cupped it in his palm and placed his other hand on her shoulder with a theatrical look of concern. "Darling, are you okay?"

Chapter 5
Grand Slam

She had sex with Adam, only after about a month of dating, having denied the invitation upstairs several times. They met randomly one night dog walking. She was wearing her usual work button down-blazer combination, and said yes to dinner on the spot, even though they hadn't spoken at all that day. She wanted him badly, especially the sharp edge of his canine on her body. She often visualized him tonguing it, something he did while thinking, and also the way it got caught when he licked his lips. They were big smooth lips and all she could focus on as he spoke. They didn't have any wrinkles; just a supple invitation to the expression of his mind that she couldn't deny.

His room was different than she imagined, and she did imagine it, nearly every-time they spoke on the phone before bed. Its neatness pleased her. His four-posted metal-framed bed, otherwise wooden in her mind, was pillow puffed with a military grade-tucking job. His tightly bound comforter, cognac recliner, and fluffy white shag rug looked as though it came right out of a Nautica catalog. She crushed carpet fibers between her toes. The smell was calming, not like the scent of a man, like something she knew but couldn't place.
She looked at herself in the mirror and became light-headed.
She smiled for no specific reason and fell onto his bed.

"What do you wanna eat?" he asked her while peeing.

"Anything. I'm starving." She didn't get up from her catalog spread. He picked up on what she was really saying and cocked an eyebrow.

"Okayyy?" he cut through their tension with deliberate resistance. They left the apartment within minutes and walked down the street to a new Thai restaurant.

"I'm going to have a Lychee martini, what about you?" he asked her with his face hidden behind his menu.

"Definitely not following suit," she laughed.

"Oh I didn't tell you about my condition?"

"Oh right," she said uninterested and turning to the second page of the menu.

"Noooouhhh," he said pronouncing no like the name Noah.
"You're supposed to say, what condition Adam?"

"What condition Adam?" she asked with a Brady Bunch inflection. Mina was getting used to him now and could tell when he was going to act out a character.

"I'm gay," he said. She fake smiled and returned to dinner options. His only audience was the green cliff-sides and ocean view printed on her menu's cover.

"Drunk Man Noodle? Why would I want to order a dish called Drunk Man Noodle? Why would they put that on a menu? Uh, yea hi, can I please have the drunken man noodle?" Adam ordered to a fictitious server.

"It's kind of delicious. I've had it before," she said.

"What! You've been here before?"

"No. I've had it though, it's a common Thai dish otherwise known as Pad Kee Mao."

"Oh cuz if you were here before, I was gonna say you know…. you know…" He spoke as if he was tough.

"No I don't know." She looked him directly in the eye.

"I just want to know, yuno…who you mighta come here with." He puckered his lips and bopped his head like some hip-hop gangster, but not in the true sense of the word, just the MTV version.

"What are you talking about?"

"I'm sayin… I'm sayin," then he stopped. He stopped with his hands and voice. The excitement for that persona left the table. "So, just so I'm clear, what you're telling me is… is that Drunk Man Noodle is a dish you can get at other Thai places?"

"Yes."

"Okay, will you please order the drunken man noodle? I want to hear you say it," he laughed at the thought of it. Mina was still thinking about the conversation prior. It was the first time he asked her a question like that. She wondered if he was jealous, or just pretending. It didn't matter, she wanted him and her apprehensive deliberations about having sex with him dissolved.

"Maybe," she smiled about it all. "Do you like curry puffs?"

"Puffs? My god," he exaggerated and spread a gay hand with pinky-extended across his chest. "Do you even listen to me? Try to remember my condition." She looked up with one hard blink. It was unspoken, but definitely clear that she was annoyed with the gay joke and wanted him to stop.

"Yes I would love to order curry puffs okay? We'll have two orders, or is one okay? One should be fine, right dear? One is good. Did I tell you that you look very nice this evening? Your skirt shows off your sexy legs. Tell you what, why don't you just order for us, since you seem to be so acquainted with the menu?"

"Really?"

"I'm in your hands. Guide me," he said. It felt like a first date for Mina, not that she had been the one to lead at all on their first date, and he was talking like a Jewish woman at the moment, but even that didn't matter. It was somehow her turn to impress him. The two of them walked side-by-side after dinner saying nothing, and then it happened: He grabbed her by the arm in the street, aggressively squeezing her by the elbow, pretending to dig his knuckle in her ribs.

"What'd you say? What'd you say to me? Don't even think about moving." He threw her against a glass door in a vestibule. "Don't make a sound. Just walk. You just shut-the-fuck-up and walk." Mina couldn't stop laughing, but did it with minimal noise and loved her body so close to his. She was getting turned on in the way humans take sex with violence. Her glands prepared her body for what was coming. The insides of her cheeks filled with saliva, like lemonade streaming down beverage fountain bins. They walked in through the grand lobby of the Corinthian just like that, her laughter shaking him, arousing him and his gun-finger poking her small ribs.

He slammed her back against the wall of the elevator hidden from the concierge. He kissed her on the mouth with his hand around her neck and open eyes. They kissed passionately under the heat of elevator lights, and his in-character hand became affectionate. They broke sweat mid kiss and he caressed his way down and around her body. The elevator stopped and they disconnected their mouths waiting for the door to open.

Once in the apartment it took all of five minutes for him to go to the bathroom and turn on his sound system. He played, "Regulators," by Warren G. She couldn't stop laughing and it was what he wanted. He needed to slow things down. He wanted this badly. With puckered lips, he rubbed her hips and legs as she slithered to the music. It was, a joke at first and for both of them. This wasn't the song she had in mind and he seriously wanted to have sex with her, but because he hadn't showered or mentally prepared, and was denied when he tried before, he wanted to take his time. He released her from his clutches to make two apple martinis and gather his wits. She resisted making fun of him for owning a bottle of Apple Pucker, and preoccupied herself examining his very religious bookshelf and un-Orthodox movie collection.

Song #8 Orange Wedge, The Chemical Brothers

"Oh I like this song," she said. He entered the living room holding two neon green liquid diamonds.

"You like this techno rave shit?" He clicked the remote towards the television to see what was playing. "Orange Wedge? What the fuck is that?"

"This is your IPod!"

"I know I love this shit," he said.

"You're so weird." There was a silence and she stood up. She knew she was being watched but she wasn't going to make this easy for him, even if he did have a bonsai. She walked towards the tree to examine it.

"Do you cut this yourself?"

"I do. It's called prune, as in the art of pruning," he said with perfect diction.

"How often do you prune?"

"Twice a year, usually, but it depends on the changes it goes through each season," he said walking closer to her with drinks.

"So wait, when a branch begins, hold on let me get a sip." She lifted her martini and pinky. "Ahhh Apple Pucker, it's been a while. Okay, so a branch begins to bud and very quickly grow, but because it's not picture perfect or in the right place you eliminate it in order to preserve the tree's ultimate design?"

"Yes, and no. The aim of keeping a bonsai is to capture its beauty and power, but to keep the tree's natural form without showing that it's been crafted by hand. There's many types of pruning."

"What's your method?" Not one character she had seen of his could compete with his intensity at that moment.

"Kajiwara. You want to learn horticulture right now?"

"Teach me something." She shrugged her shoulders.

"Okay there's two important parts of a bonsai: the sucker and the crotch."

"Shut up," she pushed his arm.

"I'm serious," he grabbed her hand and pulled her in slowly. She couldn't leave his grip.

"No you're not." She remained still.

"Okay. I absolutely am, but I'm not getting into that right now." He moved a strand of hair away from her face. "Some say...that a bonsai...develops from a combination...of what the owner feels about the tree and the tree's behavior..." He freed her hands from the martini. "...And, that the most beautiful bonsais are in a constant state of compromise."

"How'd you learn so much about this stuff?" She stared at his mouth.

"One of my mentors in Israel was part of the Israeli Bonsai Society. He taught me everything I know."

"Are you a member now that you have your own tree?" Mina laughed as she spoke, despite how much this interest of his interested her.

He moved behind her. The tips of his fingers traced along her clavicle and spread wide to press her chest into his. He snuck an index and middle finger between two buttons and cupped the side of her face and neck. His hand swam through her hair. She tilted her head back and he used his teeth to move her shirt collar out of his way. He exhaled heavily on her skin.

"Mina, may I please take you to my room?"

"Uh- huh." She was covered in goose bumps and had more of that lemonade saliva filling her mouth.

She loved the way he kissed. She lightly chewed on his bottom lip. His breath intoxicated her like truffle oil always did. They walked as they kissed. He licked the outside of her lips coating them with saliva, making them his and every time he did, she lifted her knee and tucked her foot around him. They walked half of the way with her hopping on one leg. She reached for balance, grabbing at the wall and doorframe. When he lifted her whole body to softly lay her on his bed, he said hi, as if he was seeing her for the first time. He took his time removing her clothes, unbuttoning and peeling her garments off with precision. His confidence calmed her and she knew she was never going to look at him the same. He watched her respond to his touch and shutter at each lick. He returned to her face to kiss her mouth just before opening his nightstand drawer for a condom.

She grabbed it from his hand and got on top. It made him smile. He didn't think she had it in her, seeing that he waited a month for her to just come upstairs. She kissed the top of his chest and moved her way down his torso while he closed his eyes.

"This is the sucker," she paused. "And here," she paused again. "This is the crotch." He exploded into laughter and covered the huge smile on his face.

The IPod continued to shuffle. Bass swelled against the bedroom wall and joined them in their naked dance. Each of them stared at the other as something miraculous took hold of their bodies. It changed their positions and framed their moans. He came unexpectedly but it somehow ignited pleasure in her as well and they held on to each other like they never thought they would.

"Oh my god," he said when it was done.

"What?" she asked with eyes closed and head to the side.

"Where's the condom?" he asked. Mina looked down between her legs at his bare naked body where there should have been a jimmy, and jumped up.

"Oh no! Are you kidding me?" She looked at the bed and saw nothing. He hopped off as well to search the moistened sheets.

"It's not here," he said.

"No shit Adam!" Mina was already squatting with her hands inside of her.

"You think the condom's in you?"

"Yeah!"

"Why?"

"It's not on the bed. It's not on you. Where else is it going to be?"

"How long do you think it was off?"

"I don't know I'm not the one with the dick, it still feels good for me with or without the condom," she spoke while feeling around inside of her. "Oh come on!" She was getting frustrated that she couldn't feel or remove the foreign object.

"Can you feel it?"

"No not yet."

"How do you know it's even in there? Has this happened to you before? It can't be in there."

"You find it then," she said with obvious aggravation.

"I'm going to," he said sure of himself. Adam moved the comforter and pillows, even checking the floor on both sides of the bed.

"I feel it!" Mina said in exasperation.

"You do?" Adam walked around the bed uninhibited by his limp penis picking up the clothes they had thrown on the floor. He sat down on the mattress and put his head between his hands rubbing the sides of his head. He let out a big sigh as he waited for more information.

"It keeps slipping. This is... ridiculous." Mina's tone changed as she saw the humor in the situation. "This is so stupid, of course this would happen right now," she said pulling her hand out and staying low like a tribal woman.

"Let me try," he offered.

"No." She shook her head as pitcher calls off hand signals.

"C'mon bring me your vagina. Let the doctor take a look at it. You can't see what you're doing, I have a better view." She stood up and looked him in the eye. She wasn't sure what she was going to do, but she had to stretch her legs.

"Get on the bed," he told her.

"You aren't going to be able to see it. You men hardly know the entry point."

"Not the Dr., baby. Bring it to me." He had never called himself the doctor before, nor had he referred to her as baby, but it worked. She crawled onto the bed and opened her legs for him. He attempted but his all-knowing fingers hurt her instantly.

"Stop. This isn't going to work," she stood up. She spread her lips wide and reached deep inside and threw her butt down into a low seat to dig deeper. "Oh I can feel it. It's the brim too. I'm gonna get it." He watched her with his naked body hanging off the side of the bed. His focus on her softened and he was no longer aware of her naked breasts or what she was doing. He became removed and consequently noticed how physically tired he was. His eyes gazed at the floor as thoughts of work entered his mind.

"Got it," she slapped his thigh with the slimy condom. "Here's your drunken man noodle."

Chapter 6:
Sacrilegious

It wasn't spring anymore and those first time butterflies had passed. The tenderness they shared then was ripe. But here under Augusts' sun, there was a heavy conversation pending. It referred to a serious problem, and although they were walking, silence was still between them. It was an obvious discomfort causing them to walk in slow motion. Until now, Murray Hill was a neighborhood they had called their own, but now Adam considered the many dangers of her address and she too was experiencing a state of shock. She had been warned by some of her friends about this very thing happening but never took them seriously. She was quick to say that she and Adam were only friends and often told others *not to get involved*, and even deluded them with the notion that, they were the perfect *faux couple*.

Mina was a modest woman and this was what Orthodoxy stressed, but by no means did that quality make her Orthodox. She wasn't going to all of a sudden join their community and start wearing a wig like the rest of the women just because of her feelings for Adam. What was apparent from their silent stare on the bench was that he was only willing to see things through this narrow scope.

"You want me to go in?" she asked in front of the coffee shop. This was their normal routine when they had the dogs.

"No I'll get em, you stay here." He wanted to be the one to escape. He knew the time had come to say what he had avoided telling her all along, and he always envisioned feeling this way, not because he wanted to, but because he knew that dating, fucking, and trying women on for size was going to get the best of him at some point.

Song #9 Wasting My Time, Taryn Manning

Mina smeared one sweaty palm against the other desperately trying to get her head straight. It was ten in the morning. The quiet streets alarmed her like white space between words in a sentence that didn't make sense. Those that didn't make their own coffee were sleeping to the rattle of an air conditioner, leaving Starbucks completely empty. She clicked a parking meter dial until it couldn't go anymore.

"I want to talk to you about the other night," she said as he handed her an iced espresso.

"Okay."

"I didn't mean to slap Uri on the ass or flirt with him like that."

"Okay."

"I was happy...and drunk."

"Noo?" he said with heavy sarcasm.

"Don't do that, we were having a good time, flirting and dancing. I was feeling feisty, and I admit I got carried away, but I want you to know that there wasn't any foul play."

"Okay."

"What's okay? Say something other than okay? What're your feelings?"

Adam thought about that night, especially when he slipped his finger down her shirt, playing with her cleavage and forcing her nipples to poke through material. He partially blamed himself for letting her drink so much, getting a bottle, when there were only three of them, but he loved having her dance all over him. He didn't think she wanted Uri but it was a bother that they got along so well. He even remembered them sitting in the kitchen drinking later that night after the club, chatting about the old man and his escorts, and was curious why so much of their talk harbored sex. He didn't know that any of it mattered. He didn't want to talk about it because he hadn't spent enough time thinking about it.

He noticed the white of her fingertips as they clutched the parking meter. She was wearing her favorite jeans. He called them her favorite because he hated them, yet still she wore them. They had about four holes, and were easily two sizes too big. Her eyes were especially green. They were big bright eyes that expressed everything she felt, and at that moment he looked into the face of someone that was ready to cry.

"Lets sit in the park," he said untying leashes from the pole. They walked into the Park on 36th street, let the dogs loose and sat on another bench.

"I just want you to know that I wouldn't do that to you, you know. It's really hard to talk about this without letting you know how I feel." Mina couldn't stop talking.

"That's okay. You can tell me how you feel about me," he said to make her smile and she did.

"I hate you," she joked. He at least had that, a smile to look at and remember regardless of what happened next.

"I don't know Adam...It starts with an appreciation, I guess. An appreciation of someone, or many things about someone, and then, a desire to spend as much time with that person as possible... And the more that you're with them, the more they improve who you are, and then soon enough, they're a part of you and you just want to be around them all the time." She was blushing and smiling as she lifted her gaze from the floor and brought it to his face. "I appreciate you."

"Thanks." He took her hand. "I know you do, Mina."

Rags rounded the opening of the fence, and she yelled out her name. The dog came running back inside.

"I don't want more than you're giving me, and nothing should change in anyway. It's just that since this happened with Uri, I realize that I have to let you know something."

"What?"

"I'm not interested in being with anyone else."

He too knew the feelings she described, and there were certain things he noticed about himself because of her. He was much more self aware, due to her. He was also happier. He woke up happy and had energy that he didn't have before knowing her. He noticed that he wanted to become cultured and learn things to impress her with, but this didn't pay his bills, and it wasn't logical to think in terms of impressing someone else. He became worried that he might have wasted too much time with her already. He imagined saying to his dad, 'Sorry I'm just going to travel around the world with my hot-blooded Italian trying out different cities, looking at art and eating at fine restaurants, hope you can understand and take care of yourself.' He couldn't bear the thought of it. He had a responsibility and it concerned him that someone like her, so different from all the other girls he had ever been with, had distracted him so severely. He couldn't imagine sincerely desiring a non-religious woman.

"I agree Mina that we have gotten to be really close and spend a lot of time together. But I am not in the position to be with you. I am not in the position to be with anyone. When we first got involved we both said we weren't looking for a relationship."

"Yes I know that. But, I'm not *not* looking for a relationship either, Adam. I'm not crazy, right? I mean we have a rare, and beautiful connection." It sickened her to imagine that the adoration she felt for him was in her head. She knew that there were going to be consequences for speaking like this, but she had to know.

"There really is something special about you, something irresistible, something incredible, something Mina, but...I don't know what to tell you, he said.

"Tell me you don't want to be with me."

"I can't do that."

"What do you mean you can't do that? You always have the answers."

"Not this time." He looked into his palms.

"Tell me to walk away, or don't. Tell me to stay."

"It isn't what I want, but if I had to tell you what to do, what was smart for you, it would be to walk away. I care about you so much, but I'm not ready for this. So, yes, I think walking away makes the most sense for you."

Song #10 Something Heavens, H.U.V.A Network

Part 2:

Everything has a beginning, even if you don't remember starting there.

Ch. 1
Unknown

Mina loved the trumpet. A jazzy number played and eased her cramps as she entered the museum's cafeteria. Each tour nauseated her as if the museum was on a boat. She hadn't told anyone about what happened with Adam, and even when she spoke about it with herself, she wasn't yet calling it a break-up. She leaned over the green beans and glanced past the tortellini. Even chicken nuggets and French fries were less than appealing. The salad bar's huge bin of roasted peppers made her think of anchovies, particularly the disgusting hairs that spewed in disarray. She couldn't eat any of this, not now or at all. But it was time to eat, how could it not be? She hadn't eaten anything all day. She heard her mother's voice as she often did concerning food. *Something Mina, you must eat something.*

She wondered what a safflower looked like in the middle of reading the nutritional facts on the Multi-Grain chips, but her stomach hurt. She couldn't distract herself from this. She checked to see how much time was left in the day when a sensation stabbed her in the top corner of her belly. It ripped across her midsection to the other side of her hip. The pain consumed her lower back, shot both up her spine and down her legs. She was sweating and sure she was going to pass out, even though nothing like that had ever happened to her before.

Mina thought she might have food poisoning, but couldn't even remember what she last ate. She ran to the bathroom and smacked her face with water. She gargled but that didn't help. She took an open mouth breath and exhaled in long audible moans. Still sweating she stood over the first toilet she could see. She pulled her pants down to see her inseam saturated with blood. This was more blood than one sees from an aggressively onset menstrual cycle. The pain depleted her energy and she needed to puke, and did so using the wall for balance. The sight of her own blood on everything made her even more ill. She kicked the flush-lever in between pukes and washed it down. She puked once more as new water filled the toilet.

"Ya need help baby?" An MTA security guard with a southern twang asked from outside the stall. Mina stood gasping for air in disbelief. One of her eyes remained shut as she tried the impossible feat of swallowing her own saliva. She growled out a no. She had no idea what was happening. She did feel slightly better now that she had puked, but all she wanted was to lie down. Her period was typically heavy after a three-month hiatus, and it had been just that, but this kind of stop and start was normal for her.

"Hello?" Mina sought assistance.

"Yea I'm here baby. What'dya need?" The MTA woman asked.

"Wet paper towel."

Mina smeared her face with it and patted the back of her neck. She was leaning against the wall holding the top of the stall door for support. It was the first time in her life she told someone to call 911. The medics had to carry her through the front of the museum.

~ ~ ~

"How's everything in here Ms. Luizzi?" A silver haired doctor walked into Mina's hospital room. He was drying his chubby hands with a brown paper towel. Thick white hairs protruded from his jowls. Dr. Mason was a happy doctor, smiling out of the corner of his face, pleasantly strolling towards her in a worn pair of Sambas. "Feeling better yet?" he asked her. Mina sat up from a half sleep to meet his eyes.

"Yes, a little."

"Well, I'll take a little. The good news is that you're gonna make it." He laughed at himself and to let her know he was kidding. He picked up the chart resting at the footboard and checked boxes on a spreadsheet. "You were in a lot of pain but you seem at ease now. Don't worry. We'll give you plenty of painkillers to take with you. Okay?"

"Okay."

"You were right Mina, it wasn't your period."

"It wasn't?"

"No it wasn't." He put the chart back.

"What was it?"

"An embryo."

"What!"

"You haven't had your period in about a month and a half right?"

"Maybe."

"I see. Well, what you experienced was a miscarriage, and a lucky one at that, seeing as you didn't wish for pregnancy."

"A miscarriage? How? I haven't had unprotected sex?"

"You were certainly pregnant. We expedited the process and flushed the rest out of your system and there may still be some cramping, but nothing like the discomfort you were experiencing before. You look better already. You'll need to hydrate so get plenty of fluids and rest," he smiled. "I just wanted to come back and check up on you before I signed your release. Do you have any pain still?"

"Wait? I had a baby inside of me?"

"Well, not a baby. But, a fetus? Yes."

"I can't believe this!"

"You don't know how this could have happened?" he asked with his back to her.

"No, she said in amazement.

"You always use a condom?" Dr. Mason looked at her curiously.

"Yes."

"Do you know that a goldfish has a memory span of three seconds?" he asked her.

"Actually, wait. A condom did get stuck in me one time. But I'm pretty sure it was a spermicidal condom. I mean why do they even make condoms without spermicide. I didn't think anything of it, I mean don't get me wrong I thought plenty about it, but it was too soon and I had just gotten over my period. I didn't think you could get pregnant that close to a period."

"Life can happen, anytime, all the time. You know what else?" he asked with a smile.

"What?"

"Pregnant goldfish are called twits."

"Really?"

"Yes, really." Mina started crying.

"Are you in contact with the ...man... responsible?"

"No," she became hysterical and grabbed tissues from the box next to her bed.

"You don't have to go through this alone. If you want to tell him what's going on, you should."

"I'm just so tired. I can't believe this happened. I never thought that this would happen to me. Ever. I was pregnant and now I'm not."

"But it's okay. You are going to be okay. There are literally thousands of worse situations." If he couldn't be funny at least he could provide some perspective.

"It's not possible to tell him." She looked at him with a completely twisted, red wet face.

"Let's see you on your feet Ms. Luizzi." She stood up with his help, and wiped her eyes. She reached around her swollen naked belly feeling her midsection as if it was a foreign body part under the thin hospital gown.

"I feel so weak," she whispered. She remembered all of the moments her body had been trying to tell her something in the past weeks. First it was headaches, but that she attributed to tension from crying. Her breasts had been incredibly sore, but she was expecting a period and this sensation was quite regular. "Where are my clothes?"

"Those are in that bag." He pointed to a triple bagged, tied knotted ball on the bottom of the closet. "If it's all right with you I'll have the nurse bring you some scrubs."

Song #11 Soldier On, Temper Trap

Mina called her cousin Gio to pick her up. She wasn't getting on a train. She wasn't getting in a cab. She didn't want to talk about this with anyone. He wouldn't ask too many questions and she would be home in under a half hour, unless he was on shift. He drove a raised truck that she needed help getting into. She reclined the seat, put her feet on the dashboard and closed her eyes.

"What happened to you? The first time I see you in a month has to be at the hospital?" Gio asked without driving off.

"I had a miscarriage."

"Minchia! You were pregnant?"

"Yes," she spoke softly despite his volume.

"But you're not now?"

"Correct. G, what the hell is that smell?" she asked him.

"Did you have an abortion?"

"God no. How do you not smell that? It smells like gas."

"Yea a gas can leaked a little in the back the other day. Did you know you were pregnant?"

"Are you kidding me? What's the matter with you? Of course I didn't know. How do you drive like this? I swear to god I'm gonna be sick. Who drives around with leaking gas cans inside their car?"

"Why are you wearing scrubs?"

"I had a miscarriage! I was at work when it happened and my clothes are disgusting. Actually, can you throw this bag in that garbage right there?" She nudged her chin towards the bin in front of the hospital just to the left of his vehicle. "I don't ever want to look at them again. I'm beside myself." She sat up to get fresh air from the open window.

"How'd you not know?" he asked as he opened the driver's door.

"Please G." She turned to her side and fanned her face with air from the open window.

"You know whose it is?" he asked putting the car into drive.

"I've only been with one person in the past six months and we don't have sex anymore, so yea I think I can recall. I can't believe this smell. Please, let's go so I can get some air."

"Sorry about that Meen, I must be used to it. I helped this woman the other day and her kid was holding the can in the back. That's what I get for being nice. Are you gonna tell him?"

"No."

"What do you mean no?"

"What the hell would I say? Would you want to know if your unborn child died inside someone that you weren't ready to have children with, not to mention the same someone you just broke up with?

"I didn't know you guys broke up."

"Well he's not here is he? Doesn't this seem like something he would be present for if things were good between us?" Tears filled her eyes morphing streetlights into starbursts.

"I'm sorry."

"I can't tell you how sick I feel," she said with droplets falling down her cheeks. "Just like that, life leaves you, love leaves you, and where does it go? Where the fuck does it go?"

"I dunno," he answered her.

"Of course you don't. Neither does the doctor. Fucking Goldfish. I do. It's thrown into red plastic bags in bins with hazard signs on them and discarded as nothing." She scratched her itchy face and closed her eyes. When she woke she noticed they were about to turn onto the FDR from 79th street.

"Where are we going?" she asked in desperation.

"Your mom's. She invited me to dinner tonight. I figured you'd wanna come with, no?"

"No!"

"Aw, come on. She called me on my way to you. I told her I'd bring you over. At the time, I didn't know you had all this going on."

"What! Why? I can't see her right now. I can't go to Brooklyn like this. I don't have anything with me. What am I gonna say to her, plus I'm wearing scrubs, for Christ's sake G! What's the matter with you? You ask me a hundred questions and not think to mention our destination? Turn here," she directed him to turn around.

"You fell asleep and I didn't want to bother you. But relax! We can stop at a store. I can run in and get you some clothes."

"No. I need to go home."

"Fine. Fine. I'll take you to your house, but you have to come or she will ask me a million questions and, so help me God, that woman will know if I'm lying."

"You can't tell anyone about this," she snapped.

"Who am I going to tell? Stop being psycho. You're the one their going to ask, so start acting normal and come up with a good story." Mina flung her head onto the headrest as she sighed.

~ ~ ~

"Hi Ma," Mina waved to her mom in the kitchen and reached down to meet her father's cheeks for a kiss. He was sitting in his usual chair with eyes on the television. The game was so loud, it was as if the Yankees were playing in Brooklyn instead of the Bronx.

"Mina what's eh matter with you, you look mushade?" Marzia came over and rubbed her head.

"I'm fine. Where's my sister?"

"Carmella's not coming, Baby Michael has a fever and she doesn't want to get everyone sick."

"Again? Wasn't he just sick? I talked to her like two weeks ago and he was going to the doctor."

"Babies get sick, that's what they do. You'll see when you have your own." Mina sucked in her gut. Between her recent deposit at the hospital and eternal health class textbook visuals, she was feeling pukish again.

"Mina what's wrong?"

"Nothin Ma, I'm just tired and hot."

"Sit down. Gio, Move over. Give Mina your seat so she can put her feet up in the recliner. Do you want some iced tea with lemon?"

"Sure." It made her sick to think of all the alcohol she drank and cigarettes she smoked with a baby inside her. How careless she had been with her life, now someone else's, and for what? She had nothing to show for it. Oh the irony of using *protection*, while fetus and dick bump fists! There were those one-offs that she let Adam hang out inside of her raw, but it was moments and always followed by safe-sex. Physically, Mina was exhausted and could have fallen asleep right there, yet her mind was active. She imagined a life like her sister's, but without a husband, house, or money, just a son who's likeness was everything she loved and missed about the father. Her cramping returned and she wasn't comfortable sitting, lying, or standing, not outside, inside, or resting on the toilet. She wasn't hungry for dinner. Instead, she tried her best to hide the pain.

"I have an announcement to make, Gio addressed the table. Mina had no idea what he was going to say. She thought he told her everything, plus they just drove here, and he didn't say a word about an announcement. She left the two painkillers the hospital gave her in the car. She reached for the bottle of wine, praying he wasn't going to talk about her.

"Tell us," Joe said.

"I asked Jess to marry me," he said without a full breath.

"Congratulations!" Marzia shouted as she walked over to kiss and hug her nephew. Joe grabbed Gio's face and kissed him on both cheeks.

"You didn't even tell me." Mina didn't know what to say. Heat spread itself along the back of her neck and forehead. She felt lightheaded, a sting of jealousy, and then fatigue. She was ashamed she didn't already know and that she thought this was about her. "Congratulations!!! I am so happy for you," Mina said. Jessica's presence had been stymied by how badly his previous relationship ended, and Mina knew how extraordinarily slow their developments had been for the same reason. It was nice to see that they were overcoming it all.

"Come outside with me, Mina." Gio held what was left in the wine bottle in his hand. She grabbed both of their glasses and squeezed through the doorway leaving her parents behind. The temperature was cooler now and she was in less pain than she was drunk.

"I didn't know! I was going on and on about how shitty everything is. Relationships, and love, meanwhile you're going through one of the greatest times of your life."

"Don't apologize, you've had it rough today, besides you know I've been there before. The two of them sat in lawn chairs centered between a fire pit and vegetable garden. Marzia's backyard had looked the same since they could remember. "Enough about me, you know I love Jess. I know I love her. It was only a matter of time. What happened? I can't believe you, of all people, had an abortion."

"Would you stop saying that, it was a miscarriage. Miss- Care-Itch."

"I'm sorry. How the hell didn't you know?"

"I don't know."

"Who is this guy?"

"A Jewish guy named Adam."

"Mina!"

"I know."

"You have to tell him that you lost the baby."

"No way."

"I thought about what you asked me, and I would want to know. Even if we weren't together, I would still want to know."

"What! You're not serious."

"How did you meet him anyway?"

"At the museum."

"You work with him?"

"God no!"

"How long were you together?"

"We weren't."

"How'd you break up then?"

"You don't have to be in a relationship to experience rejection."

"No. No, True. But is there a possibility of something happening in the future?"

"The future? I don't think so. You know how I start my day? Watching the news. The stupid news, and it's all his fault. What does it mean when you begin a habit, or perhaps its better to say, join someone in their habit, and then allow it to become something you now do, whether you talk to them or not?"

"I don't know, but if you felt it, you felt it. There's never a right or wrong to these kinds of things. What happened?" Mina didn't answer his question.

"He also owned these really thick black-framed glasses, she began laughing and stood to imitate Adam. "Like Malcolm X glasses and he walked around his bed with a pretend hunchback, and believe it or not, I called him Rabbi. It was one of these games we played and he talked with this heavy Long Island accent. He's totally bizarre."

"Is that where he's from? Long Island?"

"Yea. Anyway, he used to sit me down in the center of his bed, tell me to lay a certain way as he did this stupid walk, grabbing my legs and arms to examine them, all while making horrific scraping sounds in the back of his throat. He held them as if they were delicate and precious, but then cursed them because they were Un-Orthodox, slapping me and shit."

"And this turned you on?"

Song #12 I want you, Kings of Leon

"I told you it was a joke, or a thing. It wasn't sexual, but it did turn me on. I mean of course it was sexual. It doesn't make sense, you had to be there, well not really, but you know. We were friends but then the whole Orthodox-Un-Orthodox thing really got in the way, as you could imagine."

"I see that."

"Sometimes he'd ask me for advice, and he would say, *Are you sure you're not Jewish?* As if we shared the same value system; that my opinion was important to him, and somehow my years of Catholic school had moralistically aligned with his religious traditions. Jews were the original Christians, no?" She laughed for the first time in a while. "Look, despite all the problems attached to two people like us coming together, I somehow convinced myself that we were working." She looked blankly into the garden. "He just had one hell of a hold on me. I wanted to be good enough for him. She took a moment and stared at the overgrown grass. "You know we met by accident. We even began dating by accident. It all just happened by chance."

"How'd you meet him at the museum if he doesn't work there? You toured him?"

"No, that sounds funny. And perhaps I did show him a few things he would have missed otherwise in this life, but we met in the elevator. Mina laughed. "That sounds so cheap. And I only agreed to go on one date with him as a dare. I didn't have a group with me, thank God. He was making fun of the museum, you should have heard him, shouting too, and it was just us in the elevator. I thought he was insane, he must have seen my nametag when I got in because as soon as the doors closed he just started yelling. *'This is what people do? They come here, look at things and watch other people look at different things, then leave? I don't understand, and it's a suggested price to come in? A suggested eight dollars! You don't even make money on the people that come here and stare at things?"* She smiled and sipped her wine. "We spoke for a little bit beyond his rant and I gave him a walk through on how non-profits work, but then he said…" Her laughter interrupted her story. *"You know what, you're right! The museum should pay me for looking at that mole wall. What a ridiculous thing!'* He went on and on about how useless it is to see how a mole travels to its home underground? He kept on repeating, *'It's a mole. A fucking mole, and I want to see how it gets home? No. I don't think so."*

"He doesn't sound very intelligent, well at least not as you usually like them, Meen."

"Yea my first concern, until our conversation became serious. I told him there were certain things that people wanted to know or remember, and unfortunately because they're not gifted with photographic memories, places like this educate and inspire people to remember the small things they often lose sight of. He had the audacity to tell me that that's where I was wrong! He even called me a tour guide. He was such an asshole, told me to tell my next school bus that everyone has a photographic memory but because they waste their film on things like moles, they don't have any when it matters."

"What does that mean?" Gio asked.

"I don't know. I took it as, that if we wanted to, we could remember anything and everything. It is so ironic, now looking back at it, that of all things, our very first conversation was about cheap thrills.

"I can't even go on telling this story, the dare for our date came when I started talking about art, but I already wanted him right then and there.

"Of course you dared about art."

"Whatever. It was in the context of the photographic memory. I asked him why some painters use blurred strokes of color and others produce fine handcrafted photographic paintings that look as though it's seen with the naked eye. He said that we should go to a real museum and compare notes. I realize now, saying this to you, our date happened because he couldn't answer the question. He didn't mean anything he said, it was all an attempt to ruffle my feathers. The entire thing was one performance to see what I was about and I fell for it: *A real museum,*" she repeated it the way he had said it. "He hadn't been to the Brooklyn Museum, the MoMA, the Whitney, and Guggenheim, none of them, just like he had never been to MNH before that very day."

"So?" Gio asked puzzled.

"So, we started something beautiful," she said without enthusiasm.

"How long were you two together?" he asked. She covered her face in laughter spreading her fingers wide enough to hide her eyes as well. "Well?" Gio continued to wait for an answer.

"Not long."

"How long?"

"Like, three months."

"What! You're crazy over someone that you only saw for three months? No wonder you don't want to call him."

"Yea, and I almost became his baby mama." Gio snorted and raised his glass in her honor.

"Do you think he'll call you?"

"No."

"Why?"

"Because he doesn't love me. I don't know if he can love." She drank the last few sips from her glass. "I'm going to bed, but I love you and congratulations." She moved slowly, not a careful slow, but a heavy sluggish mope of a walk. Her arms looked like they didn't belong to her, but were a form of weighted punishment. She fell asleep instantly and in her dream she wore a book bag.

Song #13 Shadows, Au Revoir Simone

A giant man lifted Mina. He was easily the tallest man the world had ever seen. Gravity weighed down on her book-bag and she became dizzy and strained until he perched her on his shoulder. His every movement made her feel nauseous in the dream, like the ups and downs of a roller coaster. She asked him if she could lie down on the bed and he complied, and as soon as she reached the bed, a small boy appeared out of nowhere and covered her with blankets.

"It's okay," he said. "I'm just like you. There are a lot of things I know how to do, because I'm just like you," the little boy whispered. She began to slip into sleep, and the child put his hand on her face. "You know what my first memory of you is?"

The question forced her to lift her head and look at the boy more closely. Suddenly, she remembered him, and that the notebook in her bag kept record of everything they had ever done together. She opened her bag in search for it to recover what he had asked of her. She flipped through the pages to find the answer. He watched her in silence, peeking here and there at her scribbling. She read the word 'good-bye' and couldn't believe it. She moved a few pages forward, but then back a few more, only to come back to the same page that read: good-bye.

Chapter 2
Family Values

Mina wasn't working anymore, not as in going to work, because that she did, but being Mina wasn't working; not for her and not for anyone else that might have crossed her path. Depression is a slow and tiring process. She longed to be in the absence of people and light. It wasn't exhausted adrenal glands that ailed her. There wasn't an amphetamine or caffeine dosage that would have remedied her situation. She didn't gorge herself on carbohydrates and sugar, or accrue credit card debt loading up on facial products or handbags. Instead, she did nothing.

Any natural energy her body could have created was robbed by drinking. If she banged her knee it wasn't just the knee or that moment. It was a much larger issue, her karma, and more evidence for the case she had against herself. She was awful at remembering things now, like why she entered a room or what she was in the middle of doing. Mornings were particularly hard for her to get it right. One minute she would have everything she needed and the next screaming *'what the fuck!'* to her shadows, furiously locking and unlocking the front door several times before making it to the train.

Song #14 Honey, Honey, Fiest

She only left her apartment for work and was unable to concentrate on anything as solidly as Adam and her own fame of course, because when life becomes difficult, pretending to be grandiose makes it better. She asked questions she couldn't answer. She made up stories to fill gaps in her knowledge and retold them to herself several times a day. Her left eye started to contract on its own, an annoying tic-tic-tic, on her eyelid, reminding her that if she didn't feel insane yet, all she had to do was look in the mirror for a couple of minutes. She asked herself one night if this was her new slogan: Lose a Baby, Get an Eye twitch.

Adam and Mina's second date was at the Brooklyn museum and it was one she thought of often. They didn't have an exhibit in mind when painted footsteps on the floor led their interests into a crowded closet of a room. They stood close to each other looking at the woman on film. It was the typical white-on-white-plywood-made-room with a single TV looping an artistic video.

The film opened with a woman before mountains and bright blue skies. She looked straight into the camera where together landscape and visitors watched her in silence. Her caramel complexion suited the candy apple red of her dress. Her weathered face and ballooned cheeks took up the whole screen. Her legs came into view just as the camera zoomed out. She was patiently and pleasantly seated. She slapped her knee once commanding Earth to charge her with electricity and it did. Wind rippled her dress and her eyes rolled back into her head for a few seconds. When she came to, her gaze fluttered like wings of a butterfly and her movements increased. She shook her arms in every direction and struck the tops of her thighs with open palms and aggressively lifted her chin to the sky. She did this three more times, in that order and each time more vigorously than the time before. Her braid whipped behind her like a fish out of water and the azalea pinned in her hair lost its form. She shined with sweat and glued to her cheeks were a bunch of loose hairs. In the last stretch, she cried like her life depended on it with eyes closed and blood swelling her veins.

As viewers walked out they searched for a compassionate glance in one other. It was Adam's face Mina remembered most, and that he was already looking at her when she turned to him with smiling eyes. But that was then, Mina was now at MNH sorting out her independent existence - post Adam and post Adam's baby. Mina was a docent, a decent docent. She wasn't as scientific as some of her counterparts but the others didn't possess her charm or lively wit and humor. She had liked her job for a long time but now offered visitors the same subpar experience she had recently found in life.

Most of her down time was spent in the dark cool jungle of Biodiversity. She crawled into the oyster right at the entrance of the Hall and began daydreaming. Hiding here helped her avoid questions about her life in general, but specifically her emergency stretcher stroll the week before. It also didn't hurt her newest game: pretending to be the only woman to ever be devoured by a crustacean. She told Jack, the security guard, the one person she couldn't avoid that it was food poisoning. Sulking in her shell, she moved her head and caught a whiff of her hair. Personal habits that once brought her joy were becoming a thing of the past. Some days were worse than others. She sank deeper into her imagination. It was a little like spontaneous meditation. She concentrated heavily on herself and others in complete fantasy. She saw every scenario like a photograph and currently the image was of her falling, first down an elevator shaft, then under water, sinking deep to the bottom of the ocean as a pearl bearing oyster would.

She walked to the far-east side elevator playing in the space that humans trap secrets, digging up sadness to produce tears. This was the same elevator that she once shared with Adam. She knew it wasn't going to happen, but when the doors opened, she imagined him standing there every time, and it wouldn't be enough to have him there. He had to be wearing the same sad face she wore so well. Mina gasped at the white button down shirt and khaki pants interrupting her fantasy. She cleared her throat and hid tears behind hair but her legs didn't move. His name was Roman Arenstein and he smiled as he held the door open.

"Are you getting on?" Roman was an older gentleman in his sixties and one of the curators for the Hall of Earth. He recognized Mina as a face he'd seen in passing, but her crooked nametag helped jog his memory that he knew her at all. Mina couldn't think fast enough. She couldn't say no. This was her routine. She couldn't act like she didn't just press the button or that she wasn't waiting for the elevator.

"I'm Roman," he lifted his glasses from around his neck to put them on to read her nametag. "Nice to meet you Mina, that's a lovely name. It reminds me of an old Italian singer my wife used to love."

"Yes. That's me, and yes named after the singer. My grandmother loved her as well." The bell sounded for the second floor.

"Oh, what floor were you going to Mina?" He realized she hadn't pressed a button.

"This is fine." She stepped out first and he continued to walk with her.

"It's none of my business, but I get the sense that you are not well? Is this true?" he asked.

"I'm not." Mina couldn't lie.

"Oh? Did something happen?" Roman asked genuinely. Mina started laughing.

"Did *something* happen?" She put a hand across her forehead. "Yea, a lot of things happened." Her yawn stretched the taut salty skin of her cheeks. They reached the corridor's end and entered The Hall of Earth.

"Well what's your theory on it?" he asked her without looking at her.

"My theory? I hate it. That's my theory," she pouted.

"Well that's a good place to start." He grabbed keys from his pocket and opened a white door on a white wall.

"Oh Wow! I never knew there was a door there."

"I bet." He placed his bag on the desk. "There's so much other stuff to notice." He turned the light on a tightly packed office with one desk, two filing cabinets, and a few cardboard boxes filled with papers.

"I can't believe I never knew there was a door here." Mina opened and closed the door confirming that the white of the wall camouflaged the white doorframe.

"It's all about context, Mina." She watched Roman collect papers. "There are displays on all the walls here, so why would you notice a door? That's not what you're looking for. Tell me about your theory." He led their conversation.

"Oh. Well, you were the one saying it's good that I hate my situation. Why?"

"Because you know how you feel about it and that's an insight to why you are feeling down, no?" he asked.

Song #15 Fuel, Ani DiFranco

"Yea I guess, but it doesn't change anything."

"Ah, well you may not be able to change things. That's number one really. But I suppose I can best serve you if I knew what we are talking about?"

"I don't know," she said rolling her eyes. He stepped out of the office with a roll of papers and walked towards the back of the hall.

"Help me a minute, Roman said as he walked past her. "So it's personal," he said with his back to her. "Is your health in danger?"

"No."

"Okay, good. Did you lose someone?"

"What do you mean?"

"Did someone die?"

"No," she said.

"Good."

"Well actually, maybe something did die. Not someone, but something. Something definitely died."

"Some thing? Like a pet? Or a plant?"

"No. Not like that either."

"Okay, does this make you sad?"

"Maybe."

"Okay, so back to the beginning, what's your theory on it?" He put the papers on the ground and unraveled a floor plan.

"My theory?"

"Yes, your theory." He pointed to the writing on the wall,

THE BIG BANG THEORY.

She kept her gaze on the semi transparent wall and read out loud,

THE EXPLOSION OF A SINGLE PARTICLE IN A DEFINITE POINT IN TIME.

She walked toward the wall as if she were looking at it for the first time. She continued to read.

LIFE ON EARTH IS POSSIBLE BECAUSE IT IS JUST THE RIGHT DISTANCE FROM THE SUN TO BE PROTECTED BY ITS MAGNETIC FIELD, KEPT WARM BY AN INSULATING ATMOSPHERE, AND PROVIDED THE RIGHT CHEMICAL INGREDIENTS FOR LIFE.

Mina stared at the solar system. She didn't focus on any one planet, just the display, thinking about how connected the Universe was. How small she was, and how little and insignificant these problems were.

"What are the ingredients for life?"

"Are you asking now, or then?" Roman raised his eyebrows.

"I didn't realize they had changed."

"They didn't." Roman couldn't help but smirk. The answer is water and carbon. But now that we're the top of the food chain, the only ingredient for life is other people." Mina laughed with equal confusion and indifference.

"I don't know if I have a theory yet. I've been trying to find a meaning for a while now and haven't had a good run at it."

"Well you have to start with a theory. How can you understand any of it, if you don't have a theory, at least about the beginning? Whatever it is, just think about how it came to be and why it matters, if it matters?"

"I don't know." A theory of the beginning is all she could repeat to herself. *The beginning of what? How she started with Adam? Or maybe he meant the beginning before Adam, like how she became the person she is. The beginning of the family that created her, or something so much grander, like all that was here before her. Where does it begin?* She thought about evolution and DNA, and stories of creation. *We all come from the same basic cellular structure, and most religions deny this basic fact, but she was certain that if it weren't for the differences between their cultures, nothing would have happened between them, but she didn't know that at the very beginning, so what started this whole thing?*

"Do you believe in God?" she asked Roman.

"I do. I'm Jewish."

"Of course you are."

"Mina, there is very little room for religion in science, and yet as miraculous as science is, it is only a voice trying to understand what is unexplained, but Faith is something else. Look, the questions people ask themselves about their existence are buried beneath their feet. Everything we need to know is right there. We don't have to travel or pay money to get it, and the same goes for the answers people look for within."

She envisaged kneeling at the edge of a lake ready to dip her finger into water, knowing that if she did, a small ripple would grow, and become everlasting to spread across the world for a lifetime. *A lifetime?* She asked herself in the middle of her own thoughts. *What does a connection with the world make you think of, if it isn't Earth? And what does the Earth make you think of if it isn't the Universe, and why does this entire chain bring death to mind?* She looked at Roman as if he could hear her thoughts like the announcement of a lost child on the main speakers. Mina speed-talked with herself using hierarchical modes of thinking that had been taught to her by academia. *What can beat the world? Nothing. And when one thinks of forever, the Earth is constant. So long as we live,* she continued to herself, *and so far as we know, we're at the mercy of our Universe, the sun and everything else in space. It was here before us and will be after. It has power over everything.* She stopped, and just like that her mind became quiet.

A woman's voice released from a globe in the middle of the room: *Emotions Disappear.* The globe was made from the same glass on television screens, except it was attached to the ceiling. The globe displayed satellite photos of Earth as moving stills to illustrate the planet's changes since the beginning of time, reducing billions of years into seconds. Depending on the time period, it depicted a lifeless globe covered in brown gaseous matter shifting into bodies of water and the emergence of clouds, to then the amazing green under blue skies. She knew what this display said, had heard it for months, yet instead of the correct: *Oceans Disappear,* she heard *Emotions.*

She glanced over at Roman and felt embarrassed, like someone had made a fool of her, but she wasn't sure why. She knew she wanted to be happy, successful, and in love, regardless of how small and inconsequential she was to the Universe, but why? She stared back at the Solar System, thinking about the range of human emotion, specifically uncertainty and how individuals struggle to find an honest expression that balances their contentment and purpose, while warding off sadness and vulnerability. People long for connection; it's what makes them feel whole and in control. She asked herself, what it was they were longing to be connected to. *Vegetation Disappears*, the display persisted. She tried the best she could to form a theory on the beginning, but nothing was clear, not even which beginning, and all she could hear were the female tones of a stoic robot. She remembered Adam's words, 'they couldn't be together because it wasn't the way the world worked,' but in her mind, the world had nothing to do with his indecision. If anything, the world was what brought them together in the first place. Nature doesn't ask for help and the world makes things work, so it was naive that he should say otherwise, as if he knew anything about these systems. *Clouds Disappear.*

"You'll form one," Roman said regarding her yet to be conceived theory. "You mind giving me a hand while you're here so I can find the right plan." She grabbed the ends of his blueprints and rolled one side out as he pulled the other.

"Oh my god." She looked at her watch as she pinned down her end of the sheet. She quickly started to walk away but still facing him walking backwards. "I'm sorry. I've been gone for an hour. I have to get back. There's no one on but me today. Shit! I wasn't supposed to be gone for this long. Thank you again," she started to trot away and then stopped to turn to him. "Wait, what's your name?"

"Roman."

"Will you be here later Roman? I just have to see about a tour."

"For a little while, but I'll be coming in frequently while we are making these changes. Take care Mina and good luck."

Song #16 Skinny Love, Bon Iver

Chapter 3
Earthly

Mina raced back to the front of the Museum to find guests waiting on her: one old couple, dressed similarly in the way marriages blend characters. Next to them was a rowdy group of Japanese boys in bright colors and a woman in her late forties. The boys smelled of cigarettes and beer and were oblivious to the attempts made by the dame next to them. Obviously conflicted, she tapped her waist with almond shaped fingernails in waiting for them to look at her.

"Hi Everyone, Mina addressed the group with a warm smile. "We'll be ready for the tour in just a moment." She kneeled to grab her blue binder to find a blank form.

"You need a vacation," Jack said as he leaned into Mina with one hand on his oversized belt. He loved talking with Mina, often calling her by the pet name he had given her: *Tumblemina*. It made his day just to see her and he offered to help her with everything she ever mentioned to him.

"You're telling me." She smiled as she counted the heads of those in front of her. "Thanks for stalling them, I didn't mean to take so long." A vacation was impossible for Mina. She couldn't seem to hold onto to the dollars she spent so well on Broadway, not the Broadway that offered music and melodrama, but Broadway Liquors on 79th street.

"Okay Ladies and Gentlemen, right this way." Her bright voice and smile engaged the eyes before her. She led the group up the stairs as if the Hall of Earth wouldn't wait for her.

"Can we go to Bird Halls?" One of the younger Japanese boys blurted.

"Sure, you guys can visit the North American Bird Exhibit while we go to the Hall of Earth. If you get lost, Birds of the World is on the third floor, just take the stairs up one flight and walk straight. You can't miss it." Splitting a group wasn't advisable, especially if visitors were foreign, but Mina welcomed the opportunity to lose the misfits. She was hoping to find Roman just as she left him, but he was nowhere to be seen.

"OK," Mina said loudly to grab her group's attention. "One thing that you won't read on the exhibits here is that our Sun was created from an explosive death of another star, and from that explosion the

Solar System was created. You know what they say, when one door closes another opens." She paused frozen with excitement, like a kindergarten teacher encouraging her students' participation, holding her breath between pages of a picture book. "We all come from the same molecules in that explosive matter, so not only are we connected," her eyebrows reached for the edge of her forehead as she continued her lines, "...to the planets in the solar system, but also each other.

Mina left work that afternoon energized. She walked north out of the museum, and entered Central park without a plan. She continued past the canopy of trees to meet the Sun, this time for real. She took off her blouse revealing her yellow tank top and petite breasts in an attempt to soak up the mid-October sunshine. It dripped all over the city at this angle and baked skin with its glare. She walked towards the pond and pressed the ball of her foot onto the iron railing as she watched geese float in pairs. It felt good to stretch the muscles of her lower leg. The breeze ran up her shirt cooling her, and she breathed it in as well. She took a step back with her hands still on the railing further releasing tension from the back of her legs and spine. As she shook her head from left to right tiny yellow flowered clusters caught her eye. The golden florets sprouted in patches, too small to notice from far away, but too many to examine close up.

Song # 17 Parks on Fire, Trifonic

A bee attracted to the yellow, on her and that of the flower, or maybe that of itself, attracted to what it knows and trusts, did the only thing it must do. Mina knew this was what it meant to be connected with the world, but before she could finish her thought her insides suddenly shook. It became hard to swallow and she was in full panic. Vibration tackled the tiny flower stems and they leaned to their side, saluting what seemed to be nothing all at once. There was no wind, just this strange and powerful tremble. Bass filled the air, but was too great of a sound to be from a car speaker. It filled her and made her feel hollow at the same time. She could feel it in her glands beneath her ears, in her mouth and down her throat. She had never felt anything like this. It was disagreeable and metallic; like blood on the tongue. Her face cringed in paralysis, the face made by someone listening to nails scratch a blackboard.

Her body absorbed the bang from below, radiated it outwards but only to be soaked back in and bring her to the ground. Her hair flung as she catapulted with a speed that seemed impossible to create on her own. People of the park just fell to their knees, submissively surrendering all motor control. It ended as quickly as it came, and most everyone stayed right where they landed. They were in shock, waiting for their bodily fluids to ease. Her knees were deep in her chest and she sat in a tight ball for as long as it took and then in the next second, everything returned to normal. The muscles in her face loosened and breath fully expanded her lungs. The static ended and she had control over her tongue and throat, and just like that, the beautiful afternoon of bees and buttercups resumed.

"Is everyone alright?" A bald man wearing NASCAR style sunglasses stretched his arms out as he walked to the highest part of the grass. There was no response. "I'm from California, and that was an earthquake!" He hugged a mother and two small children. Others listened but were too disoriented to speak. Cars seemed unaffected and every building in sight was erect. Mina saw that the buttercups had become straight again, and the pond too was just as it was before. Trees stood tall and still, but where were the geese? Mina stood up, shook out her Earth legs, and walked towards the gate to see them in a tight bird huddle under a blanket of trees.

Chapter 4
Even the Score

Mina walked through the front of her apartment building, instead of the back for the first time in about a month. Her first two minutes indoors were spent ripping edges off of envelopes as she tugged her mail from an overfed slot. Even with take-out in her hand, she took the stairs instead of the usual elevator. Her movements were near involuntary. She was deeply affected by the day's events. She sorted mail between fingers, keeping C-town savings and Val-Pack coupons away from the expected hospital bills, and overdue rent. She was close to $6,000 in the hole with nothing to show for it.

Upon opening her door, the sweet smell of yogurt complemented by bits of blood was all that she could taste. She scanned pieces of herself scattered around her apartment and dropped everything to clean all 757 square feet. By the time her tasks had taken her into the kitchen, her spirit had already lifted. She began to sing. Rags couldn't help but follow all of this rhythmic movement. New York City water pressure massaged her forehead and shoulders after dinner. Steam fogged the mirrors and window. She had let it run a while as she washed over the tiled walls and ledges of the bathtub. Hints of chlorine opened her sinuses and helped to wash away any fatigue. She sat at her desk in a robe to review the unrecognizable but beautiful golden envelope from the bunch. Giovanni's wedding was now on the calendar and she decided that love was good, even wrote a few lines on it.

Rest my love
in the distance.
The atmosphere will shake and split,
lingering for all eternity.
But you—

You will rest, and
those persistent echoes and reflections will
change and in case
you go backwards
in search for what's remembered—
Just rest,
avoiding change
is fear's rage
and it too will soon pass.

Mina had just lain down in her freshly made bed. Her room had been the last of it. It took an hour to distinguish dirty garments via sniff test, stuff them into a hamper and hang others up. Then her phone rang from a private number in the middle of an almost immediate sleep. She answered without deliberation.

"Hello," Mina said.

"Hi," Adam said taking his time. "How.. are you?"

"I......'m okay?" She said, but it sounded like a question, as if she was asking herself, *am I okay?* She couldn't believe it was him on the phone. "How are you?" she asked out of habit.

"Good. I didn't think you'd pick up, but I had to call to see how you were doing, after what happened today. Did you know there was an earthquake?"

"I did." She was exhausted and closed her eyes as she spoke to him. "What time is it?"

"Close to twelve."

"That's it? It feels so late. Where were you during the Earthquake?" Mina asked.

"In my office. It wasn't that bad.

"Were you on the ground?" he asked her.

"Yes."

"Oh you were. Where were you?"

"Central Park, by the pond."

"Oh wow. Were you alone when it happened?"

"Yea."

"I wanted to call you, but I didn't get a chance. You were the first person I thought of."

"I'm okay. Mina sat herself up against her headboard trying to be formal and elusive at the same time. "It was scary but beautiful, not the shaking, that wasn't very beautiful, nor was that insane bang, but there were a few of us in the park and...."

"I thought you said you were alone?" he interrupted her.

"I was. But, Adam, there were others in the park." Mina didn't say anything immediately and he too was quiet. "It was just such a humbling experience. There we were, all of us, perfect strangers with no reason to speak or even look at one another, and then panting, feeling what it's like to be at the mercy of the world. It was like nothing I have ever experienced."

"Well, I am glad you're okay."

"When it was done this guy stood up and told everyone what it was. Otherwise, I don't think I would have known. I mean, maybe eventually, but I felt like I was going to die for a minute out there."

"What do you mean?"

"I thought it might have been a heart attack, or a seizure. It happened so fast. Even if I wanted to ask for help I couldn't."

"What did you feel?"

"This sharp pulling, a constant pulling from the ground." Mina suddenly became aware of the fact that she was describing physical pain to him. Something that she wanted him to know and for some time: one because he was the sole reason she had cried herself to sleep so many nights, not just because they weren't together, but because their break-up was unsettling, or worse that what they had been doing the whole time they were together was a fraud and he refused to discuss it. He still didn't know that she *was* pregnant, and that only after a lonely and insufferable experience, she *wasn't* anymore. It had been almost three months since he told her to walk away with a straight face and there was no way to foresee this opportunity presenting itself so soon and with such an open ear.

Adam was eager to hear her speak. It didn't matter what she was going to say. It was nice to hear her voice, but only part of him was pleased having her on the phone, the other terrified. He dialed her number several times before pressing the last digit to let the call go through. He wanted to say he missed her but had no plan of executing that. He knew that she was fine and would be with or without his call after the earthquake.

"How did he know what was going on?" Adam asked about the man in the park, avoiding the heavy.

"He just told us he was from California and that it was an earthquake. Do you even know why earthquakes happen Adam?" Her posture returned to horizontal.

"Yea, I'm pretty sure. It's from a split in the Earth, right?" he asked.

"Yea, basically." Her voice was becoming less clear. She visualized a single strand of blonde hair with a split end, curling away from itself becoming thinner and thinner until nothing.

"Aw you sound sleepy? Get up, talk to me it's been so long. What else is new with you, Mina?"

"Nothing really, same."

"Anything exciting? Have you been going out?"

"Not really."

"You don't get drunk on red wine and fight in the street anymore?"

"No, she laughed. I don't see you anymore."

"What else is new then?" he continued.

"My cousin Gio is getting married."

"Mazeltov."

"Grazie." She stopped talking, fell asleep for a second and then woke up shocked. The way people wake up after falling asleep by accident on the train. "I'm tired Adam. I have to sleep."

"You're gonna have the big Italian family wedding, just like in The Godfather, with cousin Paulie, Frankie, Anthony, and John-John. The whole crews gonna be there right?"

"You've never even met my family. Remember when I invited you to the Memorial Day party and for like a month you were coming, even bringing something, but then couldn't make it last minute."

"OY Vey! Why so harsh Mina!"

"You even admitted afterwards that you regretted flaking and called yourself something like ...*a cowardice piece of shit, scared of my goomba family.*"

"I may be a coward but let's get this straight, I'm not a piece of shit, okay? Okay? OK?"

"Okay, she said with less enthusiasm than he was looking for. "Let's get something else straight then, since we're splitting hairs. If you were to meet my family, I would be the one to get the worst of it, not you."

"What's that supposed to mean?"

"Nothing."

Chapter 5
Man Alive

Song #18 Sister Winter, Sufjan Stevens

Mina woke to a breeze that carried hints of winter in it, but what did a season smell like? She sensed cinnamon and stew, and what would soon be frost blooming on windows and the ungodly sound of the radiator. It reminded her of cold mornings, the inability to remove blankets and how dark everything stayed even after one woke. Maybe it didn't smell like anything and only made a nose cold. She could smell her clean apartment but there were beginnings of winter mixed in as well. It was the smell of moisture escaping Earth's leaves, gusts that caused them to chase each other along crosswalks, and a night that fell painfully early. She glanced out the window and with the trace of her eye caught a glimpse of crisp new sheets curled around her bed. It was true. She had cleaned. No clothes everywhere. No garbage to contend with. This also meant that she cleaned the bathroom and that none of this was made up. She reached for her phone to see that she was up an hour before her alarm went off, and actually able to find her phone. She surrendered onto her pillow and smiled. Adam occurred to her. She replayed parts of their late-night conversation, but the ending was a total mystery. Mina was notorious for falling asleep on the phone. The window was cracked open for the first time in a long time and a magical chill tickled her naked body as she hopped out of the shower.

In the kitchen, she reached for the lonely farina box in an empty cabinet and made breakfast consciously, adding a little vanilla extract and cinnamon sugar. She tried to describe farina to Adam once. He said he'd rather see her cook it and to have a taste. After it was done, he said it resembled something one picks up from the bottom of the ocean. She dressed slowly, after having read her poem with coffee. She walked in and out grabbing at things to adorn herself with. She couldn't wait to get back to the Universe and work on her theory there in the Hall of Earth. The concept that she was in the world just as much as the world was in her was going to be the basis for said theory. She checked the time on her phone before getting on the subway and noticed an alert titled MNH meeting. She had completely forgotten about the meeting. It was scheduled months ago and was sure to be about funding. The museum had meetings like this once a quarter if they remembered, but nothing ever changed: they didn't have enough money. Her phone also had a text message from ASSHOLE that read: Good Morning. She hadn't remembered changing Adam's contact information to ASSHOLE, but there it was changed, and a good morning indeed.

Song# 19 Papa was a Rolling Stone, The Temptations

"Morning Roman," Mina ran up behind him after grabbing a double espresso from the café on the third floor. He was the exact person she wanted to see.

"Ah! Good morning Mina."

"I will come by and see you later, we have much to discuss," she said bouncing downstairs. She started a new log and tidied up brochures in the front lobby. She put up a sign that designated set tour times throughout the day.

"Have you been thinking about what to ask me?" Roman asked her while sitting in his secret white-on-white office.

"I didn't know I needed a question."

"Are you familiar with the Socratic Method Mina?"

"Not really, but I know who Sow-crates is."

"It's not actually pronounced that way."

"I know Roman. It's from a movie. Never mind," Mina held her face in her hands from embarrassment.

"I suggest you practice the Socratic method of inquiry anytime you feel dissatisfied with someone or something."

"Okay. You have to tell me what the first step is in adopting this method." She would have done anything he or Socrates suggested, seeing as Roman had already aided her in a prospective transformation.

"Have you been thinking about your theory?" he asked her.

"Yes."

"Then do you have a question for me?"

"Maybe. I wrote some things down last night."

"Oh, what did you write?"

"I don't know maybe a little poetry and then a list."

"I didn't know you were a poet."

"I'm not sure what it is, other than my emotions. Some people vow to stay committed to someone else, but I am vowing to remember that I have a place in this world, and I can't just stop because something unexpected happens. Oh! Speaking of which, did you feel that earthquake?"

"I didn't but I saw the news. These things happen. I remember we had one around this time last year, came from Canada. But we are lucky. This city has some of the greatest fault lines in the country, and if we were to get hit badly, one earthquake could destroy this whole city. But for now...what's your question?"

"My question," Mina laughed and looked down to sort her thoughts before she spoke. "...may not come out immediately, or even clearly. But I will try to relay to you all that I have been discovering in bits and pieces, half sentences and trains of thought that even I can't keep up with. I told you I started writing them down and even that's difficult."

"Good! That's good news," Roman said. "A teacher once told me when I was much younger, 'If a little bit of you isn't everywhere then you might as well be nowhere.' She just looked at him unsure of what to say.

"I'm just questioning everything. The usual things people probably think about I guess, like am I making decisions that are truly in line with who I am, and who I want to be?"

"Well, are you?"

"I don't know. I am still trying to get the questions right before I kill myself answering them. What I do know is that we create a world in our head that resembles the world we live in and as our existence changes, because change is our only constant, we have this need to constantly adapt. Meaning, there's no right or wrong, no one way for anything."

"Okay, but where's the question?"

"Hold on. What I am saying is that when and if we are to undergo self-analysis, we are essentially looking at something, a fracture of our existence, and we are also kind of playing god as we look, for we have suspended time to examine it. But, there can never be a pause, like ever. No matter how self-destructive we become, unless we die, nothing around, between, or in us stops. We're forever spinning energy very much in the same way molecules spin and bounce off of one another."

"Yes, this is true," he confirmed her thoughts.

Song# 20 Kingdom, Chevron

"I think I am talking about paths of life, fate, and spirituality, Roman."

"Fate? Roman made a bewildered face. "You asked me about religion the other day, and I told you science leaves very little room for a system of beliefs like that. Scientist's don't set things in stone, that's not what they do. Their efforts give a voice to the interpretation of what would otherwise be incomprehensible. And, if something, anything, big or small, can be explained through experiment, then fate," he made air quotations with his fingers. "...is no longer reliable."

"Right, I get that Roman. What I am saying is that it is dependable. I am not using it to determine anything or even live by. It's just that for the first time I am trying to understand why we as people are predisposed to being a certain way. Before going home last night, I got takeout and this guy came up to me stroking his hair, already in conversation that in the time it took to make eye contact, we were talking about cellular division, meanwhile every television covered the Earthquake! He was so involved in what he wanted to say that nothing else mattered, not even an earthquake."

"You met someone?" Roman asked his questions separately. "A complete stranger? Last night?" He paused. "While you were getting takeout, who wanted to talk to you about cellular division?"

"Yes, but that's not the point. That was just where he was stuck."

"What was he saying?"

"Oh God how should I remember, the whole time he was talking I was thinking of how much effort people put into understanding one other, using their dull and narrow findings to make sense of who they are, and what they think they know. Like I said, this stuff that I have in my head may not make sense when it comes out, but I'm trying Roman. And, I think I understand one thing now that I didn't before. People are conflicted, divided, and unhappy, mostly through their own doing. They pin themselves up against a wall with expectation, a line in the sand, extreme exaggerations of the truth resulting in war, but none of this mirrors our existence. We should just do what feels right, listen more, and trust ourselves. Like in the park yesterday a crisis was happening: our planet's floor was opening and shaking everything on it, and right before I fell to my knees, I was watching a bee search for pollen, doing the only thing that makes sense, the only thing that matters, in spite of everything else." She looked up at the clock. "I have to go Roman. I can explain more later."

Chapter 6
Back to Basics

Mina found herself in the center of a bustling lobby full of people. Docents, cashiers researchers, even retail staff she wasn't familiar with, chatting between T-rex and the Brontosaurus brothers. Their anxious eyes bounced back and forth between the great-coffered ceilings and conversation. They shifted their weight from left and right legs, neurotically sipping on Starbucks in an airy prison of massive columns and beasts. It was the first time Mina heard of this fear of lay-offs that everyone else seemed to be consumed with. Of course she remembered the museums transition to an *At Will Employer* and the packet of legal nonsense that followed, but was convinced it was going to be more of the same. Besides, she was eager for the miniature blueberry muffins and croissants sure to be at the meeting. With one hour to meeting time, she took visitors through the wonders of natural history starting with the beginning: Dinosaurs. She pulled out the old fun facts, '*A Tyrannosaurus rex only has a life-span of about 28 years!*' Most of these were lifted word for word from mandated videos downloaded from the MNH website. *Africa was the cradle of humanity*, she paraded through corridors spewing off this kind of jargon in the way Korean manicurists sing pop songs. The cognition is subterraneous like the learned hand positions and muscle memory necessary to type well on a keyboard. It sounded easy, but in order to do anything well in a complex society, adaptation has no end. Each experience becomes a manageable part to a well-organized system, in the way keystrokes become words and words build sentences to express something as non-linear and formless as thoughts.

~ ~ ~

Song # 21 All The Little Pieces, Louis XIV

She was asked to clean her locker but couldn't leave without one final walk through. She put on the lonely sweatshirt once forgotten in her small cubby. It had the perfect sized pockets for stolen grapes she took on the way out. Her head was beginning to ache from a caffeine crash, lockjaw, and disappointment. The minor detail that renting an apartment is one small step away from homelessness is the other side of the shiny coin that attracts people to a city like New York.

She made her way up the stairs with cinderblocks for shoes. She wanted to talk to Roman. She needed to know certain things and it seemed like he was the only one who could figure them out.

"Cold? Roman asked her.

"No."

"Why are you wearing your sweatshirt and hood?"

"I can't wear a hood?"

"You can. Just asking why. I haven't seen you wear a hooded sweatshirt at work before."

"Well I don't work here anymore so right you are again, Roman. How do you hit it on the head every time?" She pulled out a new stash of grapes from her left pocket. "Want a grape? I should warn you. They're pity grapes. They're the kind of grapes you give someone just before you tell them they no longer have a job.

"There were lay-offs today?"

"Yea. The museum doesn't have the money so they're downsizing."

"I know that," he said to her obvious statement. "They've been crying broke for years now."

"Yes well today is the day they decided to do something about it. Lucky day! It just keeps getting harder. I can't catch a fucking break man!" She turned to the side to look away. It wasn't so much that she didn't want to be seen crying. It was too late for that, but she was determined to not let this bring her down. She focused as hard as she could on one rust colored stripe in the image of Saturn's rings to the point that it was no longer the likeness of a planet. "My grandmother used to say, 'Oh man alive!' in moments of exasperation, and although I've never used it before, I keep repeating it in my mind. I'm trying hard to keep it together but it just seems like nothing is working. What does it take to just live? I'm not one of these robotic fools taking up space in a cubicle. Sure I can learn more, but I don't think I'm worse than any one else that all this shit should be happening to me like this."

"Slow down Mina. It's every department. Scientists are experiencing the same thing. It's scary on all fronts. And it's not great, but nothing is easy and that is just the way it is. Don't get bent out of shape, or kid yourself that you could have done something to prevent this."

"You knew there going to be lay-offs?"

"Not today, I didn't. But, yea sure, it's the only way to get an immediate solution to a long-standing problem. Now, if they were a bit more organized or proactive rather than reactionary, these kinds of upsets wouldn't be so devastating, but that is not the kind of organization we work for. They've even talked of cutting spending on projects they've only approved last year," he threw his hands up.

"One year is no time at all to get something done. Getting funding isn't easy, but allocation is much harder, but this shouldn't stress you out. You are young and these things happen. I've been fired and laid off several times and in the end, it was always for the better. It's opportunity presented in a slightly different package. Take what you've learned here and move on. You can always come back and volunteer, and it's not like you can't visit. You'll find something, especially with this on your resume, besides these days it's really more about who you know rather than what you know, and I am sure a woman like yourself is savvy on the internet and social media. You must have a long list of friends, surely some big shot can help you find a great position with one email."

"Even my time with big shots has come to an end."

"Is this what we've been talking about? A break-up?"

"Yes. Although I would hardly call it a break up, in fact, it was a lot more like a lay-off. It's safe to say I was laid off twice this year." Mina cracked a smile and grabbed more grapes. "That's exactly it! He was of a financial mind and I was too volatile for investment."

"Mina, break-ups are extremely painful, but the sooner that you realize there's nothing you can do to change the way other people feel, the better things will be for you. You know that bee you mentioned before? Do you know why bees do what they do?"

"No." Mina's eyes swelled with tears.

"Don't be sad. This is how we grow. When height can no longer be measured in lines on a bedroom wall and the same shoe size can be purchased with regularity, there has to be a way for us to continue to evolve. But of course you understand this because I heard it in what you were talking about before."

"You did?"

"Yes," Roman began to laugh. "You were trying to discover why we are connected or drawn to others and the reasons we act the way we do. I want to give you an answer. I don't think it's the only one, but it's certainly one answer to your question: Hormones. They are in everything and a part of what charges us to be connected to others. They digest our food and send messages to all of our cells so that our biological systems function. Plants, flowers and even trees have DNA and this is what allows them to release hormones. They even ripen the fruit we eat! In nature nothing is inconsequential. We, at the top of the food chain frequently forget this. And to your point, hormones are responsible for the behavior of bees. If a bee, any bee, stopped getting hormones from the queen bee, it wouldn't know what to do. She renders all other female bees infertile with a steady release of hormones so that her colony isn't compromised. Pretty remarkable, right?"

"Yes, and that you know all of this."

"Hormones and DNA are the greatest creators of life Mina. They are the divine intelligence that connects us all. They are responsible for everything as we know it. Don't speak too soon, you did catch a break: the world shifted and parts of the Earth moved for you to witness. It might have been just the break you needed to understand that human suffering is kind of a self-perpetuated experience and at the same time infinitesimal in the grand scheme of things."

"I don't know what that means, Roman."

"What don't you know? The meaning of infinitesimal?"

"Well yes, but also I just don't understand how to get along, how to fit all of me into one category. I don't want to be one way or another, and why do these types of decisions burden our life? I wish that I, or we weren't so conflicted with this way of thinking or behaving. It may be selfish, but I just want to trust that people are who they say they are, that they mean well, and not just to me, but to everyone."

"This isn't something that can be rushed, and not that I am wishing you bad luck in love or personal experiences, but try to remember the things we've discussed. Don't get discouraged if for some reason you feel like this yet again, because this is a process and it happens at every stage of life, in fact several times in one life. Remember to write down all of your theories. They are good, and that part about change being constant, and our effortless spinning mirroring tiny molecules; you are right. We are constantly changing and so keeping the eye, or interest of one person is a challenging prospect for all of us, even staying fond of our own personality is a tall task, but this may be too much to take in right now. Just go home and think of today as a day off."

"Day?"

"I was laid off."

"Yes, but just take the day off from everything."

Chapter 7
Say When

Song # 22 Smell Memory, Mum

One day off turned into several days. She had to fight the three strongest words she ever knew: *not good enough*. It didn't even sound right to her, but it was all she could say as she packed her things. All of her adult efforts were, just not good enough. Not her degree, earned by teeth gritting coffee binges and note card memorization. Two years submersed in the less than artistic efforts of the East: Chinese Dynasties, the colors of India, Africa, and Persia, all gray to her now. She was going to be living back at home like a child, despite all else. Purging, as is done when downsizing a 1 bedroom apt to a single room is like re-watching a chunk of one's own life on a timeline. She was reminded of prosperity through photos, clothing, and just collections of stuff. So many useless items had been purchased just because she could. This is what humans do, create and consume things in order to bottle up an experience and keep it forever. The restaurant industry had been good to her back then. She was young, starting out as a hostess smiling for no reason, looking pretty as she did her best to impress those that frequented her resume's upscale eateries. But she soon bloomed, carving her own epicurean intelligence, still wearing an apron and getting the most out of a fine dining wallet, to then one day making an amazing connection and scoring a job at MNH.

Negativity lurked and moved in on her perception, asking her in its subtle way, to do things for it. Close inspection destroyed any glimmer of freedom this kind of de-cluttering could provide. Sometimes she muscled through it, like the anticipation of a hill on a regular jogging route, but even that proved especially difficult because it was her voice in her head. Some days passed without a word, yet even fighting depression became a pattern and her resistance magnetized more reason to be upset. One tireless night in her new home slash old bedroom, after kissing her parents goodnight and feeling like she owed them her life, she wrote a poem determined to leave this bullshit behind her.

Adverbs fill the void —
on billboards and inside, reducing all that is—
to just one image— justified, and privileged.
Neon's burn in daylight, lyrics educate, butt plugs and bootleggers
inspire an –ism so great.
It capitalizes each letter, N then Y, and C, for a most criticized city.

Jumping yellow jacks buzz a price for duty,
while the performing community
catch waves of change in the subway.
Quarantined in a state of renting. Symbiotic and small
It's a jump and shuffle made musical.

Sailors make the most of their hours—local dry cleaners kill themselves
for a dollar.
People eat publicly and on foot
Bells sound doors of shops while protestors shout.
Nike sneakers hanging and graffiti encases whole buildings—
like pigeons on stonewalls or puddles 'round fountains:
These things and their belongings.

A photograph prints it all, but there's more:
a winter burn, summer's stench,
screeching trestles and steam coming from underneath.
Pristine public profiles still mix like liquor in and around the dirt-poor.
Pennies and metro-cards, a single boot, gum, and free art sparkle—
Even glass shards find home in the floor.

Hydrants and yellow curb, commercial vehicles only
No standing in front of church, holiness and limitation.
Couples take turns moving cars for night regulation.
Living in scaffolding and poles that construct,
A landlord waits for pay and there is none.
Like licorice on the tongue, it's too much at once.
A lint-filled land of lust, losers, and luck, magically monotonous,
moronic and moot, majestic as Mecca, but a money making mogul.
Noteworthy, no, more like needy. Each one here dreams to be.
Saying you're someone you're not, while roaches feast where you walk.
Concierge, terrace views, door-to-door delivery — all just temporary.

Simple pains long for permanence
in stalls of love and rhyme—
now or never in this transient ogre.
Her story is scratched in wood
and telling you why, right there
between a God's letter
and numbers for a good time.

~ ~ ~

Joseph her father was a curious man who didn't ask any questions. That was left to his wife. He had opinions and judgments but they came from listening to Marzia's conversations with his daughters. Joseph didn't help Mina with her things. He rarely if ever ventured out of Brooklyn. He paid for the movers that did it for her, and Mina helped them more than she needed to. To their surprise she traveled to Brooklyn with them in their box truck. Riding with her things just made sense and didn't occur to her as odd. With one long exhale she walked up the same staircase she'd known since she was a child. Nearly everything about the house was the same, save for that dreaded new sound system. She carried the last of it and with a final knee crawl onto her bed reduced six years from her life.

It didn't deny all of her capabilities but it wasn't that far off either. It was about to be November. Carmella had come over to help her get organized and adjusted, and to talk about her first-born, Sophia, and her many accomplishments in first grade. Carmella advised Mina to live rent-free. She was in a selfish pursuit of assistance to aid her with her two small children. Mina woke up the next day completely unbothered by her mother and father. She gazed at the honey locust tree from her bedroom window. The golden teardrop leaves flickered brilliance. It was unusual, but maybe her parents understood what she was going through, or at least understood that she was going through something and let her be. Williamsburg was at one point a scary neighborhood, but by now had turned into a cool place to live. After college, Mina stayed in Saratoga for three years and yes, she noticed the influx of a younger more artistic breed in the people of the L train in her home visits, but hadn't thought of her neighborhood as a place to be. As she looked out her window at the tree, still half asleep, she knew it was time to get reacquainted. It was the last stretch of 2006: family and holidays. In the first couple of weeks, she spent the better of her morning hours just walking with Rags learning new sights and smells.

Song #23 This Charming Man, The Smiths

She made her way to the river, zigzagging through unrecognizable streets. There were people and shops, restaurants, bars, galleries, woodshops and glassworks studios, and to her surprise colorful graffiti everywhere. Beautiful women and other characters took up entire walls and repeated messages and inside jokes. She even started to recognize autographs. The impressions of spray paint lured her and each frame of the eye had its own special composition. Playful street side bathtubs had been repurposed into planters. They shouted things like, *save me, keep me, take me home, and make me yours*. Random freestanding toilets were additional homes for colorful flowers and gave this once industrial neighborhood an ironic sense of community. Hydrants were painted colorful patterns and seemed to sprout from cement like flowers ready for a photograph.

She turned around at the bridge to walk back on Berry St, passing Brooklyn Bar, never to be confused with B Bar. The folks that partied here were the original bikers, even before the gays cultivated this neighborhood from the wasteland it was fast becoming in the eighties. Their wind blown tattoos were blurred from years of drinking. The neighborhood's shift had made their love for beat up leather and handlebar mustaches the minority. The people that she glanced at now in the daytime seemed to say, *pick me, pick me, pick me,* and other such desperate things, but not pathetically. Cafés and restaurants were always lively with the young and they sat in sidewalk pens for the best pastime: people watching. Like her, they wandered on Bedford at all times of the day, borrowing apartment stoops for seats.

The word hipster may have started because it was hip, but also Williamsburg was just too long of a word to add anything to it. The one thing these inhabitants did not look was healthy. Their blood did not meet the backside of their skin for a natural glow of pink. They were long, lanky and white, like the awful winter sky with no sign of recovery. They ventured to New York from places like Ohio, Minnesota, and Wisconsin, and it drove Mina mad. She wondered why on Earth nobody stayed in Ohio and repeated a joke that perhaps it was a state of grandparents and other elders left behind, now holding signs that said:

BROOKLYN → THIS WAY

Women tried a bit too hard for her taste, squeezing into skinny jeans and clicking their heels thin against cement. There were a number of professionals living there as well, but after a few PBR's and white lines they just as easily fogged Union Pool's windows radiating their stench in dance. They were creators of looks; bloggers reiterating what was in, or gossip queens who gained notoriety spending their day writing half-witted sentences about who was who and where they could be stalked in New York. This generation used social media as a selling point for themselves and brand awareness on something they called a global scale. They hopped on the L every morning and collectively created the quintessential NYC consumer experience for the time they had their hands in it. They created what was accepted as cool, ate as delicious, desired as a function of convenience, any look that was bought and sold, even forecasting what retrograde unforgettables would return to the limelight. They retouched photos, wrote book and food reviews, dressed mannequins and filled blank space on nearly everything a commuter could glance at. Some were lucky enough to have an expertise in shoe and jewelry design, or spent hours on digital media making such designers popular through cross marketing in cosmetics, fashion, publishing, retail, and the ever-growing not-for-profit industry. It worked for the most part: coolness sold, regardless of how out of touch and little access these wannabes had with the globe.

They were for the most part non-conforming conformists, yet instead of noticing their own irony, sitting pretty in cubicles face-booking hometown friends to keep up the presentation of NYC, they focused on a subpar class struggle with newcomers. It was similar to the mentality of those leaning on a bar-top with a drink in hand, still refusing to accommodate thirsty attempts from others to get a bartender's attention. There was no end in sight to Williamsburg's growing population. Mina could sense that this was just the beginning, like the process of growing out one's hair: so much effort to reach chin length but beyond that, the weight of itself was a cause *and* effect to sustained growth. Naturally, Williamsburg had its veterans. These folks had had their fair share of shitty apartments, mice infestations, but were finally in a place they called home, making good money and actually involved in the world, perhaps starting a business here to give back to a community they loved so much. McCarren Park was a good sized park on both sides of Driggs and a meeting place for all. The west side was the concrete baseball field mainly used by sculpted Spanish and African American men, cut in half by a basketball court where the Hassidic Jews ran and flapped their Tzitzit like bicycle streamers as they took their shots. The grassy east side of the park hosted weekly football or soccer games and a brand new track for the athletically inclined. And just like every high school lawn, it too was comprised of cliques. The break-dancers practiced flips and one-armed handstands on the turf next to the Italians throwing curses with bocce balls in a cloud of cigar smoke. People took cues from each other and went wherever there was a crowd, at least for now before winter really started.

Despite this diversity, almost everyone had a tattoo, if not a collection, one in progress, or a well constructed plan for their sleeve. All too often though, they were hackneyed wall images like sailor's sparrows, anchors, or unintelligible stickers of things like a cupcake. These simple blue-black images, whether a memory of particular fondness or reminder they needed, started conversations and gave birth to love and understanding. And for a minute people did fall in love, with the night and each other, with Williamsburg and themselves for being there. They forgave debauchery, bad poetry, caffeine crashes, and slow roasted pork contaminating the vegan air. Brooklyn Bar, now Mina's favorite, probably because they had free refills on their peanut bowls and also the no-name boxer that frequented the bar made her think of Adam. The floor and sidewalk out front were always covered with a fine layer of crushed shells. But these weren't the only things left behind on the sidewalk and street. From corner to corner throughout the Burg, there was always someone wishing to sell their neatly organized goods on a blanket that they would at the end of their sale take home to sleep on. Not just because they needed the money, but this act was their public cleansing and passersby couldn't help themselves. Trying on dirty hats and shoes, they showed their friend just how cute some used ashtray was and that friend was already holding a book that they loved so much and had somehow lost years before. The lunchboxes and old backpacks that were in style when Mina was in grade school were everywhere as was all of the nostalgic plastic jewelry, snap on bracelets, retro game systems, old clothing, fixtures, and books. Things she nearly forgot about, had they not popped up in this new place that she had always called home. She didn't know why anyone here would want these things, but here they were desired and showcased in windows as if they were new. No amount of silence could break their bond, like a sister that returns after moving away, Mina accepted Williamsburg and every square under her feet, in front and around her belonged just as it was.

~ ~ ~

"I'm glad you came over. I never got to see you when you were in the city, plus I could really use your help," Carmella said as she opened her front door. Carmella's brand new jeans were pleated and were the first thing Mina noticed. She was also wearing a loosely knitted pumpkin colored top. It was of course the quintessential color for the fall season. Carmella was good at being festive to the point that she may have been obsessed with presentation.

"Yea, well I'm a wreck," Mina said looking at her sister's family photos. "When was this?" She held up a photo from the hallway.

"Mimi!!" Sophia, Carmella's only daughter ran to squeeze her aunt's legs.

"Sophia be careful you don't want to knock her over," Carmella said as she pulled her off. "Why don't you show Aunt Mimi your pretty dress?"

"You have a pretty dress?" Mina feigned enthusiasm.

"I do. I picked it out all by myself. Do you wanna come upstairs and play fashion show with me?"

"Oh boy," Mina said with wide eyes looking at Carmella while Sophia's small fingers lead her upstairs.

"I'm wearing it for Aaron's birthday party," Sophia said in song as she twirled and grabbed beads from her dresser to put around Mina's head. Mina bowed without a word to wear princess jewelry. She peeked around the very pink bedroom to see a plastic wrapped pink polka-dotted dress hanging on a closet door.

"Is this your dress darling?" Mina was now speaking in song as well.

"Yes. It's hanging in the car."

"The car?" Mina asked.

"Yes. We're going shopping, and you're big sister. We're playing house, and you have to help me get the babies in their car seats so we can drive." Mina looked down to see two baby carriers stuffed with dolls and lined up perfectly.

"Okay," Mina said as she sat cross-legged on the fluffy pink rug. She felt just fine pretending she was big sister, taking a ride in this plush pink room. Sophia made car sounds as she turned an imaginary wheel. Mina released one of the babies to inspect the doll's details.

"You can't take her out now big sister. We're driving." Sophia got out of her pretend driver's seat, and put the baby back in her car seat.

"Where are we going?" Mina couldn't stop laughing.

"We're going shopping, silly."

"We are?" Mina had no experience as a big sister.

"Yes. We have to buy things for the house. Make sure you have your seat belt on. We don't drive unless you put your seat belt on." Sophia put her hands on her hips.

"I can't go shopping now though, Soph. Mom needs my help downstairs. Can you put your dress on for me? I'll get it down and you can be in a fashion show."

Mina and Sophia walked downstairs to find Carmella on the phone, but the minute she saw Sophia wearing her party dress she ordered her to go upstairs and take it off.

"Who's Aaron?" Mina asked Carmella as she hung up.

"Oh, a friend from school. I swear to God these parents make such a big deal out of everything. This kid is having his birthday party at DanceWave. Aha! Carmella laughed out loud. "Look at your face." She pointed to Mina and hit her own forehead. "You're like what in the hell is DanceWave?"

"What the hell is DanceWave? And can I go?"

"It's a dance studio slash party room that rents out space for kiddie dance parties. You can choose from all these different musical themes. But of course that wouldn't be enough, Nooooo. The Bergman's are hiring a DJ. He's turning seven, Mina."

"So..."

"So, it's a little ridiculous! You have any idea what kind of money they are spending?"

"No."

"A lot!" Carmella shouted.

"Well, she is going to be pretty in pink, literally. And Aaron as her Duckie?" Mina asked.

"Duckie?" It was over Carmella's head. She took out a whisk and didn't think anything of it. "Now, I have to bake, because Soph volunteered to bring treats to school tomorrow. Wasn't that so sweet of her?" Carmella rolled her eyes.

"How's Baby Michael?"

"So much better, finally able to sleep. Actually he's napping right now. Let me check on him. Can you beat two eggs into this bowl, after you put the mix in though." She opened a cabinet and placed a brownie box next to her blue bowl. "I'll be right back." Mina opened the fridge for eggs. There was so much food, all in their separate corners. It seemed as though all twenty-four water bottles from the case were there. She popped open blueberries and helped herself. Finally locating the eggs and balancing them between tiles on the counter, she read the ingredients from the back of the brownie box.

"He's out like a light," Carmella said returning to the kitchen. "I am so happy. I think he's finally over this cold, and thank God Sophia didn't get sick."

"Yea he's been sick a while now, huh?"

"Yea but its fine. I went through the same shit with Sophia when she was his age."

"But so what's up with you, didn't you say you were a wreck?"

"Oh yea, I'm alright though, played big-sister upstairs with a pink dress. Somehow it doesn't matter that much anymore, ya know."

"Bullshit, tell me what's wrong. You only call me when you need to talk, so out with it!"

"I don't even know where to start."

"Is it about a guy?"

"Yea, there was that. I was seeing a guy, but I'm not anymore. I was also pregnant with his baby but that's also not the case anymore. What else...? Oh right, remember I got that awesome job at the museum. I'm not working there anymore either."

"Jeez. Give me that bowl. I don't want you making my brownies with that kind of luck." Mina just stood there feeling worse than before she started talking.

"Ohh I am kidding." Carmella tried to rectify her comments with a smile. "Did you have an abortion?"

"No. I miscarried." Mina walked to the other side of the counter.

"Oh no! I had a miscarriage, once, before Sophia. I'm so sorry you had to go through that. It's so bad. I thought I was going to die. I didn't even know if I was going to be able to carry again, but then we kept trying and all was fine. It's quite common actually."

Mina patted the top of her own head, unsure of what to say. She fingered the crinkle in her forehead and felt a tiny hair protruding from between her eyebrows. She heard an audible vibration as she rubbed it with her fingertip.

"Mina? Where the hell did you just go?" Carmella asked snapping her fingers in front of Mina's face.

"Shh! Listen,"

"To your forehead?"

"Yea listen." Mina walked closer playing her hair instrument into Carmella's ear. Carmella just stared at her, not sure of what to make of the entire scene and the face of concentration that had Mina cross-eyed. Mina just kept on stroking as she walked back to her seat and then started laughing hysterically.

"Maybe you could just get waxed so you don't have hairs growing out of your forehead?" Carmella said as she opened the oven to see if it was on. "There's tweezers in the upstairs bathroom, if you want to take care of it yourself."

"This guy I was just mentioning, Adam. He was the worst, a really hairy Jew, both on his chest and back and in strange patterns. He used to get his whole upper body waxed."

"He had to wax his whole chest and back?

"I don't know actually. I never saw him that hairy, but it must have been bad for him to have to get waxings. He used to get so red too. I once saw him right after a waxing. Wait, I think I have a photo of what he looked like."

"Nooo! Let me see."

"He let me take one." Mina grabbed her phone from her back pocket to browse through her pictures. "It's sick."

"What the hell is this? Mina was talking to herself as she selected a video recording that had no image, only darkness. She pressed play and heard Adam's voice.

"HULLO, There appears to be a receiver off the hook."

"Oh my God, do you remember that recording? It played when the phone wasn't hung up correctly?" Mina asked as she paused the recording.

"I don't think so. Carmella wasn't laughing. She didn't understand what was funny. Mina resumed play on the video.

"Please check all extensions, hang up, and try your call again later. Thank you."

"You really don't remember the recording that used to play when you left the phone off the hook?"

"No!" Carmella shouted because of the questions she was being asked.

"Here's really great at impersonations like this."

"Why would he record that on your phone?"

"He's a maniac. I have no idea."

"You make music with eyebrow hair and he records off-the-hook messages on your phone. Thank God you're not having kids," Carmella said.

"You're so right. But, I still want to talk to him," Mina exhaled. "I want to call him so badly."

"When was the last time you two spoke?"

"He called me a couple of weeks ago. Shit I don't even know. When was the Earthquake?"

"Maybe a month or so," Carmella shrugged her shoulders.

"So, we haven't really spoken but that doesn't mean anything? Actually, I can't remember how we got off the phone when we did talk. But I don't want to have to tell him that I left the city to come back home."

"Speaking of which, how has it been?" Carmella asked buttering her pan.

"It's fine. I am probably going to gain like thirty pounds with Thanksgiving around the corner, then Christmas. I'm just gonna let myself go, Carm. I'm just gonna let my uni-brow grow really long until I can braid it, and maybe while I'm at it I can be like everyone else in the burg: I'll boycott shaving. Maybe connect my uni-brow braid to armpit hair. It will be a totally new look.

"Stop it. What's your plan for work?" Carmella lifted the bowl to pour out her batter.

"Some café not far from the house, and I met this guy that owns a gallery that may need me for events. It's a shitty gallery, but I haven't even tried that hard to find anything better. We'll see."

"So wait, the last time you spoke to Adam was right after the Earthquake and he hasn't called you since?"

"No."

"Not even a text? Does he know about the miscarriage?"

"No, thank God. No. Wait, he did send me a good morning text the day after we spoke."

"And you didn't write anything back?"

"No," Mina laughed. "That was the day I got laid off."

"Do you love him?"

"I don't know, anymore."

"Did you tell him that you loved him?"

"No. I knew I loved him though, when I realized I wanted him to tell me."

"When you wanted him to tell you that *he* loved you?"

"Yes."

"That, and I was going to tell him what I saw when I rubbed my eyes to scratch them," Mina said.

"What?" Carmella stopped rinsing her dishes and faced her sister.

"You know when you rub your eyes to scratch them? Mina asked sincerely.

"Yea."

"You know what you see?"

"I don't see anything," Carmella laughed. "My eyes are closed."

"Well, I see black and white circles, and spirals, and rows of geometric shapes repeating hundreds of times. It doesn't matter, when I found myself wanting him to know what I saw from rubbing my eyes I knew that, while we weren't perfect, I wanted to share everything with him."

"Mina you might be insane. How did things end if you felt so strongly?"

"They just did and it sucks. I don't always think of it like I did when we first parted, but times like this, when the memory of him makes me laugh and talk about him as if you care to hear these pointless stories." Mina pointed to Carmella. "I just want to call him and be like, *Hey, remember that time when you did that thing, how are you? That was really funny. I really miss you. When can we see each other?"*

"Show me his photo," Carmella demanded.

"Oh right, duh." Mina scrolled through her phone's photos. Carmella opened the oven to slide the brownie pan inside. She waited for the picture resting her head in her hands.

"You know, Meen, you don't have to tell him anything at all about your life." She paused collecting her thoughts. "When you call him, you are living the life of your dreams, for all he knows. And he's the one missing out." She made a face as if she had said something brilliant.

"Here I got it!" Mina turned her phone towards Carmella so she could view the awful photo. They laughed at how red and spotty he was.

"Well he is very attractive despite the blotches. How old is he?"

"My age."

"He looks older, not in a bad way though." Carmella handed the phone back.

"I know. He's probably the prettiest man I've ever dated."

"I can't believe what I'm hearing. I've called you a man-eater to maybe every single one of my friends. You always have a new someone that you're seeing."

"They were all just friends Carmella! You know that," Mina defended her past.

"Friends my ass! This one seems a bit more vain than the others though," Carmella pointed to the phone. "You don't want a man like that."

"They really were friends," Mina said again. "...And Adam is super vain."

"Do you have any more of him?" Mina shook her head no. "You know, I always wanted to be more like you, completely independent, not at all bothered by someone else's wants. I couldn't imagine things not going right for you, Meen. You always seem to know exactly what you want and why, and then go for it."

"Maybe I should just email him?" Mina asked.

"You see what I mean? Here I am talking and you're figuring out the best way to do what you want anyway. Maybe you should call or email him, but remember that you owe him nothing. Don't concern yourself with what he thinks of your life. I can guarantee that he's the one that misses you."

Song #24 Fly, Holly Miranda

Part 3

"There's nowhere you can be that isn't where you're meant to be..."

—John Lennon

Chapter 1
The Invitation

November's sundown chased people into the next day making her first afternoon shift at Atlas café an easy one. She drank espressos while she worked and opened cabinets just because she could. She ran fingertips along grooves in the wooden counter top and watched people do what they do. The place had one large antique mirror, a few street signs, and maps covering every last bit of wall space. Even the tables had old maps shellacked to them. It was a traveling café even though most of the regulars lived within walking distance. Beth, her fellow barista, was so ghastly white that her skin barely veiled the blue running underneath. She wore a sensible black bra with straps as thick as a sweatband under a black tank top to hold down the ten extra pounds she knew as breasts. Her hands produced skinny feminine fingers that were marked with hundreds of tiny wrinkles. They were like beat up leather bought for the second or third time, as most everything was in this part of town. A bluish black residue lived under her fingernails permanently from her weekly hair dying sessions. The space behind Atlas' counter was extremely narrow. Mina either plastered Beth with her backside or slammed her own back into the counter to make room for Beth's bulbous breasts. A French bulldog and owner came by like clockwork for one cappuccino, a fried egg and water in an aluminum container. It only took a few weeks for Mina to anticipate orders. Late morning around eleven on weekdays brought in the rush. Atlas easily housed ten construction workers at once, but that was pushing maximum occupancy. Their arrival was always unwelcome and disrupted those plugging away at their keyboards. They came in exhaling their last drag of tobacco wearing matching neon yellow vests talking into their Nextel phones. The bleeps and chirps of their walkie-talkies bounced off the ceiling and punctuated their requests. Mina could hear cement delivery times, four bacon egg and cheese, marble and granite slab measurements, 4 iced coffees, three light and sweet, one no sugar, three tuna salad, 2 pesto chicken, and the consensus in their upset: General contractors, real estate investors, and Bloomberg himself were hungrier for these new condos to be sold than these builders were for lunch. Williamsburg was facing a carving of sorts. Construction companies, large and small, as well as young entrepreneurs had taken out hefty loans with plans of building and selling modern luxury high-rise condos at Manhattan prices. These plans never had current residents in mind and were steadily being implemented as savagely as some of American history's infamous relocations. Mina walked into her house after happy hour to find her mother on the phone. This was usually the case now that the wedding was every conversation. Grace carried on uninterrupted into the receiver while Marzia had full conversations with Mina.

"You got a letter today in the mail, Marzia said to her daughter. Mina unraveled her scarf grabbed the letter from the counter and walked upstairs. The envelope had the same forwarding label as the rest of her mail but no sender.

Dear Mina,

I miss you so much, but that is not why I'm writing though. I have wanted to tell you that for some time now, and I've spent enough time writing and rewriting this letter to know that there is no good time to write it, or to add it to a sentence. I just have to put it at the beginning and then say it once more. I miss you. I wanted to write you an email, but after much debate I knew that requesting to see you in person was going to be better than any email would have been. I hope you can understand. Allowing myself to be vulnerable is something I am currently working on.

I thought about a lot since we last spoke or rather I have been thinking about a lot because we no longer speak. I am sorry that I did not handle things between us well. You deserve so much more than I gave you and for that I am sorry. But I am requesting that you come meet me at an event. I will be honored to have you there.

I really want you to come, but completely understand if your wishes are to not talk to me, and if that is the case, please allow me to express to you again how sorry I am that I left things the way I did between us. You are an incredible person, Mina. You deserve everything you've wanted from life. I mean it, and I hope to see you there.

Take Care,
Adam

A post card invitation was attached to the letter and stamped from a company called Landmark Education. The event was in a week.

~ ~ ~

Her father walked in and filled the downstairs with sitcom voices and canned laughter. Landmark's website was a bunch of copy about living an extraordinary life and melodramatic testimonials from people who had participated in the workshops. Her search for real reviews only brought up exaggerations from those fond of ranting and over-usage of the word *cult*. She gave up reading through the stupidity when her mother called her down.

"So who sent you a letter?" Marzia asked.

"Oh just a friend.

"That's nice, they sent you a letter. No one sends letters anymore, it's always email and that texting."

"Well, not this one, they keep it kosher."

"Kosher, they're Jewish?"

"No," Mina felt like an idiot for making such a joke, but why, it wasn't like Adam was going to meet them. She tried her best to fix the conversation. "It's an expression, Ma."

"No it's not. It's what Jews eat. That's what kosher is, ask your father he knows. Joe, we're gonna sit down for dinner."

"Your father knows what?" He asked taking his seat.

"Ma, I know it's what Jews eat, I'm not confused. I'm just saying..."

"Jews?" Joe interrupted Mina. "Why are we talking about what Jews eat? Gefilte Fish. Gross," he made a disgusted face. "Who eats fish from a jar?"

"Dad, have you ever heard someone say, 'Keep it kosher?"

"Yea, Jews."

"Oh my God. Look sometimes people say, keep it kosher, as in keep it right in the traditional sense of things, and they don't have to be Jewish to say it." The family ate from their plates without saying anything for a few minutes.

"Well Jewish or not it's nice to have friends that write letters. What's their name?" Marzia asked Mina.

"Who?" Joe asked.

"Her friend," Marzia caught her husband up to speed.

"Which friend?" Mina shoved rigatoni through her face.

"How is your friend from back in the day? You's two would never go to sleep and drove me and your mother crazy." Joe waved the air in front of his face.

"Francine?"

"Would you stop changing the subject, Joe?"

"So, who wrote the letter?"

"His name is Adam."

"Adam! He is Jewish." Mina hated herself for not changing his name.

"He's allowed to talk to you?" Joe asked.

"Yea. Dad, we're not living in ancient times."

"It's still the same for them Mina. You know that. They don't like change," Marzia said.

"That's why all their people are a little... ya know... cookoo," Joe said curling his index finger around his temple. "They like keeping things in the same gene pool if you know what I mean."

"He's not Hassidic, Dad."

"Did you like this boy Mina? Marzia asked with a tone that suggested she knew something, like she had read the letter and resealed it. Mina rolled her eyes to say no, but was caught up in the possibility of her mother having actually read the letter that her head-shaking was unconvincing. "Well you're sticking up for him, like you do," Marzia grabbed some bread and laughed at herself. "So..."

"Who are we talking about Marzia?" Joe asked.

"Adam, a friend of Mina's, wrote her a letter today, probably telling her that he misses her. They knew each other from the city.

"Ma! How would you know what he wrote to me?"

"Jews don't like Italians, Marzia." Joe poured himself wine.

"Mother's know everything."

"Well, what is he doing now?" Joe asked.

"Still living in the neighborhood, working, I guess."

"When's the last time you saw this boy Mina?"

"We haven't seen each other since I moved."

"You's two can easily take a train if you wanted to. It isn't that far. If he wants to see you, he should take a train to see you, and meet your parents," Joe softened his tone and getting to the heart of the matter.

"My God, the two of you are unreal."

"God has nothing to do with this," Joe added.

"Things aren't like that between us, okay?"

"Well he wrote you a letter didn't he? What did he have to say?" Marzia asked.

"Nothing!"

"That's how you talk to your mother?" Joe asked without looking up from his food.

"Well...?" Marzia asked again without re-asking the question.

"Well nothing, he invited me to some event. I don't really know a lot about it."

"Well that doesn't sound like nothing. What do you think Joe?"

"Does the boy work?"

"Of course he works. He's in finance."

"Finance! Where was he when you needed financial help?" Joe asked.

"Oh my God! Guys, things aren't like that between us."

"Alright, enough with the Lord's name. You're smiling that kind of smile like he's makin' the smile and we're your parents, so don't think we don't know, when someone is makin' our daughter smile," her father said.

"How many other people did he invite to this event?" Marzia asked.

"I have no idea. I suppose his friends and family. Mina thought this was a good way to make her invite seem unimportant. She pushed her plate away from the edge of the table and gulped down the rest of her wine, upset with herself for lying and knowing the truth. It was highly unlikely that Adam's family would attend any function she had also been invited to.

"Have you met his family?" Marzia asked.

"Of course she's met his family, how else would she know they're going.

"He probably wants you to go so he can show you off to them," Marzia was pleased to be right all along. "Are you going to ask him to the wedding? He should meet your family if you know his," Marzia stabbed her fork into white space on her plate and just held it there to make her point.

"Ma, he's a friend, and Dad I don't know anyone in his family, you guys are playing the worst game of telephone and we're all sitting right here!"

"What's the matter with bringing a friend to a wedding?" Marzia asked.

"Nothing, I guess."

"You're being silly now. I have to tell you when you are being silly and right now you are being silly. You think your cousin, the Romeo that he is, wants you sitting alone at his wedding? Come on, Mina!"

"Your father's right, but maybe you should wait to see what kinds of friends Gio has invited to the wedding," Marzia brought her napkin to her face.

"Gio's Friends! Are you kidding me? I don't want to be wrapped up with some Gumba."

"Gumba? Gio doesn't know any Gumbas," Joe defended his nephew.

"That's not a very nice thing to say Mina," Marzia added.

"Look Dad, Gio's friends are all a bit old school for me and that is all I'm saying." Mina stood to collect dishes and silverware. "Besides, I am not the kind of girl they're looking for anyway."

Chapter 2
Nametags and Tissues

Song #25 Santa Esmerelda, Gotan Project

Adam was waiting for mina outside the main entrance. He was wearing a suit and looked just as she remembered. Her foot travels in Williamsburg had its moments, but mostly the scene was crowded and trendy with overgrown hair, flannel of a red and black plaid, so many more bangs than forehead or eyes. Their 27 inched hips sported a ring of keys and skeleton legs under their only pair of black jeans. An occasional curly haired passerby caught her attention, but the majority of those that populated the neighborhood were either too full of themselves or already sporting women. They proudly stunk and walked around smoking, pretending not to see anyone else on the street, but not Adam. He looked at someone in passing, stranger or not, straight in the eye and smiled a tiny smile, so small that if it suited him, it could be denied and he could convince the new acquaintance that he wasn't smiling at all. But his eyes were dead on, that one wouldn't question it. They'd prefer the smile, and if it wasn't the semi-permanent dimple in his cheek, it was the pucker of his lips that demanded attention. His salt and peppered hair sparkled light from somewhere unknown. His mouth was like a lifeboat and the only way to avoid the ocean of his eyes: two portholes with a view of deep waters, blue and black at the same time, blending and separating, calm and clean yet wholly deserted; water that doesn't break on land but forever swirling salt and oxygen, splitting and rejoining, grabbing and giving joy in the perfect rhythm of a wave.

"Hey," he said. He was instantly warm and threw his arms around her to hug for a good amount of time. She didn't have her hands out at first and only hugged him back after it was already too long of a hug.

"It's so good to see you. How have you been?"

"Good, thanks." Mina curbed her smile.

"You're not in the city anymore are you?" he asked.

"No I'm not. How did you know that?"

"I went by your place today to see if you were coming. Someone was coming out of the building and I got right in, but when I knocked on your door, it wasn't you who answered." She laughed at his misfortune.

"Who answered?"

"I'm kidding, I checked the name on the door before I knocked."

"Really?"

"Yea."

"What would make you do that?" she asked him.

"I didn't. I didn't knock either, but only because there was a Tweety-bird mat outside your apartment door. I knew that couldn't have been yours."

"You didn't think I would show?"

"I didn't know. I thought you might not want to see me, or maybe you were nervous about seeing me and needed some motivation."

"I am a little nervous," Mina admitted. "But, I'm nervous because I have no idea what this event is all about, and the little bit I did eventually find out about it online wasn't good."

"Don't worry. It's going to be great. We're a nice cult. You're gonna get up there and sing all the songs on the program. Everyone's heard about how talented you are. You're going to make a great sacrifice." He opened the door and waved her through.

"What! You're joking!"

"Mina, stop being modest. You know you're an amazing performer and I packed the audience for you today, so let's not disappoint." She stopped dead in her tracks and refused the nudging of his open palm on her back.

"I'm kiii-dding, I promise you won't have to do a thing except sit there and watch me make a fool out of myself, sound good?"

"Yes, very."

"You would like that, you're still such a little..." He trailed off without ending his sentence. "Now my dear, can we please go in."

She clicked her heels on each step, brushing the tips of her fingers on the railing as she descended. They both smiled without looking at each other. He handed her a nametag.

"Do I have to wear this?"

"Just put it on. We're all wearing nametags." He showed his.

They entered a room with 100 chairs in neat rows all facing the stage. The back of the room had a few tables and more chairs also facing the stage. He stood in the aisle looking around, giving acknowledgement to random members amongst the crowds, waiting for her to take her seat. A tall dark skinned woman tapped him on the shoulder from behind their seats.

"You ready?" She bent down to speak to him, but he stood anyway.

"We'll see," he answered. "But first, please meet the love of my life."

Mina was horrified. She didn't know what to do. Her cheeks went fiery red and it hurt to smile. Her jaw remained open. This was certainly unexpected.

"You must be Mina," the woman said to her. Mina extended her hand to greet the amazingly tall all-knowing woman only to spot her nametag: Joanne. Mina sat down feeling foolish for assuming it was Adam's proclamations of love that had given Joanne knowledge of her name. Things aren't always what they seem, and every nametag she could read added insult to injury that she too was wearing her name across her chest. Joanne made her way to the stage after a few winking hellos and extended hugs.

"Okay everyone let's get settled down. Its here... the time is here. You have come a long way and I want to thank each and every one of you, because it's this day I dread. I hate leaving all of you beautiful people especially after everything we've shared together. So, I like to make it as fun as possible. I know that some of you have breakthroughs you want to share and I want to hear all of them, but first let's put our hands together and welcome our guests this evening! The room filled with applause and hands started one by one to reach for the ceiling and almost immediately someone was standing and talking into a microphone.

"I just want to say that I'm so thankful for having completed this program," Jerry began only to be interrupted by Joanne.

"Jerry please introduce yourself, so many people don't know who you are or why you've come here."

"Hi everyone," he smiled and faced the crowd before turning back to Joanne. My name is Jerry and I came here because a great friend of mine completed this program a couple of years back and... I guess he got sick and tired of hearing me complain about the same things." Jerry turned to his friend in the audience and smiled. "Well, anyway I wanted to thank you, all of you, for sharing your own situations and giving me guidance throughout this process. I have since made many changes and amazingly, the things that made me unhappy have changed dramatically. For those of you that don't know, or maybe feel the same way, I too didn't think I was getting paid enough for the time I was putting in at work, nor did I like the person I was working for. I wanted to be treated better, but I didn't once examine how I was treating anyone, or the story I was building about my job, about my boss, and basically my own unhappiness. I was letting it bring down the rest of my life even letting it negatively affect my relationship with my wife and kids." Jerry grabbed his own face in shock and paused because he was too choked up to talk. "We were thinking about separating."

"Does this sound familiar to anyone here?" Arms lifted in affirmation. "Well tell us Jerry what did you do differently? Joanne asked for everyone in the room.

"I stopped making meaning out of what was happening, did my job and asked for a raise."

"Great." The entire room applauded him along with Joanne. Mina did not bring her hands together. Instead, she sat amazed that so many people congratulated this guy for doing something so simple. She wanted to say something in Adam's ear, but when she saw how invested he was in the speaker, her comment seemed rude and inappropriate.

"And what about your wife, have you talked with her?" Joanne had the incredible ability to have a personal conversation with one person in a room full of strangers.

"I have. I told her I was unhappy with my job and how foolish I had been for not addressing it sooner, and how sorry I was for letting it affect our home, which I know she doesn't deserve."

"Oh Jerry what a romantic you are! What did she say?"

"Well, she cried." He started laughing and looked at his wife sitting in the aisle, holding a tightly clenched fist over her lips, declaring her love with a stare. "She's here, right?" Clapping and whistles competed to give Jerry praise.

"So do you see what Jerry did?" Joanne addressed the group and walked around adjusting her clip on microphone, but her rhetorical question received no answers. "He stopped looking for validation for his feelings. He just did what he would normally do otherwise without making a story about it. How did the raise go Jerry?"

"Great!"

"This is what I am talking about people! Thank you Jerry. Who else has something to share?" Adam was luckily called among the many eager to speak.

"Something that's present for me right now, is that like Jerry, all of us have something we want, or something we feel we deserve, and yet if we were to just ask for it we would have a conclusion, but so often, we are fearful of our own desire or the idea of failing at it, that we don't just go for it." He paused. "I never thought that I would be able to have Mina by my side tonight, but I asked her to come and here she is. The whole room once again filled with applause. This was too much for Mina and she wondered where his family was? She looked at him glow with excitement under fluorescent lights. It was surreal. "I just want to say that I am so thankful for this woman, because for some time now, I have wanted to be completely self-expressed, it was one of my initiatives when I started this program. She doesn't know it but she has been my inspiration, because she already understands how to do this." He looked down at her. "It's hard to imagine that she hasn't already been in this program," he laughed, as did others. "But she gets it and I brought her here today to tell her that I finally get it."

"Excellent Adam! Thank you so much for sharing. And to you women who have supported and accepted Jerry's and Adam's possibility, thank you. You give hope to all of those who have not yet had such courage to fully express themselves in their relationships. Today, we have one last truth to uncover and for all of you who have been invited here today, I hope that from what you get, you can uplift your own life and begin journeys of your own. Start your Landmark experience here and now and feel what its like to live powerfully." Joanne sat down in a director style chair. "Remember when I told you two nights ago, how difficult it would be to enter the world, after leaving the community you created here in this room." Nodding individuals murmured acknowledgement, and it was weird for Mina to see such a large crowd agree on nearly everything that was said.

"But this is just another task for you," Joanne continued. "Go and create a community wherever you are. That is part of the work people! What you have gained here, that power you have to create your own happiness, is not just something you deserve, but what you must share with others as well."

The program lasted another hour, without a break, one Mina took without hesitation. Nice or not, it was totally a cult. She excused herself to the bathroom and admired herself for a while in the mirror: her smile, cheek bones and the joy in her face, her dress, new stockings, and recently purchased suede heels. She had a new sense of fashion. Before they could leave, Adam hugged nearly everyone that had also been part of the program, even shaking hands with their guests as if stories about them had sealed their friendship. Mina stared at the ground as they exited. She did not want to be the first one to make the next move.

"So what do ya think?"

"There's so much I'm thinking Adam."

"I bet you didn't think I was going to say that huh?"

She stopped walking and slowly brought her eyes to his, not to notice the lovely things she usually paid attention to, but just to make sure that this was really happening. Here he was mentioning how he had called her the love of his life, or the rant where he basically said the same thing as if it was no big deal. She closed her eyes tightly as she reached the corner and envisioned a tiny woman, in her likeness, flowing out of a rocks glass saturated in its golden liquor contents.

"We could go somewhere warm and just talk for a little," Adam offered.

"Yea, we can do that, but I have to get back to take care of Rags."

"Oh how is she?"

"Good."

"Where are you living these days?"

"I'm in Brooklyn."

"Oh really, what made you move there?"

"Finances."

"You like it?"

"Yes actually, it's very hip. There are a lot of young people there and it's not as pretentious as the city. There's always cool stuff going on too. Artists' making use of old spaces and recreating culture."

"Sounds like its right up your alley."

They walked into a place neither of them knew. It was filled with memorabilia of the sea. The walls had anchors, fishnets, sails, and paintings of great ships and beautiful seascapes. She followed her intuition and ordered Tullamore Dew on the rocks. He was caught off guard, and as usual wanted to taste hers before he followed. After one sip and a wretched face he ordered a French martini.

He did not take his eyes off of hers and waited patiently before he spoke. Their silence wasn't awkward and he was blatantly smiling.

"What is so funny?" she asked.

"Ah nothing really. I mean I'm happy. I'm happy that you're here, that we're hangin' together. Can I just be happy?"

"Yes of course you can. Sorry it's just..."

"You know, it feels good to be so present. When I think back to a few months ago, so many times I wasn't present to what you were saying or doing, and I just want you to know that, my God, I think I am getting choked up talking about this." He was slightly red in the face but there were no tears. She wanted to see him cry and then furrowed her brow when it didn't happen. She didn't need to see him cry to know that he was telling the truth. "I'm curious about your thoughts on the program," he asked.

"I don't know. It seems like you had a good experience with it, but is that what you were just about to say?" she asked.

"Kind of. I just meant that I've learned so much, and feel so different, that it's hard to imagine why you would have hung out with me before. I have become a better person with my sisters and my family. Even my religion, I have taken on a completely different role with it.

"Really? How so?"

"I told my dad that I can't have religious conversations with him anymore, and that I'll integrate religion as I want it to fit into my life, and that I won't answer his questions on the matter."

"How did he take it?"

"So far, so good. My mother tried to lay on the guilt, but then she told me that if it wasn't for the Rabbi that married them, they would have never been as religious as they are."

"Did you know that story before?"

"Not exactly, but see that is what this program does. It opens up lines of communication that you never thought were possible."

"Is this why they refer to it as your *possibility*?" Mina had learned so much of their rhetoric in two hours.

"Yep, you understand. I knew you would jump right on it. You should go through the program. You deserve all that comes from it. You are an amazing person and with it, you just feel like you have the support to do anything."

"I think I'll be all right."

"Of course you will." He put his glass up to hers. "I know I dropped a bomb in there, but I meant it. You are incredibly close to me, even though we haven't spoken in so long. There isn't a day that goes by that I don't think of you. Something you said or did. I still have a note from you on my fridge. Mina thought of the good morning letters he used to write that she too saved in a box."

"What does that mean though Adam?"

"Everything. It means that you are important to me."

"Okay."

"Okay? Am I not important to you?" Adam asked her.

"I don't know. I don't know what you mean by important. Do I think of you? Yes. But, I still find all of this very odd."

"What is?"

"The way we left off, the way we are now, the bomb you dropped and keep dropping. What does your dad say about you not being with a Jewish woman, did you guys discuss that?"

"No need."

"So then is that a no?"

"No I told him that I didn't want to discuss anything regarding my religion, so that includes everything down to what I eat and what I do with my free time."

"Right."

"Yea it was kind of amazingly easy, once he got what I was saying, he was extremely disappointed, didn't say much for two days, but then he wrote me an email saying he respects my decision. He was worried that I wouldn't be around for holidays or Shabbos, but when I assured him that nothing about that would change, he was all good with it."

"That's good, I guess, but what does all of this really mean for you? How did you get involved with this program in the first place, it doesn't seem like you at all. Sitting and talking about other people's feelings," she started laughing and then covered her mouth to quiet herself. "No. I'm serious, how did you find yourself listening to a room of 100 or more people talk about their life?" She dipped her nose into the aroma of whiskey.

"Well, my dear if you must know, I've had some minor setbacks. I advised some of my clients to shift around the money they had in auto investments and I got fucked." He nervously rubbed his forehead. "I lost the firm a good amount of money, cost them some clients, lost clients myself. It was a mess."

"What happened?"

"Well its finance bullshit, do you really care?"

"I asked. Right?"

"I thought you didn't have a lot of time?" He smiled and put his arm around her shoulders. "Look at us hanging just like old times."

"I don't have a lot of time," she said as she shook from his grip. But I have about three sips left and at the moment minor setbacks for you, regretfully, bring me joy. I'm kidding, sort of. I'm just really curious what about it brought you to the program."

"Well actually a friend told me about it."

"A friend? How close are you and this friend? Was she a friend like I was? Are you two still friends?"

"Mina..." he said softly.

"What?"

"Nothing." The two of them sat quietly waiting out the other. "I don't ask you about that part of your life because I don't want to know and I don't feel comfortable talking about that kind of stuff with you.

"Why not though?"

"Because."

"Fine." She was less than satisfied but dealt with it. The bartender asked if they would like another round. Mina wagged her finger no and stood up. "I'll be right back." In the bathroom she tried to find ways to leave without asking what the point of all of this was. She couldn't believe that this was actually happening. After everything he stood up for on that bench not even six months ago, tonight's charade didn't add up. Why did he want to call her the love of his life, but not actually talk about his life? Was he dating someone? And if so why didn't he just invite that girl to his stupid seminar.

"I have to go," she said as she returned and pulled her coat off of the wall hook.

"I know I figured. Let's do this again soon please. I would like for us to see more of each other. I told you, you are very important to me." He waved down a cab and handed her a twenty-dollar bill. "Get home safely. It was great seeing you." He hugged her tightly, as tight as she felt inside for not fully expressing herself.

Chapter 3
Inequity

Song #26 A change is Gonna Come, Sam Cooke

The cab traveled over the Williamsburg Bridge and Mina was exhausted from such an unfulfilling evening. The ultimate opportunity to say what was important to her arrived and yet nothing came out of her mouth. She didn't tell Adam any of the things she imagined saying to him, and for so long. It was foolish for her to not tell him how angry she was but at the same time she didn't share a word about missing him, and under no circumstance did she describe her painful hospital visit.

She woke rotten. Pissed as well about the oreo-stained mug on her bedside table. She walked downstairs and the sight of her mother bothered her. She took a hot shower but was still unable to feel better. Her Atlas shift didn't start until later, but she went there anyway. She began typing with headphones on facing the wall. It was a cue she learned from dedicated patrons.

I believe in love,
the tireless tongue of a dog,
and kisses from the morning sun.
A mind that creates outcomes and families that give it ground.
I believe in heritage and biochemistry—
in acceptance and rejection.
I believe in prejudice and poverty, and that many of us suffer
wars with no conclusion.
In unhappiness—
shutting down every prize to be won
in the games we don't speak of.
I believe in caffeine and ocean's salt, conflicted thoughts
and sand's will to be in everything.
I believe in promises and forgiveness.
But all of these—my beliefs
are unresolved and challenge
calm lakes of antipathy—
where we're all scared
of what comes from
the freedom to believe.

She came out of her poetry haze with twenty minutes before her shift. One cup of coffee and a cigarette she smoked in halves is all it took for her to get complete with what was important to her. She left her computer and bag on the table and went to the bathroom. She read her creed once more when she came back and upon pressing save, Word crashed. It just shut down.

"What the fuck!" She restarted the computer hoping that the program would recover her words, but the monitor only showed a blue screen of death.

"What the fuck!" Her second outcry was followed by a conscientious glance to see if others were paying attention, but they were involved in conversation and fully functioning computers. There was no way she could deal with this and was now even angrier than when she woke.

"What up?" Mina curtly addressed Beth as she joined her behind the counter.

"Not much, I have to stay here for another couple of hours to do inventory. Fun Fun Fun."

"Well, I am on now, so take care of what you need to."

Mina grabbed a rag and wiped down the steamers on the espresso machine. She always did this when starting a shift. There were some things that even the tidiest of people let go. Someone could be totally anal about nearly everything, except for one detail that of course, matters to someone else. A quiet older guy, frequently in and out of the café, approached the counter from his usual table. He had been sitting just two seats from Mina's temper tantrum, but he hadn't looked at her then and did not give eye contact now as he ordered a latte. She bent down to open the fridge.

"Whole or skim?"

"Whole." Mina clicked twice catching coffee grinds in a hand held filter.

"What's wrong with your computer?" he asked. She turned her neck to make eye contact but her body remained opposite him. He was clean-shaven with small eyes brown eyes.

"I don't know. It went blue." She frothed his milk. He paid with exact change and gave her his business card for a company called Big Boy Computers.

"Big Boy Computers?" Mina read out loud.

"I mainly work on MAC's, but there's nothing I shouldn't able to help you with. I can probably restore what's on your hard drive. Its not a new computer by any means, and you might want to think of upgrading, but I can at least save what's on it for you."

"How do you know it's gone right now?"

"I don't. But, if it went blue, and you can't get it to restart, I'm curious how you expect to recover your files."

"Okay, but I can't buy another computer or pay a load of money to fix what's wrong with this one."

"Just call me and I'll look at it. If I can do it, it'll take me two minutes. Call me sometime over the weekend though. I'm too busy during the week."

"What's your name?" Mina asked unsure about the entire conversation, his ability to fix her computer and the lack of funds to make it happen.

"Phil," he pointed at the card in her hand, and walked out.

Dépêche Mode kicked in. Beth always played Dépêche Mode. It was easily her favorite band. The song started:

I'm taking a walk with my best friend. I hope he never lets me down again.

Mina thought of Adam.

"Beth, I need to meet a guy."

"Oh yea?" She made tally marks for sleeves of cold and hot cups on her yellow notepad.

"I saw an ex last night, and he was the last one and a while ago. I think I'm in need of some special attention." Mina raised an eyebrow and batted her lashes to clarify that she was talking about sex.

"Well you can come to a party that's going on in my building tonight," Beth laughed. "But I can't guarantee that you'll find a guy there that's worthy of special attention," she made a similar face. "I don't even know what kind of guys you like. I see Computer Geek gave you his card. Maybe he has some of what you're looking for?"

"Are you serious, I doubt I'll call him. It'll probably fix itself. Sometimes computers just crash but they come back to life. What's the party for?"

"Nothing. Once in a while bands show up and start playing in the courtyard and people follow. It just somehow became a thing."

"That sounds cool. I can't believe you weren't going to invite me if I hadn't said anything," Mina joked. The co-workers had never hung out before, and this was the first time Mina had opened up to her.

"I didn't know you needed a guy so badly."

. "Do me a favor and count how many bags of chai powder we have?" Mina did as she was told.

"Four plus the open one we've been using."

"And the Nesquicks."

"Three."

"Alright! I'm outta here." Beth handed the notepad to Mina over the counter. "So, you wanna come by tonight? I can introduce you to some people if you'd like, then you won't have to fuck computer geek."

"Don't say that?"

"I find something about him enticing and strangely fuckable. I think it's because he has no interest in being nice and yet today he not only notices that you had some issue with your computer, but hands you his card to help you. Just how long do you think he has wanted to talk to you?"

"Gross, creeper. I don't know. I never noticed him notice me."

"He used to always come in with this big-haired blonde, total bitch, but that was a while ago. I'm sure it was a bust."

"What time does the party start? I just realized I'm closing. I might have to wear what I currently have on." Mina waved her hand up and down at the subpar outfit she was sporting.

"It won't matter. It's not really a party. Just come after you close. I'm on Kent and North 8th. Text me when you get there so I can meet you downstairs."

Song #27 The Denial Twist, The White Stripes

It was a night full of hot chocolates, sometimes these things happened. As if a glittery chainmail demanded people from the neighborhood to sip hot cocoa or none of their friends would love them anymore. And no, these saps didn't come in all at once, but evenly separated by a latte, so that each and every hot chocolate was made to order. Stainless steel cleaned easily, but espresso machines were composed of removable parts that revealed another two more parts, making closing a laborious task. Mina had never hated milk so much until she worked at Atlas but still not as much as the marshmallow bag. Regardless of how carefully she retracted pillowed squares, that bag's plastic always toppled to one side spilling contents on the floor and making everything sticky.

The smell of fire scented the air as she crossed Berry Street. She came to what looked like the back of a tall industrial building but with no entrance on the opposite side, which should have been the front. She did a double walk around. In fact, she gave the front enough of a look-see to notice how much it resembled a jail. Beth peeked her head out of a single door made from what was once a freight elevator shaft. It was the only door into this strange building. Beth was done up. Mina hardly recognized her and by now the smell of fire was overwhelming.

"I didn't know you had bangs."

"I didn't. I cut them tonight. Well, my roommate cut them."

"And I've never seen you with make-up on. You look like a totally different person. I mean you look great, but it's so different."

"Thanks. Would you like to come upstairs and have a beverage before we see who's playing?"

"I would love to."

The doors of the hallway were very close to each other like offices in a building. The floors were filthy wooden slats splattered with paint and plaster, and laughter and music could be heard from each of the apartments they walked by. They pushed through Beth's apartment door. One wall was the kitchen and a living-dining room combination made up the other end and Christmas lights bordered them like a holiday card. Two girls with similar cropped asymmetrical haircuts welcomed Beth and Mina when they entered, and farther into the room were two guys smoking by the window. Mina noticed a small wooden ladder that climbed to a curtained crawl space on top of the shortened wall of the living room.

"Is that your bedroom?"

"Both of ours," Beth pointed to her roommate, one of the girls. "Leila, Mina, Mina, Leila, and that's Tiny, who kind of also lives here." Mina smiled and looked around the kitchen. The place was too small for anyone, let alone three women. Smirnoff was the only thing to drink in the room and without asking, Beth poured Mina vodka and grapefruit juice. Mina asked for ice.

"Where's the bathroom?"

"Down the hall."

"Outside?" Mina asked in disbelief.

"Yea," Beth answered.

"You walk down a hall to use the bathroom?" Mina asked again.

"This is how we do," Tiny said. "Where do you live?"

"I live on Skillman over by Graham."

"You live in a house?"

"Yea. Well, I live with my parents, so..." Mina trailed off realizing how different things were between her and the rest of these people.

"We cut Beth's bangs right here in the kitchen," Leila said as she kicked the garbage bin. "You don't always need what you don't have."

"How was the rest of your night?" Beth asked Mina about work.

"Hot chocolates," Mina said with a smile.

"That's how I know you, Atlas." One of the guys said, mentally confirming with a head nod as he cut behind Beth to get to the fridge. The countertop in the middle of the kitchen was on wheels and kept moving half an inch in the same direction. Tiny pulled it back but the attempt was futile. It was cluttered with take out menu's, a few beer cans, one disgusting ashtray and drinks.

"Yep. Good Ole' Atlas," Beth said as she pat down and realigned her newly cut strands of hair.

They walked down the hall to a different set of stairs than the one they ascended to join the party in the courtyard. It was a keg party without a keg; thirty people drinking from cups they brought from their apartment. An amateur band played in front of a well-lit fire and people were dancing in groups. Despite Mina's vodka and grapefruit, she was completely sober and chain smoking. As she lit a new cigarette, groups of people moving about were eye candy for her otherwise hermit life. Hipsters were definitely a generation of performers; they entertained and competed for attention. Mina noticed the similarities in the accoutrements of their look, how they moved, the words they used and what they thought was in good humor. Their consistency in managing an awkward air even amongst their own party was not something she was familiar with. She felt outside of herself, looking in on a party she didn't belong to. One particular group of boys caught her attention. They were sitting in lawn chairs against a brick wall. They were eighties styled chairs with plasticized tubing running in horizontal folds. Mina moved in to listen to them debate extremely unlikely scenarios where zombies challenged robots. It was obvious that there was a distinct split in the group. Zombie fans were unable to comprehend the limitless ability of robots in settings such as traffic, eating contests, or miniature golf.

"Are you guys really talking about this or am I in a very bad movie? And by bad I mean"...Mina smirked as she took a long pause and blinked her eyes profusely. "God-Awful." The group's reaction was half confused and half intrigued. It was hard for them to grasp the familiarity of her forthright words combined with her disinterest in a topic they held so dear.

"You don't like Zombies?" An average Mediterranean man asked. He had big blackish eyes and thick hair, a wide nose, and big lips. Every feature was swollen and their arrangement under his rippled forehead made him look gaudy. She looked away from him as she answered.

"I've never met one, but if we're talking metaphorically, I suppose we're amongst them all the time." She deliberately paused. "Even right now," she said looking around with fear, as if somewhere hiding behind a bush or tree, zombies were going to attack them.

"What would you like to talk about then?" The only one standing found his voice.

It wasn't Mina's intention to insult them. A little perspiration squeezed its way through her pores. She looked into the open mouths and hungry eyes of a close-knit group that had just been disrupted. She knew whatever she said had to be good, and long enough to debate and as ambiguously uneventful like Zombies vs. Robots.

"I don't know."

"How about your name? You are?"

"Mina." She had no idea what she was going to say, and suddenly the stakes rose. They knew her by name. Her hands experienced the same swampy result as her armpits. She looked upwards and pulled her scarf away from her collar so air could cool her salivating skin. She noticed the wall of each building surrounding this party patch of grass, and it reminded her of medieval living, and suddenly the history of what happened long ago seemed to fit their current state. She knew the rising investments in this neighborhood were not intended for the majority of the people living there, because no one was doing anything for the structures that already existed. Despite how happy they were to share a hallway bathroom, what they called home would be another condemned building torn down to make way for a modern luxury high rise. Those that worked barely made $30K annually and would certainly not be enough for the application's income requirements once these projects' began to fill vacancies.

"Did you guys ever notice how this building looks like a jail? I mean right now we're sitting in a community courtyard. I've never been to jail, but they always look like this on TV, but it also makes me think of the Middle Ages and feudalism," she laughed. "I'm probably taking you back to Global studies. I mean aren't we all overworked and underpaid and searching for... something. I don't know if this is right, but perhaps the word I'm looking for is zeitgeist. I don't think we have one. We drink and smoke. We numb ourselves from truths we can't escape. We sample from the past because nothing satisfies, and we're too condescending, too self-absorbed, and too dismissive for true ingenuity."

"What's a Zeitgeist?" Patrick asked.

"Is that like poltergeist?" The man with the large features asked. Mina looked at them as she searched for her words.

"No, although spirit is a good word to describe it, like a spirit of our times. It's the driving mood amongst people, like the commonality between us and how we are living right now would be referred to as zeitgeist."

"I'm sure there's something common between us." One of the quiet-up-until-now hipsters spoke in a heavy accent. "We enjoy ourselves," he looked around at his bandmates. "We create music and are enjoying other artists that are doing the same thing. He pointed to the woman-led band on the makeshift stage." Mina could tell that English wasn't his first language. "Do you know German Literature, Mina?" She laughed almost too quickly.

"I studied it for a semester in college."

"You're talking about Weltschmerz, but that is just one way of seeing it."

"What the hell are you guys talking about?" Patrick had been dethroned as the speaker of his ensemble and didn't like it.

"I don't know Weltschmerz, what did he write?" Mina said humbly.

"Look it up and come see our band. We play next weekend at the pool." Pool parties in Williamsburg were at an old community pool that had been drained several years ago. It was easily the size of a football field except it was a pool. People stood in and around the tub to watch music, spin hula-hoops, play dodge-ball in teams among other art centric activities. Clear Channel had been threatening to close it down for the past two years, but nothing yet. The European stood up and towered over her. He was wearing a wool hat and blondish tufts stuck out behind his ears. He handed her a promo card for their upcoming show and sat back down. She locked eyes with him as she tucked it into her jacket pocket only to find Beth's arm around her interrupting the exchange.

"We're going back upstairs, this music is lame. Mina looked straight ahead into the direction that Beth had turned her body to see the two dames on stage barely making their voice audible through the microphone. She could see Tiny and Leila waiting by the side door they had come out of less than an hour ago.

"I'm probably going to get going too. I'll see you tomorrow maybe."

"I'll be there," Beth said as she unraveled herself and walked away. Mina turned back around to face the boys.

"So, are you the singer?" Mina addressed Patrick.

"How'd you know that?"

"I didn't. I just asked," she said with a smile. "Maybe I'll come check you guys out this weekend. Thanks for the card."

"Hey where ya going, you can't just start a conversation and then leave!" Patrick did his best.

"I have to, I have work early tomorrow." She was lying. "Come see me at Atlas if you ever wanna have a coffee. I'm sure you can pick up a few fans, plus I'll be there."

Ch. 4
Williamsburg: An Answer For

It was a sexy crescent moon that winked at her as she turned onto Skillman Ave. Beth was right, save for the German, those weren't the kinds of people she was interested in. She didn't actually know if he was German, but that is what she was calling him to serve the irony of a Jew followed by a German.

Mina could hear Rags running towards the door as she unlocked it. This reminded her of tomorrow. For starters she had to clean all of Rags' droppings in the backyard. Her father asked her to take care of it last week. It was the least she could do in exchange for all of their help. She had a new appreciation for them and the convenience of a private bathroom in her house. She also needed to restart her laptop and hopefully restore intellectual properties from the past seven years. She longed to talk with Roman. The next day was the start of Thanksgiving week. She promised her mom she would search for

Mamaw's serving platters. Grace really wanted to use them this year, but didn't want to put an ounce of energy in getting or cleaning them. That would be everyone else's contribution since she was cooking. Grace was used to having things done her way. She was the only woman in her home and charged her husband and son around like workers. The laptop was still blue before bed, but perhaps like Adam, it needed a period of silence before returning to its senses.

She rose earlier than expected, poured a cup of coffee and rested her mother's nerves by looking for the platters first thing. Despite the smell of wet dog and disintegrating sponges, it wasn't a true basement. It had small rectangular windows on the top third of the wall. It was used mainly for the stuff they couldn't throw away, like old records, books, an antique pasta maker and memorabilia from who knows when. Mina couldn't help herself. She kneeled down by the metal crate to scan records: *Fox Trot, Baltimore Society Orchestra, Words and Sounds of 1971, 72, 73, etc.* Some were unopened with horrific designs from the eighties, but there was also a whole collection of Italian records, maybe ten by *Mina*, the singer. She reveled in lightheadedness seeing her own name printed on these dusted squares.

The smell of old things brought her back to beanbags in the loft of her middle school library. Mina the singer looked out from her 1974 record cover. She had a thick head of brown hair, large opaque eyes with perfectly arched eyebrows. They were painted. They must have been painted. The two stared at one other, and before Mina knew it, she was holding the complete record collection in her arms.

She continued to search the room for the stack of platters that her mother said would be *right there* when she first walked in. There was nothing. She walked further into the maze of boxes. An old rug tied with twine leaned against the wall, a small two-seater table that used to be in the kitchen and large plastic tubs encircled her. She pulled boxes down to begin her search, but knew the platters were too large for boxes. She found books, yearbooks, almanacs, and old magazines that for some reason were being archived in this lovely basement. The second box she opened held every lost family photo. She laughed out loud at the hair-dos and don'ts and outrageous outfits that people happily wore. She inspected the signature seventies upholstery patterns that were backdrops to most of these photos, when out of the corner of her eye she noticed golden gilt-edged pages from a small leather bound book. It was strapped to a larger one just like it, but she only managed to slip the smaller one out. The first page read in the center:

This book belongs to Mina Luizza.

She had never seen or held this book before, yet suddenly it was hers, or not so suddenly, as it had always belonged to her, but this wasn't her writing. She flipped to a random page to see *Baby's Name* printed at the top in cursive. Her mother had written down poetry or lyrics to a song Mina had never heard before. When she was done reading the bits of Italian and English, 'Amor Mio, Mina' was em-dashed at the bottom. She put her baby book on top of her records and was lit up like she hadn't been in a good while. This was better than shopping at a vintage store. She was shopping from her own family's memories and this one was about her. She scoured the room for the last hope of finding the fateful platters that brought her to these new gifts, but didn't see anything. As she carried her stuff towards the door she noticed a commercial sized garbage bag behind the door. Sure enough, as her mother had said, they were right there.

Rachel Ray was on the television seducing American households with a morning rasp most people clear up with coffee and a shower. Marzia removed the white cloth from the dining room table while she waited for Mina. She also brought out all the old polishing tools: a tiny little brush for dusting, a ratty bottle of polish that didn't have a label anymore and shredded dishtowels. Mina pushed through the basement door dragging a bag behind her like a beat up Santa.

"Oh, you found them thank God."

"This bag is heavy, Ma. She really needs all of these?"

"I doubt it, but I haven't looked at them in ages. They're probably a mess. It's good to clean them, anyway."

They admired the craftsmanship and imagination from years passed as they handled each piece. Mina pulled out a water jug with rolling waves embossed along the base. She examined the work for some time, and together they discovered dishes designed with ivy and leaves from olives and grapes. Some of them were being seen for the first time, but Mina recognized the next large oval platter she pulled from the bag.

"Make sure you clean that one real good," Marzia said. She explained that the beveled image resembling plant roots in the middle of the platter was the Tree of Life, and it represented good luck. Grace had specifically requested this one. The last item Mina pulled out was a pewter tray. Its small size made it more of an astray or collectible than an actual dish. It featured a woman of pure beauty with hair flowing behind her as if she traveled with great speed. Her left arm was tucked behind her head and resembled a sail. She was only carved a profile but this didn't reduce her beauty. The illusion of water folded into itself like pillows under a blanket, right below her navel hiding her naked parts. Her torso was bare and above water, with a perfect line down the center of her abdomen. Both of her legs were visible but tangled in a blanket of sea unwilling to let her go. Mina traced her fingers along this tiny monument of beauty following the realistic curvature of her hips.

"Ma, why don't you listen to the singer Mina anymore?"

"I don't know. We don't play records anymore. Mamaw was the one who loved her anyway. What makes you ask?"

"I was just curious. I saw a bunch of her albums downstairs and we have the same name, ya know?"

"Well she certainly had a beautiful voice, and so many great songs, but that's old Italian music, Mina. You don't listen to that?"

"I would. Do we still have a record player?"

"No." Mina couldn't wait to read the rest of her baby book. She smiled at her mom eager to read her secrets.

"Her voice bothers me so much. How do you watch her, Ma?" she asked about Rachel Rey as she lowered the volume.

"I think she's cute. I don't know how her food tastes though. I never make anything she makes, anyway."

"Trust me you can't learn anything from her. How are we cleaning these? I want to help you before I clean the backyard and take Rags to the park."

"There's two buckets, one's soapy, and the other's for rinsing. You see I used to use toothpaste but Grace told me to use dishwashing soap, but I don't know about that, so I mixed the two. So make sure that when you dunk one in that you get a chunk of toothpaste and rub it over the whole thing. Get it in the cracks too. I don't wanna hear her complain." She handed Mina a washcloth. "Don't be too rough or you'll scratch them. Not that these are in the best shape anyway, but be gentle."

They continued to work in that fashion. Mina tossed her minty silver into the rinse bowl where Marzia would then dry and polish.

"Ma," Mina broke a long silence of cleaning. "How did Zizi Grace and Uncle Leo get their money?"

"They've always had money. Leo was a steelworker and did well. He worked under big Tony Mazzocchi and he still does things for the union here and there. I don't know, he's all politics. Just wait 'til Thanksgiving. I am sure he will have so much to say. I don't even think my sister knows what her own husband does. All that man ever talks about is how things used to be. He's such an old man." The sky was bright with no reason to be. Mina poured herself the last of the coffee and walked out back holding the door so Rags could follow. She winced lifting putrid pieces of poop under a sun so faint it resembled a bleach stain in a powdery grey tee-shirt of a sky.

She took Rags down Manhattan Ave crossing Meeker under the BQE and into Greenpoint: the Polish part of town. It wasn't a very different neighborhood than Williamsburg and bordering lines were hard to distinguish, but by day there were always a few brown baggers drinking next to their shopping carts. McGorlick Park had a great dog park filled with sculptures. Mina sat with her baby book while Rags ran free with the others in the run. The first few pages were filled with old stylized drawings of baby girls, little rhymes of what girls are made of, floating ribbons, spoons wrapped with bows, and tiny sparrows carrying dress clippings. She found it odd to read that Aunt Mariella, her father's sister, was the first person to find out that her mom was pregnant, but even stranger was that Marzia wrote she had a feeling she conceived on March 1st. Mina read her mother's sentences over, each time pausing on the words March 1st. This was Adam's birthday. Here she was thinking about what Thanksgiving was going to be like, seeing Jessica and talking about the wedding, getting stuck with Uncle Leo and politics, and wondering whom she might see for that special attention, meanwhile exactly nine months to the day Adam entered the world, she was conceived. She considered the possibilities of two lives meant to be together and couldn't read on at that moment.

Song #28 The Noose, A perfect Circle

~ ~ ~

Her thoughts came in a whisper. It moaned, *he loves you, you're the love of his life, you heard him, he said it and in front of all those people. It's you he loves.* It didn't fade and she decided to take a walk with Rags, baby book in hand, and taking direction from Brooklyn's lovely whisper. She stepped lightly but the whisper continued. The echoes of her subconscious faded and she remembered a dream she recently had about Adam's bonsai. She didn't think of it once until that moment and even then couldn't recall when she had the dream, and trying to recount the when caused the dream to flee from her mind. The sounds of Williamsburg continued like the subtle ew's and ah's a singer adds to their song.

Bits of blue leaked through the sky and cleared Mina's urban hypnosis. Something was coming through. She could feel a message. The neighborhood wasn't new to her anymore and maybe this plea had always been apparent but she hardly noticed it when she first arrived. At the time, Mina was insensible and distracted and for so many reasons. Their exchange was a mutual one, in the way two people may excuse an awkward door grab or hand shake, or just say sorry because they think apologies are a polite thing to do. But the Williamsburg that she had just gotten reacquainted with was changing yet again. On certain blocks the deterioration of long standing stone and brick made tiny individual graveyards out of the neighborhood, and each week there seemed to be a new development of construction. Cinderblocks formed hollow squares and raw materials were brought in by the truckloads. Residents had little defense against these efforts swallowing this *almost* great city. The structural skeletons spread like weeds sometimes twenty feet high, all sporting that same blue plastic tarp. The East River winds grew strong whipping it to shreds and turning these sites into a crinkling cacophony of flags, saluting the neighborhood for what it was and wasn't. She wanted to see Adam. Maybe it was the serendipity implicated by her baby book, or the attractive couple walking towards her, but maybe she just wanted to see him.

She brought Rags home and the ex-lovers met at a place called Sea. Mina sipped her Lychee martini holding a fashionable will-vibrate-when-table-is-ready beeper. Sea was an extremely popular Thai restaurant with enormously tall ceilings to house the oversized Buddha sitting in a lily-padded bath in the center of the restaurant.

"This place is great, how did you hear about it?" Adam asked.

"I live here," she said. Mina was still trying to figure out how to act in front of him. The shifting from happy to angry and back again was exhausting.

"Mina...Um, what is that may I ask?" He pointed to her drink. "Is that a loogie in your martini?"

"It's a Lychee." Mina was already bored with his ignorance. "You've never seen a Lychee before?"

"I guess not, I used to drink those all the time, but I never got one of those in it." He pointed again with a repulsed face. Mina then remembered his terrible taste in drinks.

"I forgot that you drank these all the time. I never order things like this, but I know they put the fruit in it here and I wanted one. Do you want to try it? It's very good. I think they use rose water too."

"Rose water? Never heard of it, Um, is this Thai Food? You didn't take me here for another drunken man noodle did you?" They both laughed. "Because..." He started laughing again. "Ummm," he uttered with tight lips.

"No." Her smile ended abruptly as she remembered the grave effect that noodle had on her. Their table was ready almost as quickly as their food arrived.

"What are your plans for Thanksgiving?" she asked him.

"We don't celebrate Thanksgiving. Well, we kind of celebrate it, but not really."

"What do you mean kind of, but not really?"

"Well we get together and have a meal and of course we give thanks. Jews are always giving thanks."

"But not you," she interrupted. "You're no longer required to give thanks right? Candles? Forget about it. Who needs candles, right?" She teased him.

"I still celebrate High holy days you little shit. I've been doing this for so long. It would be weird to just stop. I don't think I could. You did miss one of our greatest holidays though. Remember when I showed you pictures of the sukkah?"

"No."

"Yes. Remember I told you that we build a small hut in the backyard? I took a photo of the one from last year and showed it to you. It was on my phone. I showed it to you once when we were talking about the Jewish calendar at my apartment." He waited for her face to give acknowledgement, but nothing happened. "Ugh. It doesn't matter. Anyway the point is, that this year's sukkah was way better." She couldn't move her napkin fast enough to cover her open-mouthed laughter. He just continued. "I took pictures," he said and then paused. "For you, my dear." He put his chopsticks down to grab his phone.

The sukkah looked as if it had been constructed with sheets of bamboo, but she wasn't sure. There were several photos to browse through; some were of posters his family hung on the sukkah walls, and others were of the table inside. Hebrew symbols she was unfamiliar with were printed on posters, many homemade glittery Stars of David, along with random Gourds hanging from the ceiling.

"That looks totally bizarre, you built that?"

"No, we bought it."

"What!" She shouted in amazement. "Aren't you supposed to build it yourself as a family, and then enjoy it as something you did together? I mean doesn't it represent the struggles of your people, having to find shelter while they traveled through the desert for some ridiculous amount of time?"

"You sure you're not Jewish Mina?" She smiled. "You're a hundred percent correct, but get a load of this." He opened photos on his phone and handed it back to her. She now looked at two different pictures of pick up trucks with sukkahs strapped to the trucks' bed.

"Oh my god, people have businesses selling sukkahs?"

"Selling, transporting, storing. We're Jews Mina. We always find a way to make money, or to not have to do manual labor. It depends on how you look at it. But bottom line is we're not builders," he laughed at himself.

"What about the pyramids?"

"That wasn't us."

"Jesus!" She gave him back his phone. "Did you sleep in it?"

"Well, you're supposed to, but we didn't. As a kid we used to camp out, but now we just say our blessings and eat inside. But, enough about this. What are your plans for Thanksgiving?"

"We're all going to camp out in the backyard." She laughed loudly and continued to look at him with a shining smile until he smiled back. "I'm just kidding. We're going up the street to my Zizi Grace's house and we're going to camp out in her backyard."

"Nice, who's we?" He skipped over her jokes.

"Me, my sister, her family, my parents, and then at Zizi Grace's house there will probably be her son Gio, his fiancé Jessica and her family, and whoever else my uncle Leo invites."

"That's nice. You get to see your parents a lot since you are living down here?"

"Yea. I live with them Adam."

"Oh, I didn't know, I'm sorry. What made you move back home?"

"A lot of things, but basically I just didn't have enough money to justify living where I was."

"That's smart. I wish I could do that."

She thought about his parents and their home, and realized she had no idea what they or it looked like, where it was, and who lived there.

"How are your sisters?" she asked him. He was surprised by the question.

"Well, one of my sisters is going through a tough time right now."

"Yael?"

"No, she's in therapy, but now that you mention it, maybe both her and Syrah are going through tough times. Syrah's not like Yael at all though."

"I wouldn't know. I've heard very little about your family. I only know that you have two sisters and a brother. So what's wrong with Syrah?"

"Health-wise she's fine, but she's not married. She's getting older and she still lives with my parents."

"So? What the hell does that mean?" Mina was astonished by his obliviousness. He was literally describing her situation.

"Well the problem isn't that. That is fine, although maybe it is a bit much on my parent's wallet, but its fine. The real problem is that she's just going through a rough time. She's lonely. And Yael, well, at first everyone was really happy about her talking to someone, but it's just, he paused to find the right words, "It's just getting in the way, and my poor mother. My god."

"My god, what?"

"I don't agree with Yael's therapist. Instead of teaching absolution and forgiveness, she's advising her to express everything. Like the other weekend we were talking about a charm bracelet that she really wanted as a child! And apparently it was around the same time a certain necklace was purchased for my other sister," he dragged his voice as if he could still hear his sister's whining. "I mean ridiculous things that have no bearing on our current adult lives. It's nearly twelve years after the fact Mina! But, at the same time, I now know from some of the other things she's expressed how I've played a part in how she feels about me, the stories she has created about me as the reason she doesn't have a voice with the family. It's heavy and complex, but I'm listening to her."

"Do her feelings have any validity?"

"I don't know. That was then. I can't do anything about that, even if it was true. But, since our little discussion, I've promised her and myself that I won't cut her off, and that'll try my best to be what she needs from me. Her biggest thing was that I never listened to her, so I let her go on and on about this charm bracelet." He paused and they both laughed. "I mean I even told you last time we met in the city, I own it. I wasn't aware of my surroundings then, like I am now."

"Okay. But what's wrong with your other sister, and how old is she?

"Syrah's like 27, between me and Yael."

"Oh my God! She has plenty of time to get married. What's the rush? The waiter came over with the check in hand, asked them if they would like anything else and upon receiving a no, dropped it and left. Adam quickly slipped in his credit card and held it out to the side. Mina noticed his hands were better at paying for dinner than eating it. She thanked him as he signed his receipt. It was an early date and as dark and packed as it was inside, the sun was just about to set when they hit the sidewalk.

"Hey how's the museum going?" he asked.

"Oh, I don't work there anymore either."

"Oh okay. Quick question Mina, is anything about you the same?"

"Some things," she said with a smile. "Please, go on about your spinster sister." They walked towards the south side on Bedford.

"Where was I?" He twirled a toothpick in his mouth.

"I don't know about how she's lonely, unwed, and draining your parent's wallet."

"Right, so dating for Orthodox women is very different from let's say you dating me." He attempted to drown her with his seaside blues but Mina avoided the current by looking away. "You see they go through a matchmaker, which is what we call a *Shadchan*. Say it with me now." He said it again and she willfully repeated. He grabbed her hand and she froze before shaking him off.

"Wait, is the *Shadchan* a woman or a man?" She learned quickly to walk with her hands out of his reach.

"Well they can be male, but that would be rare, unless he was a Rabbi, because it isn't modest for young women to be talking with a married man. Anyway, they are usually middle-aged women, like this one and they basically act as an agent would for an entertainer. The *Shadchan* is the only contact for both parties for everything, like dates, messages, everything. Once a decision is made, she is the one who arranges a proposal.

"Really? A proposal for marriage?"

"Yes really," he said definitively. "Mina, men and women are not allowed to touch one another until they are married. Which is why Orthodox marriages happen so quickly in my opinion. So, Syrah, my sister has never been with a man! Do you know how sad that makes me? And it makes her sad too. We joke all the time that we are going to kill ourselves."

"What?" Mina was amused.

"Like, I'll ask her how she's doing and she'll say, *oh I am ending it tonight - I'm just going to kill myself in the bathroom right after a nice shower.* Sometimes I tell her I'm so heartbroken that I'm going to blow my brains out in bed after dinner."

"Heartbroken?" Mina's emotions switched from tepid to angry. "How are you heartbroken?" She didn't give him an opportunity to answer. Her ears and neck radiated heat. "I've been nice enough, quiet enough, patient even, but now you are going to tell me that you're heartbroken. Who broke your heart?"

"I don't know that anyone broke my heart, I was sad for a while, but also it was just what I would say."

"Sad about what?"

"I was just sad, Mina."

"I'll tell you what's sad," she continued in a softer tone. "What's sad is, you didn't fight for me. That it wasn't important enough. That I wasn't part of your plan, like your bonsai, I didn't fit the way you needed me to! But you know what, none of that matters now." She paused. "What I really want to know is why you told your parents you didn't want to be religious? And why you waited so long to tell me after you told them?" She looked at him nearly panting. "Unless... it

117

didn't have anything to do with me?" She had forgotten about the other woman he mentioned on the night of the seminar, and suddenly became aware of the possibility that his heartbreak and pretend suicide had nothing to do with her.

"Well part of it did," he said a little taken back by her uproar.

"Part of it?"

"No. It did. Of course it did."

"Adam, you told me I was the love of your life, but that's where it ends. You don't really know what to do about it, so forgive me but I feel like you're feeding me a bunch of bullshit."

"Maybe you're right. You're so ahead of the game when it comes to understanding these types of things. I'm not that smart. About some things I am, but I'm still figuring a lot of it out. I did what I thought I had to." They stopped walking. Mina sighed.

"I'm sorry..."

"Don't apologize." He interrupted her. "You have every reason to be upset with me. Look if I tell you what I am used to, how my family works, and what they have taught me about relationships, you would understand. Before you, I never had a real relationship," he said the word relationship with finger quotes. "They were just women. I never cared or thought about them and I had no idea what I was doing. You see, Syrah doesn't really know any other way either. This is the life she subscribes to. It was the life I subscribed to."

"What are you saying? You had plenty of relationships!"

"Yes. But I was never a friend to them, like I was with you. And I was cheating them, cheating me, cheating my religion. I was running around like a maniac! I can only move forward from that and have. I've decided to take what I want from my religion and that's it. I don't know if you understand the guilt that I have lifted by doing this. The talk I had with my father was so important and that he gets it is huge for me."

"Fine," Mina said. This was moving far from her point. She mobilized their conversation. He followed keeping his eyes on her. They were no longer speaking about their relationship, but about him being fully realized and she couldn't argue with that being the more important detail.

"Fine what?"

"Fine. I get what you are saying, but I am curious what you mean about what was taught to you about relationships. Finish your story about Syrah."

"What do you wanna know?"

"Adam! You were telling me why she's sad. Remember?"

"Yes. Well she recently went on a date. The guy's a little older than her and you have to realize that my other sister, Yael, is six years younger than her with two kids already. Orthodox women usually have children by 24, and I'm sure spending time with her niece and nephew is a constant reminder to her of the things she doesn't have, and may never have. Plus, she's a financial burden to my parents. She's never told me this, but I know it's gotta be on her mind. But whatever, this guy seemed nice I guess. I never met him, but he came to the house twice to see her. My father said he liked him, and our Rabbi knew his family. Everything about it seemed good."

"Where do your parents live that their community is that small?"

"They live in Long Island, but it's not just their community. This is how Orthodox people live. They keep everything within their circles. You know this."

"Yes." Mina shook her head remembering all too well.

"Anyway, so Syrah and this guy went out twice. On the third date, I think they went to the movies and then... nothing." He finished his sentence by throwing his hands in the air.

"What do you mean nothing?"

"Nothing. No calls. No more dates and not a word. They can't find him."

"What?"

"Yep, he just disappeared. I told you they don't keep each other's information. He has to contact the *Shadchan* if he wants to see her and vice versa."

"But why?"

"This is how they do things. It's a modesty thing. The man can't call the woman directly."

"But, can't Syrah contact the *Shadchan* herself?" They reached the Williamsburg Bridge and Mina led their walk up South 5th Street to the George Washington Memorial. "It's so strange they can't connect on their own."

"She can and she has but there's nothing that can be done." He looked around at the statue. This is pretty cool he said admiring the patina of GW on horseback at the mouth of the Bridge. The sun was setting on them and she took a seat at the base of the small monument.

"You look so pretty. I want to take a picture of you. He stepped back and caught her apprehensive smile with his phone." When he looked at the photo he noticed that, *Don't Lie,* had been graffiti'd behind her. He showed her as they sat on the small steps, and together they turned to look at the actual writing on cement.

"Okay I won't." He grabbed her hand.

"Won't what?" she asked.

"I think about you all the time Mina. I was afraid to call you because I didn't know what to say. I didn't know if you wanted to hear me at all. So, I did nothing. But that's not what I want either." Mina wasn't sure if she should speak. She watched silver clouds eddy in his blue eyes. She didn't want to interrupt anything that he was ready to say to her, but staying cool in this moment of heat was so difficult.

"Okay." She looked away. "I don't know what I'm supposed to say Adam," she said quietly.

"You don't have to say anything, it's just that I haven't connected with any woman like I've connected with you, and although I still don't know what that means exactly, I know I want you in my life."

"Right," she said after a slight pause, feeling the weight of his hand in hers.

"You know I call you my ex girlfriend and I don't even know if that's what you think of me?" In Mina's head she answered with, of course I think of you as my ex boyfriend, but it didn't come out. She didn't want to admit that to him. "Don't liiiie," he sang shaking his index finger and pointing to the spray painted cursive behind their heads. She thought about the recent earthquake, her sudden move to Brooklyn, how quickly things pass, and how good she felt next to him. She imagined the computer guy and the many bleak prospects of men that were ready to absorb her life's minutes. She wondered if things could work between her and Adam, and without trying, her memory of the bonsai dream came to her. It was much clearer now. She was tiny in the dream, small like the woman she saw imprinted on pewter earlier. She climbed to the top of the bonsai trying to pull heart shaped fruits from their stems. Some were red and some purple, and were shaped like human hearts but were impossible to reach. It was the same smallness she always felt when she was with him, the right size to fit in his pocket and tiny enough for that perfect dollhouse memory.

"I carry you around with me all the time," she said looking back at him. She couldn't help to think of the miscarriage the minute she finished her sentence. "I mean I think of you too. But I don't think you know what you want and that scares me, because you already hurt me once."

"I know. I'm sorry I want to know how you feel about spending time with me, and if we could do that... this..." He opened his hands, swirled them around their mini huddle and let them fall between them, to signify the here and now. "If we could do things like this more often?" She could feel her heart warm like an engine, uneasy at first but transforming her breath to a purr.

"I have something to tell you," she said with all of her heart.

"Please go ahead, tell me."

"I found something crazy today."

"What?"

"A baby book my mother created for me."

"Ok?"

"In it, she wrote the date she thinks she conceived me."

"Oh. That's pretty cool."

"Why do you think that's cool?" Mina didn't expect him to say that.

"I don't know. It isn't often that I hear stories where people know the night they got pregnant. Usually my friends are trying to have a baby, and have so much sex that it all rolls into one."

"Right. Anyway don't you want to know when it was?"

"Of course."

"Your birthday."

"My birthday?"

"Yes, your birthday. Meaning nine months to the day you are born, I am starting my way out into this bright world. Pretty interesting, huh?"

"Certainly is curious. How does your mom know she knows?"

"Because she's an old school Italian that keeps a calendar for these sorts of things. Are you questioning her?"

"No, Mina. God no. Forget I said anything. I just don't know how to react is all." Lampposts illuminated their periphery and the sun melted into fiery layers partitioned by buildings. "So what do you want to do now? You done with me?"

Mina shook her head no.

"You wanna play ski-ball?" she asked him with that smirk he missed so much.

"Sure. There's a first time for everything," he said as he stood and extended his hand to help her up. They walked to Red's to find two loners at the bar and not one person occupying the Ski-Ball game.

"It's great because if you get over 450 points you get a free beer," Mina told him excitedly.

"450 huh? Is that hard?" He felt around his pockets for change.

"I don't think so, but then again, we're talking about you, so I really don't know."

She took four quarters out of his hand and slid them into the tray. The machine lit up and bulbs flashed on and off. A digital song sounded and the scoreboard set to zero.

"Do you wanna go first?" she asked him.

"After you my dear. I'll watch the professional." Mina grabbed her balls, one by one, and threw her usual: up the middle, with a slight spin off the bank to aim at the 100 buckets in the top corners. She maxed out at 400 and Adam was ready to go. He rolled up his sleeves and unbuttoned his top button all with a permanent smile stamped on his face. When his score of 290 did not impress her, he was charged to play again. He got change from the bar and ordered two beers, and they fell into similar habits. They went for another round, without defending her title, she lost 320 to 400.

"Do you wanna go outside and have a smoke before we play another round? Maybe I should ask," he cupped his chin to act out curiosity. "Do you still smoke after a few sips, like you used to? I feel I have to ask these kinds of questions now since nearly everything about you, except you, is different."

"Sometimes, I do. Yes, let's." She swung her jacket around her body and slipped her hands through it. She led him to the bar's decent sized backyard. It was decorated with one of those large signature bathtub planters as a non-operative fountain. He lit the cigarette and handed it to her. Two squirrels grabbed their attention as they chased each other along the edge of the fence that bordered this yard from the next.

"Do you wanna share? I barely ever smoke a whole cigarette," he said.

"Okay."

"Meeenah!" He exhaled her name with great victory. "Tell me what you do. What do you spend your days doing here in Brooklyn?"

"Why?"

"Because, Dammit. I want to know."

"Alright, I work at a coffee shop. I started writing a little also."

"What's a little?"

"Just a little poetry."

"I didn't know you were a poet."

"I'm not, I just have been taking down notes on what I think and notice. It's a new thing, although my computer just crashed, so I don't know if I'm gonna be able to recover the small bit that I did write."

"What happened?"

"Oh I don't know the thing just died. It's old. This guy said that he might be able to help me, but I don't know if I can trust him, he just gave me his card at the café."

"Where's your café?"

"Here, not too far from where we are."

"Can we go there?"

"No."

"Why? You don't wanna be seen with me?"

"Shut up, that isn't it. I'm not working, so I'd rather not go there."

"Okay understood."

"And you? You were all, giving up on finance last time we spoke," she asked taking the spotlight off of her. "Still the same?"

"Yea I guess. I haven't left it completely." He pulled out a metal chair and sat down. "Although I have been talking with a friend of my mother's. This guy seems to know a lot about real estate and he makes a lot of money."

"Residential or Commercial?"

"Residential sales, but some rentals in the city too, but I would be working in Long Island. I've already started working a bit with him, just trying to learn the business. I think I would rather sell houses within the community. I mean people are always trying to move in, and this market can only go up."

"Is he Jewish?"

"Of course he's Jewish, and everyone I will be showing homes to will be Jewish. Have you been listening to a word I've said?" They laughed a bit. She looked at the end of the cigarette between her fingers. He pulled her into him by her wrist and tossed the burning filter. She shouted with excitement collapsing onto his lap.

"What are you doing?" Their faces were just about touching but with a tilt of her neck she angled her mouth away from his.

"Seducing you." He put his arms around her. Her internal warming was back again, same as she felt by the bridge, except this caress brought more tenderness, and she was close to crying. His chest rose attempting to breathe her in and she slipped into that same relaxation.

"I've missed you so much," he loosened his grip.

"Ditto...Do you wanna lose again?"

"Oh you think you're big time now don't you, Ms. 400, but what happened to you last game, you didn't do so well, now did you?" They stood a bit awkwardly and walked back into the bar.

Somehow the bar had accumulated a crowd in their small smoke break. Ski ball was still available and Mina quickly beat him by 20 points. Neither had scored a free beer but were content to walk in comfortable silence.

"So you're taking me to your meet your parents?" he asked.

"Are you out of your mind?"

"But that was the only reason why I let you win."

"What! You're such a liar, she said defiantly."

"No. I want to meet them though. Don't you want me to?" he asked with concern.

"Let's not get ahead of ourselves. I haven't even agreed to see you again and you are asking to meet mom and dad." He grabbed the lapel of her coat and pulled her into him as if she was weightless.

"Well what do you want Mina? You called me today." She pressed her hands against his arms and shoulders. His body was firm to the touch. She could make out the definition of the muscles in his arm through his jacket. The delicious smell of his skin coupled with his strength disarmed her. She could smell beer on his breath and wanted to drink his sweetness. He was so close to her that if she had moved her face towards his, they would have been lip-locked.

"So?" Mina asked without a care.

"So!" He tugged on her coat again. Her torso was now up against his and she rose to her tippy-toes. His eyes lowered and softened his grip. Her heels returned to the ground, and his tone changed. "You wouldn't have called me if you didn't want to see me." His mouth was a centimeter from hers, the same mouth she had been staring at all afternoon. Mina moved in and kissed him. She gave him an open mouthed kiss surrounding both of his lips with hers.

"I have to go home now," she said with a huge smile.

"I know. I'm coming."

"Stop it."

"Okay. I'm kidding." He hugged her in one of his usual extra long hugs. "When can we do this again?"

"Call my Shadchan," she said as she crossed Metropolitan Ave without him.

Song #29 This could be beautiful, Metronomy

Chapter 5
Swan Dive

Rags jumped off the bed to soak up the heat from the sun in its usual spot in Mina's bedroom. Her black coat shined colors like oil pools on a mechanic's sidewalk. Mina lay in bed enjoying the slowness of a holiday morning. She smiled to herself feeling Adam's words and kiss and opened her door to the smell of cinnamon and nutmeg. Marzia was pulling a tray of sprinkled lemon ball cookies out of the oven when they met in the kitchen.

"Good Morning Ma. Lemon balls, don't mind if I do." She grabbed a cookie and poured herself some coffee. "Do you need some help?" Mina tilted her head back and fluttered her eyes at the joy of a coffee dipped cookie.

"Well, the cookies are done. The squash is in the oven."

"What's Carmella cooking?" Mina asked detangling her hair.

"I don't think anything. I think it's going to be too much for her to cook and bring the kids. It's too much even with Michael's help. Call her please. Find out because I'll make some broccoli or cauliflower, you know I don't even know what I have. I might need you..." Marzia walked to the freezer without finishing her thought. Mina phoned Carmella.

"Oh no! Is he okay?" Mina spoke into the phone.

"Who? Baby Michael? What happened?" Marzia asked the air. Mina waved her off and turned her body giving her back to her mother. Marzia grabbed a hold of her own hip and watched Mina dip another cookie in her mug.

"Oh No! Why did she do that?" Mina asked with food in the back of her throat.

"Who Sophie?" Marzia was upset. Her eyes had begun to squint with dislike as she watched Mina's every move.

"Don't tell me no! I want to know what happened," Marzia was still talking to no one. She opened the oven to check on her squash then let the door slam as it closed. The sound shot Mina's eyebrows to her hairline.

"Okay, you want to talk to mommy?" Mina asked. "Ok. Wait, we wanted to know if you're making anything, if not, we could make something for you." Mina reached for another cookie but her mother moved the tray and blocked her hand.

"Yea, not a problem. Okay so what time are you gonna get there? Okay. See you." Mina hung up, grabbed a napkin and reached for the now available cookies.

"What happened with the baby?" Marzia asked.

"My God Ma! Nothing. Sophia was holding him in the bathroom and he banged his head on the sink. There's no blood. It must have just happened when I called, so he was hysterically crying and she gave him to Michael and was yelling at Sophia, so needless to say, she would love it if we could make a dish for her.

"But he's alright."

"Yea, he's fine."

"So, what are we gonna make?" Mina tried to take the severity out of the situation.

"I don't have enough broccoli. Can you go to the store? We're gonna need like four bags if you get frozen. I doubt you will find anything fresh now."

"But what do you want me to buy mom?"

"I don't know what they're gonna have, it's Thanksgiving Day Mina! Mina walked towards her mother to hug her. It was funny that the one person who made her was also the one person smaller than her.

"It's gonna be okay Ma, Happy Thanksgiving." Mina kissed her mother's forehead.

"Happy Thanksgiving to you too, Amor Mio." Mina took Rags with her, as it was time for a walk.

"Wait, Wait. Marzia opened the door and held it with her leg. "Get me a plunger from the hardware store if they're open."

"A plunger? We don't have one?"

"It's not working right.

"Gross." Mina grabbed the twenty-dollar bill from her mother. She left the house in the same lobster pajamas she slept in. Ace hardware store had a whistling parrot that was on a roll as Mina scanned aisles for a plunger. She checked on Rags through the window when she got to the counter but as usual she sat poised like a statue on the curb.

"Anything else?" The cash attendant asked Mina. A plunger only had one purpose and everybody knew it.

"No. I think this may even be too much for such a morning," she said with a huge smile.

"Good luck!" Mina walked towards Graham Ave resting the rubber end on one of her shoulders like the fat of a baseball bat. D'Agastino's only vegetable option was brussel sprouts. She turned onto Skillman carrying her shopping bags and plunger when her phone received a text. She pulled Rags to the side to read it as she saw someone coming towards her in her periphery. *I need the Shadchan's number?* Sent from: ASSHOLE.

"Hiya." Phil, the computer geek said happily.

"Hey," Mina put her phone in her sweatshirt pocket. "What are you doing in this part of town?"

"I live here," he said as a matter of fact.

"Get out, on Skillman?"

"No, just off it, two blocks that way," he pointed past her on the other side of Graham.

"Oh, cool! I'm right here," she pointed down the street. "Happy Thanksgiving!" Mina spread her cheer.

"Yea you too, that's funny that you live so close. Did you ever end up getting your computer fixed?"

"No, not yet," she said with disappointment.

"Bigger problems on your hands?" He pointed to the plunger. Mina laughed and failed to form a response.

"Yea and those are some pants. You are in rare form this morning!" Mina laughed and pushed his arm away It could have been for no reason associated with him, but she wasn't freaked out by him as she had been in the café.

"Cute dog," he bent down to rub the underside of Rags' neck.

"Alright, well you have yourself a nice holiday," he said standing up.

"You too Phil. I have your card. I'll call you."

"You should, I'll only be around for the next couple of weeks so if you want to get it restored let me know." Mina walked home thinking about what she was going to wear to dinner, and if she should text ASSHOLE back, or maybe just do the right thing and edit his contact information. Unfortunately, before she could try on what was draped over her bed as possible outfits, her mother needed yet another favor. Grace and Leo lived on Conselyea St. between Leonard and Manhattan Ave, just up and over one block in each direction from Marzia's house. They lived in an archetypical brownstone with huge ornamental knockers on their ten-foot doors with a grand foyer at the entrance. It was always spotless with the sitting room separate from the living room, as well as the dining room and the small windowed room off of the kitchen. Leo made a comment at the sight of Mina's pajamas the second he opened the door.

"Why do you look like a homeless person with a makeover? He asked seeing that make-up had been applied and hair had been straightened, but that she hadn't changed out of pajamas. Leo was short with hair on both sides of his head but none on the top.

"I was just bringing these over for Zizi Grace. Don't worry, I'm gonna change." Mina held out the two steno containers and thankfully Grace squeezed past him, because he didn't reach for anything.

"Leo, take this to the dining room please and put it on the buffet," She gave him an order. "You look beautiful darling. Don't listen to him. He's never learned how to talk to a woman. Will you guys be long?" Grace had an edgy short hairdo, one that would have better suited someone half her age.

"No we'll be right over." She wondered if the color in Grace's hair was new. Gio walked in behind Mina startling her with his signature Donald Duck growl of a hello.

"Mina why didn't you tell me you were gonna wear pajamas? I would have worn my shark ones? Babe look, she has lobsters just like my sharks you love so much," he said to Jessica. She covered her mouth in disbelief.

"I'm sorry I don't mean to laugh, but does this run in the family?" Jessica asked.

"Ya know if I had known they were gonna be such a hit I would have found a way to dress them up with heels and not Uggs. I'm gonna change and be back, so hi and bye." She kissed her cousin, but more people were still pouring through the door. "Hi, I'm Mina, Gio's cousin, you must be Jess' parents." They said hello, shook her hand and discreetly checked out her pajamas. "I'll be leaving now, see you in a little bit." Mina walked home.

Grace was still wearing her apron when the Luizzi's arrived. She matched the carefully picked earth tones of her décor very nicely. There was a huge cornucopia on the table that caught Mina's eye as she stole a piece of sopressata. Grace of course called her back into the kitchen after she had left. Mothers always waited for one to leave the room before saying something they could have said pre-exit.

"Take these out and make sure everyone has a glass." Grace handed her a plate.

"What the hell are these?" Mina was laughing and Grace's face became evil for a tenth of a second, yet changed when the doorbell rang. "Who's that?" Grace asked as if she wasn't entertaining.

"Probably Carmella," Mina said with a silent duh.

"Shit!" Grace exclaimed. She was making gravy and burned her finger. She looked at it and shook it in the air. "Alright hold off on those, go say hello. I don't know if there are enough bottles of wine on the table, so come back, but go help your sister with the baby." Mother's were obligated to carry a bag of things like toys and other such occupiers for their children, in case they inevitably started to act like children. Marzia held the baby following Carmella and Sophia upstairs to Grace's spare room. The room hardly saw children, but a child could certainly make do. Mothers were required to claim a space for playing, perhaps with the contents of such a bag or a nap, or a time-out if need be. Mina followed Grace's orders and carried a bunch of jackets to the upstairs closet.

"Hi Guys!" Mina said happily to Sophia and Michael and then looked at her sister. "These have to go in here," she mimicked Grace's tone. She walked back into the playroom to find Sophia handing coloring books from her bag to her mother and Marzia mid-diaper change.

"Oh that's pretty Sophia," Mina commented on the very stiff and clearly brand new Cinderella backpack.

"Mina!" Grace yelled from downstairs. Mina raised her eyebrows, enlarging the whites of her eyes.

"Oh...My...God. This woman!" she reversed from the playroom to where she was beckoned, and poked her head into the living room. Gio sat on the couch next to Jess and next to them in a love seat of their own were Jessica's parents, Eddie and Marisol. Eddie was bite size. He had small hands, a small frame, even a small face. Like Mina, he was dressed in brown; his being a suit and fedora, with the latter resting on his kneecap. He was a cute old man and Mina found herself wanting to talk to him and his wife. Marisol was reserved and squeezed herself into a tiny posture, taking up as little of the couch as possible. She had short brown hair and dark skin. The only thing that one could remark on was the amount of jewelry she wore. Every digit besides her pinkies and thumbs were adorned with rings.

Mina turned the other way to find Grace. She was apron-less in the dining room and glancing at herself in the mirror. She began whispering her plan to Mina.

"Okay I want to make a toast before we sit down, so go make sure everyone has a glass."

"I did already."

"Just check again, Mina." Grace sounded bothered and Mina began to feel similarly.

"Oh Mina!" Grace called her back yet again.

"Yes?"

"Take the meatballs out of the oven, and put them in the platter on the counter." Mina brought the tray out of the kitchen lifting it above her head with one hand, and with that she suddenly realized that she had cleaned this very *tree of life* platter herself. She then got the sentiment, good luck platter with good luck wedding meatballs. She made sure that everyone who was drinking was topped off. Grace walked in with shiny lips holding her glass up for a toast.

"Are we gonna eat yet?" Sophia asked as she ran into the room pulling at the bottom of her red corduroy skirt. Carmella opened her mouth in embarrassment and grabbed her daughter.

"How rude you are Soph. I'm sorry Zizi Grace, she's always starving.

"Yes, yes we are going to eat." Grace was happy to serve. Jessica and Marisol stood at the same time.

"Grace, can we help you with anything?" Jessica asked.

"No, no. Thank you so much for asking. It's all done, anyway, why don't you just bring your mother and father into the dining room." Mina was especially thankful the moment Leo landed the largest bird she had ever seen on the table. Everything was overdone in this house like Texas and their ridiculous way of being big. She reminisced of her grandmother: their all-day baking sessions, standing on kitchen chairs just to reach the counter and getting covered in flour.

"Where are your parents? I thought they were coming?" Joe asked Leo. Leo sat at the head of the table facing Michael and Joe at the other end.

"They couldn't make it. My brother's with them in Jersey," Leo cut into the turkey.

"Please serve yourselves. That's smoked ham and under the foil is salmon," Grace said. Hands reached for serving spoons and plates began to shift while platters made their way around the table.

"Oh also Eddie and Mari brought some pastelas, am I saying that right?" Grace asked.

"Yes that's how you say it, like pasta except with ellas at the end. They are made with meat and plantains. I don't know just try them," Jess said nervously.

"Yes. Don't feel bad if you don't like them. I just thought I would bring something that we always have at our Thanksgiving. The ones with red string are spicy," Marisol added.

"Where's my tray?" Grace asked Mina, but Mina didn't hear her. "Mina, where's my tray?"

"What tray?"

"The one I told you to take from the kitchen."

"Oh I brought it into the living room."

"Go get it," she said curtly.

"What was it?" Marzia asked her sister.

"You'll see they're so cute, I should always make them like this."

Mina walked back in with the platter in question. "I made Italian wedding meatballs for good luck, but I didn't fry them Jessica! I know you don't like to eat fried foods." Grace addressed the family and moved her hands around as if the meatballs were going to magically fill the air with good spirit. "I know it's Thanksgiving, but it is also a very special time and I am just so happy for my Gio and we look forward to their wedding day where we will celebrate even more."

"Lord, thank you for this food, which we are about to eat. Thank you for my family: my wife, my son, his engagement, our health and the health and happiness of our family and friends, especially those that are here with us for this blessed meal, Leo said for the table. Guests mouthed a barely audible amen and began eating. They soon complimented Grace on the flavor and juiciness of the turkey and even the brussel sprouts, which was handed off to Marzia, who then handed it off to Mina.

Marisol whispered something into Jessica's ear that made her chuckle. Gio asked Jessica what it was, but Marisol was already repeating it to her husband. Eddie nodded his head in agreement. Jessica started laughing again and passed the turkey along the table. Grace smiled at the interactions but wanted more information.

"What's so funny Jess?" Grace asked hiding a bit of evil.

"Nothing. My parents think they look like matzah balls. I'm telling them they're not." Mina coughed wine into her hand. "I know it!" She wiped her mouth with her napkin. "Thank you Eddie. I thought the same thing. I was like, why the hell would you make matzah balls for Thanksgiving?"

"Mina, when have you ever sat down to matzah balls in my house?" Grace was annoyed.

"She might have sat down to matzah balls and that's why they're on her mind," Marzia said. Carmella shot eyes at Mina. It was a shock that Marzia knew about Adam, or that there might have been developments she didn't know of, and that the whole thing was said so nonchalantly. Joe caught Carmella's look.

"Oh so you know she has a Jewish friend from Manhattan?" Joe asked. "Looks like there's more to this story than we were told, Marzia."

"Who knows a Jew from Manhattan?" Leo asked.

"Mina, don't tell me you're dating a Jew?" Grace asked.

"She's not," Gio answered. He filled Jessica's wine glass. Mina was sitting on the other side of him and lifted her glass so she too could get a refill.

"You know too!" Joe cocked an eyebrow at this new information.

"They used to call Laguardia, the Jew from Manhattan," Leo said as a grand opening sentence to no one. He looked at his son for some way to go on, but nothing happened. Carmella was cutting Sophia's food into tiny squares and Michael tried to feed a piece to the blue-eyed baby.

"I'm not dating a Jew and I've never had dinner with matzah balls," Mina put down her fork. "But I've had matzah ball soup before, just as Eddie and Marisol might have." She paused. "It's..ah.. mezzo mezzo." The table laughed.

"I didn't know Laguardia was Jewish?" Joe asked.

"Laguardia?" as in the airport? Marisol asked.

"Yes, he had a short stint at the job but was a great one still."

"Here we go," Marzia said with exaggeration. "Leo, where do you store all of this useless information?"

"That was just what they called him," he defended himself.

"So how'd you know she wasn't dating him? You have time to keep tabs on your cousin Mina, but not come see me?" Marzia said to Gio.

"But of course I don't miss a thing."

"Okay," Carmella sighed and looked up from her parental cutting, unaware of anything else but her hunger. She took a healthy sip from her glass and reached for food. She grabbed a meatball and bit it in half. "Mmm, why don't we give Eddie a matzah ball, once he tastes them I am sure he won't think they are mezzo mezzo." Carmella said staring down the table for food she wanted to put on her plate.

"They're not matzah balls!" Grace was not happy, but Carmella didn't understand what the big deal was.

"Oh shit, I meant meat balls. Matzah balls, meat balls, they even sound the same," Carmella laughed looking at Michael and her sister.

"Funny enough Laguardia was Jewish and Italian, but his mother was the Jew. You know this is how Jew's pass their heritage. Even though it's fundamentally a religion but... We've lost sight of this anyway...A Jew is only a Jew if the mother is Jewish. Mina was learning something new from disconnected memory of Laguardia. Thanks to Uncle Leo, she learned just how flawed the pedigree of her and Adam's unborn baby was from the start. "Speaking of Italy, it was a big year for us eh? We housed the Olympics AND we won the world cup," Leo did everyone a favor and changed topics.

"What a game that was, man. I was rooting for Italy the whole time. She loves futbol too," Eddie said pointing to his wife.

"Did you guys hear about the scandal with the referees? The Italians were trying to fix the tournament," Gio said. No's shot across the table from feeding mouths.

"Really?" Marzia asked.

"Doesn't surprise me. They're animals out there," Grace said in her usual tone.

"Well someone's got to run things? Beats the hell out of me why they're always crying," Leo said smirking. "You watch baseball Eddie?"

"Oh yes. I love baseball. I used to play in my country."

"Puerto Rico?"

"Yes. I came to the U.S. when I was four," Eddie said.

"We've never been to Puerto Rico," Grace said.

"No? You should go its very beautiful."

"We go all the time. We both have a lot of family still living there," Marisol added.

"Yea we're thinking about going for the beginning of our honeymoon, to see her grandparents, plus I've never been, but we don't know where after that, maybe Mexico," Gio said admiring his woman.

"Mexico? Why do you want to go to Mexico?" Grace asked with judgment.

"I don't know the pictures of the beaches look beautiful, and the resorts are all inclusive and gorgeous," Gio said.

"Don't drink the water," Joe warned.

"Montezuma's revenge," Leo added and their women laughed.

"There's a lot of great history there too. Jess is into the ruins and Mayan culture." Leo shook his head and looked at Grace who was content to listen to their son.

"I've always wanted to see the ruins. I've only seen pictures, but it's incredible to see how advanced they were and so long ago. They built entire communities based on where the sun and moon were," Mina said.

"You sound like her," Gio said. "Maybe it won't be Mexico. We haven't decided, yet." He put his hand on Jessica's lap. "There are other places we're thinking of as well."

"Michael where did you guys go for your honeymoon?" Leo asked.

"Venice." Michael held a juice box for Sophia to sip from. "But that was easy it was a place both of us said instantly as our first choice. Well, actually she said Florence, so we traveled to both, but we were really lucky that it worked out that way."

"I loved Venice!" Mina said. Baby Michael joined in her enthusiasm and shot out a sound and everyone started laughing as if he was trying to be part of the conversation.

"That's right Michael. Woppa Italia!" Joe shouted with joy.

"Mina, weren't you in Italy for a year?" Leo remembered this detail.

"Yea it was great. I loved it, but it was a bit different for me. I was a student and the single life over there is not like being on honeymoon."

"I've thought about Europe, and if we can afford it, I don't see why not. What did you like most about it?" Jessica asked Mina.

"The art. Everything about the culture there is founded on art. And at the time these masters were creating, they weren't just artists but geniuses. And so, so much of their culture respects creativity and it shows in how they do everything. From their dishes, to architecture, to how people there try to impress you, just what is important to them is completely different from our American way of living."

"Yea and how do you like it living back at home with your parents, a bit different, eh?" Leo asked Mina. She was agitated by his questions?

"Yes, very different. It's alright, I guess. Williamsburg's not what I remember, but I'm liking it."

"You like all the construction and young people spraying graffiti everywhere?"

"I do. Don't you? It keeps the interest here and the culture up to date, plus you get to rent your basement out for a nice penny. But, there's something weird about it too."

"How do you mean?" Leo asked.

"Yes Mina, what's weird?" Grace asked.

"I don't know, at any point in the day you can see so many people walking around and maybe they have something they're doing or a place they're going to, but it just seems as though, people are doing nothing. And even those that call themselves artists. Like the new art I see at galleries, or PS1, it's just lacking substance." Mina hadn't realized she felt so strongly.

"Well nothing is the way it used to be Mina, and it won't ever be," Marzia said.

"That's so true. Did any of you hear about this year's commencement speech at SUNY New Paltz?" Jessica asked no one in particular.

"No. Who spoke?" Leo was interested.

"The publisher of The New York Times, I forget his name."

"Yea what happened?" Marzia and Carmella asked in unison.

"Poor guy was awarded the worst quote of the year. He was only being honest, but no one wants to hear the truth. It got a good amount of press and of course all the teachers at my school were making a big deal about it. That was how I heard about it, anyway. I'm going to paraphrase because I don't remember it exactly, but he basically deflated a room full of newly graduated students, telling them how it wasn't supposed to be this way, that they weren't supposed to be entering a fighting America, one in constant disagreement, still fighting over things like human rights, the rights of immigrants, the rights of gays, marriage, abortion, etc. He even slandered the government for letting oil drive their policy and honored environmentalists in their plight to make people see what really matters. It was kind of amazing and rare. Here people were happy to begin their careers and hopefully enter the workforce, and off he sent them with an apology from all of us who ruined it for them."

"How did the students take it? What was said?" Mina asked.

"Well they just wrote about it and it passed, like most things. But it was nice, ya know for my line of work."

"I don't know even know what you do exactly."

"I'm in social work."

"You have your own practice?" Carmella asked.

"No not yet, maybe not ever. Right now I migrate between different city high schools. I see all kinds of situations and this was an interesting concept that is being heavily researched and written about. We can't disregard the world we live in. It affects all of us, whether we think it does or not. Sure we all have personal matters, but every bit plays its part."

"Well despite these things, people are still making money and finding their way," Grace said. Her husband was a political man, and this was not his position, plus there were certain things not to be discussed on occasions like Thanksgiving and this was definitely one of them. "Times may be harder now but we've been very lucky. We've had the same couple renting from us for four years now, and people are still finding ways to make money. I mean just look at this neighborhood as an example. Those condos are going up and people are gonna live in them. The whole waterfront is gonna be redone and for the better."

"Enough," Leo said loudly. "Enough with this. If people aren't happy with their life here they can leave. But they don't, because there are too many handouts. This country makes it too easy for those who don't want to put in the effort. We didn't have anything and we made it! There is nothing I hate more than people who don't help themselves."

Mina didn't want the conversation to end but they weren't discussing the same things. She was reminded of Weltschmerz and made a mental note to look it up.

"Excuse us," Carmella grabbed an agitated baby Michael from her husband and brought him into the living room. She called her husband within seconds to help her construct the playpen so that she could put him down. This was another item that mother's had to bring with them, in case their child was not able to walk, or stay awake for prolonged periods of time. These were all truths that Mina was now extra aware of having missed the bullet with a child of her own.

"Who wants coffee?" Grace asked. Carmella came back and did her best to remove stacked plates. Mina and Jessica got up to participate in the clean up.

"You don't have to do that."

"Oh stop it. Just get the coffee started and please tell me you have canollis," Mina begged.

"Of course I have canollis. What kind of house do you think this is?" Grace was successfully redirected.

"I love canollis," Jess said with a great big smile. She was pretty, Mina mentally agreed with everyone else. She had long silky black hair and flawless caramel skin. She was petite with brown eyes that closed when she smiled. She was just who Gio should be with, if one could foresee that sort of thing. The kitchen was big, but certainly not big enough for Marzia when she continued to bring platters from the table.

137

"I am so glad that Gio has a cousin like you, someone close to my age, and female. I've met his friends but they are just a group of guys, ya know.

"It's nice to get to spend time with you too. I mean you guys have dated forever and it's a lot better to see you than just talk about you all the time," Mina embellished.

"See, I never get to hear these things. I don't say much to his boys from the firehouse. They must think I'm so boring," Jessica laughed.

"I doubt it."

Dessert was fun-filled and far less formal. Night fell and lamps on both ends of the couches lighted the party. Joe and Leo were out back smoking a cigar. The television was on and sitcoms were experiencing their own Thanksgiving mishaps. Guests grabbed sweets as they walked to and from rooms. Napoleons and sfoigtaelles were on a platter of their own and brought into the living room but more food remained on the actual dining room table. The whole bottle of Sambuca remained on the dining room table next to the restaurant-sized carafe of coffee, yet another example of how overdone everything in this house was. If only that homeless guy that sleeps on Macri triangle could get some of this good stuff. Grace and Marzia chatted with Gio and Jess at the table about the wedding. They chose a reception hall overlooking the Sound in New Rochelle. Jessica was in the middle of describing the outdoor chapel that she fell in love with when Mina swooped in to grab a cannoli. She sneaked a peek at the pamphlet in Marzia's hand, and flipped the cover over to read, GreenTree printed in gold.

"Ou Fancy," Mina commented as she left the room.

"My God, it's hard to believe I went nine months without this stuff," Carmella said pouring a cup of coffee.

Mina searched for Sophia. She didn't want to talk about a wedding and considered what it meant to be *ready* for marriage, or how Jessica knew it was *time*. She was only just now getting to know Gio's family despite how many dates they had been on. She pictured Adam and it seemed impossible for the vision of a wedding to materialize, even comical, if it were to happen. She found her distraction and flipped Sophie to hold her upside down. She let out a squealing laughter and together they moved out of Marisol's way to enter the living room.

"Too much wedding stuff for you?" Mina asked sitting next to Marisol. She tried to make conversation with the only person she felt she hadn't connected with.

"Ay no. I just already talked about it with Jessica." She pronounced her daughters name, Jess-ee-kah.

"I see. Did you say hi to Marisol?" Mina tucked Sophia's hair behind her ear as she included her in adult conversation.

"Please call me Mari," her mouth pronounced Madi.

"Hi Mari," Sophia said.

"Do you know who Mari is?"

"Yes," Sophia answered.

"You do, who is she?"

"She's your friend," she said playing with Mina's hair to return the favor.

"Well yes she's a friend of all of ours, but she's also Jessica's mom. You know who Jessica is right?"

"Yes, she's sitting with mommy. She has long pretty hair."

"That's her," Mina said.

"She's always had long hair, since she was a little girl like you," Marisol said. "How old are you Sophia?"

"I'm six," Sophia answered Marisol.

"Six years old? That's so big!"

"Say yes it is, I am so big!" Mina bobbed Sophia up and down on her bouncing knees. "Tell her how you're a big sister, and how you help mommy with the baby?" Mina's enthusiasm quieted Sophia. "How old are *you* now Mina?" Leo asked as he entered the conversation and stunk up the living room with remnants of cigar. Mina didn't like his tone. It sounded as if he had just finished a conversation about her place in life, which made his opening question a set-up. As if he was only asking questions to get her to say something he already knew and state his unwelcome opinion. This was usually how she felt about conversations with her uncle. His stink nose was given to him by birth for a reason; he was either thinking stink thoughts, or saying things that stunk.

"I'm this many." She put up all ten fingers flashed them twice and then tucked an index and thumb to show eight.

"28 huh?"

"Well 29 in a week, but yes, the only age of a woman, as Mamaw used to say."

"That woman said she was 29 and a half every birthday she ever had," Leo remembered.

"And I will do the same. Although, I really do turn 29 this year."

"So close to Thanksgiving," Mari said.

"Every year. Neither of us are changing the date, but no worries you'll have plenty of time to recover for my party."

"You're having a party?" Joe asked his live-in daughter with an alertness that wasn't present before.

"No dad I'm kidding," she laughed through her mouth making a pfff sound.

"You're a Sagittarius. My sister is a Sag. Good people, great energy." she paused. "But they have such a sharp tongue."

"That she does," Joe said.

"But, they'll never lie." Marisol held up her pointer finger. "That's what makes them such good friends."

"Do you know a lot about this stuff?" Mina turned towards Marisol.

"I learned from my mother in Puerto Rico. People come from all over the island to see her."

"I've read a lot about my sign and most of it, and what you just said is spot on. Mamaw still has some of her old books in the basement, actually." Mina realized after she said this that Marisol had no idea who Mamaw was. She turned to see if her father was listening but he had checked out. Michael and Carmella walked in and noticeably interrupted Leo and Eddie's gaze into the television.

"What are you guys talking about?" Carmella asked with an exhausted face.

"Me." Mina laughed and then put her arm on Marisol's shoulder. "She was telling me about Sagittarians."

"Oh that's right this is a big year for you, 30 right?" Carmella adjusted her pants at the waist line. "Ugh, I am so full."

"Not yet Carm, don't rush me just because you're feeling old, I'm only 29."

"Is being a smart ass true of her sign?"

"Yes, they can be, but that is part of their charm. They are usually the life of the party and people love them."

"Oh, don't tell her that," Michael said.

"It's not about her. All signs favor Sagittarius."

"Who am I best matched with?" Mina asked.

"The best match for fire is fire, or air, air could work too. But all the other elements will either be too sensitive to your heat, or will drown you. Water is no good for you."

"What are the water signs?"

"Water is Scorpio, Pisces, and Cancer, Marisol took a moment and looked at the ceiling collecting her thoughts. "They're not impossible as matches. It could be good in the right situation, but what do fire and water make? Mina didn't know what to say. She looked at her sister, but no one else was really paying attention.

"I don't know a boil?" Mina put her hands up.

"Right, if fire is strong enough, but even then, as steam evaporates so will the love, or if water is stronger like Pisces, they will know your feelings, y la voltier la tortilla."

"What does that mean?" Adam was a Pisces.

"It means they'll turn things around. It is problematic and emotional. They're highly sensitive one minute and then not at all. They can estimate your feelings. That is their nature, but it doesn't charge them to act and if they are pushed, and you'll probably push them, they will be ah...how do you say it, Marisol spoke Spanish to her husband in Spanish. He answered her, and she turned to Mina to finish her thought. "You say, a wet blanket, in English."

Rain fell like tiny stones against the window. Mina wanted to continue asking more questions about Pisces but wasn't interested in another third degree about the Jew in question. Grace and Marzia were in the kitchen making to-go containers for their guests. Eddie glanced out the window as if they could visually gauge the force of raindrops.

"I don't want all this food in my house," Grace said moving around the dining room table organizing individual towers of food for people to take. The downpour was enough of an excuse for everyone to seek comfort in their own homes, and soon enough the children were neatly wrapped in the layers they had arrived in. Michael loaded the car and brought it out front. They were the first to go. Sophia was a little upset to leave grandpa but managed to do it with less tears than usual, and within twenty minutes the only thing one could hear in the house was rain.

"Eddie was really nice," Grace said. "But Marisol didn't say much."

"Maybe she's quiet," Marzia defended her honor.

"I didn't think she was that quiet. We had a long conversation."

"You did?" Grace asked Mina.

"Where was I?" Marzia pointed to herself.

"You's two were planning a wedding in the other room."

"That's right, she left the table right when we were talking about Jessica's plans. That's weird," Grace said to her sister.

"Don't you think they already talk about it non-stop and maybe she wanted to give you some time alone with her?" Mina suggested.

"You excited for the wedding Mina?" Grace asked.

"Of course, I love weddings."

"What about you, eh? You ready to find the right guy?"

"Guy? She may want to find a career first?" Marzia said.

"Maybe, I'm gonna go. Thank you for everything Zizi Grace, it was wonderful." Mina kissed her mother and said bye to Joe and Leo on the way out.

Rags barely made it down the block. She kept blinking and looking up at Mina as if acid rain had been burning her coat. Mina was drenched on her return and showered the second she got back. She enjoyed the hot water and did some sort of non-religious negotiation-style prayer as she washed. Listing and promising all the things she would do, if and when her laptop turned on, but it was unsuccessful. In her dream she was marked by a number, not inked or burned skin, just the likeness of a number formed at creation and written in her veins. It was located right below her knee on the inside of her calf. It was the number five and represented the fifth house of the Zodiac, which in Astrology is ruled by Leo. But it wasn't on her as if to say she was part of that house, but rather signified her destiny. This fifth house wasn't a true house, but an island and the only land where she could find her soul mate. Mina was a warrior in this fantastic dream and accepted her quest. It was the fifth successive mountaintop she could see when she looked out into the horizon from where she was, but the only way to could get from one house to the other was by grabbing and climbing ladders that hung from the sky. This was what people did here in this strange archipelago. Many did not make it, but it was their only hope to having true love and love to these creatures, was life's greatest purpose. She was muscular in her dream, like that of a horse, wearing animal skin and her hair reached her feet.

Between any two houses there could be one to four ladders she had to jump from. She acrobatically swung with great strength to catch and climb rungs without slipping or stepping on her hair. She had to move quickly. The ladders lowered her into the sea like quicksand the second her grip weighed them down. Waves reached for her and the mist from their break wet her face and mane, sinking the ladders even more. She woke up mid swing feeling wholly disconnected from reality.

#30 Aqueous Transmission, Incubus

Part 4

"Without self-love,
the one you think you love and the one who loves
you
will never be the same person."

Chapter 1
Expectation

Song # 31 Breathe (Chill Out Mix), Dinka

Rain was an enjoyable tune at first. The isolated sound of each drop hit the roof like footsteps on snow, but as the days continued to crawl across the calendar, the weather failed to change. Bright gray clouds turned on and off like faucets twisting out regular rain, freezing rain, snow, and sometimes all three. If it stopped, solemn faces lifted their necks to the sky. The reprieve energized the body, and filled the swell of each goose bump with hope that the sun would return, but only gray remained. Beyond precipitation, the city was presently too cold for fingertips to thaw. They didn't even belong to the hand they dangled from. Night shift or day shift at Atlas, it didn't matter; the whole week after Thanksgiving was a dark wet cold day. They were long tiring days that made the whole body yawn. The feeling didn't pass, nor did the yawning or tearing that accompanied it. People were desperate and looked like they were hemorrhaging vitality. Hands quickly learned to comfort one other in front of a warm mouth. It was an act better saved for days of skiing, riding lifts and looking at mountaintops, not the subway or walking in the splash back of the city taking a winter bath.

It depressed Mina and her mind wandered while she walked under this blanket of filth. She imagined a giant with fingers the size of couches squeezing monster-sized fists around Earthly faucets making everything miserable and wet. She described these fantastic details mostly as a joke to Lizzy, the greasy haired blonde running the cash-box at The Gallery. That was how Simi, the Croatian and owner of The Gallery, had introduced them.

"Mina, this is Lizzy, she'll be running the cash-box. Lizzy, this is Mina, she'll be cocktailing."

The Croatian had long legs and reminded Mina of an ostrich. He cupped his chin in conversation and his nose and lips stretched out when he talked. He laughed at everything and usually ended his laugh with a snort. It was nearly impossible to have a serious conversation with him because he kept on taking breaks to laugh. He had a thick accent and terribly bloodshot eyes if he opened them enough for one to notice. Mina didn't know him but didn't like what she knew. For starters he named the space, The Gallery, but beyond that she knew that he only hired attractive women to work his art shows, like it was some club. It cheapened the experience, and bothered her that years of studying art history had amounted to fine slices of cheddar cheese. Her extensive education afforded her the grace and skill to display crackers like fallen dominos or stand behind some desk, because that's what it was, that and pouring sensibly-priced piss looking liquid, labeled *Just White,* into hard plastic. Not only was she turning 29 in just a few days but this was the closest activity she had that served her passion.

It seemed that while regular family people were enjoying the coming of winter, the rest of the community was bent on turning the neighborhood into Christmas overnight. The Gallery followed suit and Mina was in the middle of spraying that lovely deflated shaving cream to resemble snow in window corners while Lizzy mounted artists' names and titles of pieces on the wall. An art gallery feels different when no one's in it. It's somehow nicer. It was the first time that Mina had been called to work for one of their shows and she was eager to be part of the set up, before she got placed on cheese detail. This particular show was titled, The Calling. It was an homage to purpose, as the subtitle read, and from the likes of Simi, she questioned who came up with it. There were oil canvases, photographs, and some mixed media, including a mosaic of very different subjects. Some of the pieces were of agricultural landscapes, beautiful photographs of cornfields with accompanying poetry. There were others of cityscapes, as in the city was a calling and destination, and an inordinate amount of bird paintings.

"I can't stand this sky. It's so Goddamn blinding," Mina grunted to Lizzy but there wasn't a response. "It looks like a piss poor attempt of an artist wishing to make clouds, except not one cloud has any color or form, just a bunch of different gray's blotting what looks like water stains on white paper." Lizzy let out a pathetic laugh. "Sometimes they're really dark and other times they're not there at all. The Ether Giant can make things go *either* way. Get it?"

"At least it's not snowing. I hate the snow." Lizzy made an unhappy face.

"How could you hate the snow?"

"Simple. I can't stand it. I can't stand walking in it. When I drove I couldn't stand driving in it." Mina thought about her travels in the rain and snow and she agreed. Everything was less pleasant. Birds didn't soar in the rain, instead they flew vigorously, partly because their weight was measured in mere ounces and no match for pelting water. And Mina watched them, not just now through the window or on canvas hanging on the walls, but replayed the mental notes she took of them on her walks to and from work. As she regretted each squirt of this foolish decoration, she thought about how much water had been pouring from the heavens and the whole elemental conversation she had with Marisol about Adam's water sign.

"Ether? Ether is the Fifth Chakra's element?" Lizzy seemed to ask and say at the same time.

"What?" Mina asked.

"That's what this says here." Lizzy was referring to the strip that she had just mounted under a painting of a crowned bird. The bird sang a universe of colors from its beak. Mina walked over with her can in hand to take a closer look.

"It's a pretty cool painting. It kind of looks like a peacock right?" Mina asked. It was a well-crafted piece and the two of them gazed into the swirling magma pouring from the bird's throat.

"I think so. Peacocks are the only birds I know that have crowns," Lizzy moved onto her next title. Mina finished Christmas duties and even threw in a special *Ho Ho Ho*, a secret jab at the Croatian and his desired employees, but he'd love it.

Adam only knew the date of Mina's birthday from their most recent conversation about her baby book. He found it curious that

that they were both born on the 1st, his being March, and hers' on December, but that was where his thoughts on it ended. He bought her a card with a big number one on it, and a group photo of nearly every muscle-bound maniac from Marvel Comics, wishing her a happy first birthday. They were spending nights talking on the phone as they did before and little by little he was getting her to drop her guard. He had a pre-celebration planned this weekend, and another one on her actual birthday.

He was back in the habit of not letting her get off the phone when she tried to say bye. He would say, 'Wait, one more thing,' and they would discuss that one more thing, and then would say it again prolonging the conversation for sometimes twenty minutes. She would fall for it nearly every time until it hit her, and she would shout something like 'Oh my God!' and hang up on him.

Adam dove right into Christmas spirit, thinking of her as he made each new Christmas habit. He even set his tiny AM/FM shower radio to 103.9, the only constant Christmas music station. He listened and sang along as he went through his morning routine, even brought up individual songs to Mina as if they were something worth discussing.

"Do you know that song, *Do they know its Christmas time?*"

"I don't know Adam," Mina said without interest. He sang the chorus for her. "Yes I think I know it, it's sung by little kids at the end right?"

"Maybe, but their group is called Band-Aid. I bet you didn't know that."

"I bet you're right!"

"Are you excited for your surprise?" he asked with a lit up face.

"I am…"

They ended their phone conversation to resume in person. He met her at the opening of his lobby sitting pretty in front of the Corinthian's fountain. It was strange to find him outside but he looked gorgeous. Yellow floodlights transformed the fountain water behind him into bubbling liquid gold.

"I'm pretty sure that's my favorite Christmas song. What's yours?" He was still on it.

"I don't know. That's a tough one for me. I grew up on this shit, you're just getting into it now. It's totally different for you. Of course you, the Jew, would ask me such a question." They hopped in a cab.

"Where are we going that we're headed uptown?"

"Oh wouldn't you love to know..."

"Yes, tell me."

"Can't." He sat quietly looking out the window while they were stopped at a light. "We're going to Queens."

"Is that where your parents live?"

"Close enough."

"Where *do* they live?"

"Far Rockaway, why?"

"Because I don't know anything about your family. Where you come from? And why you are the way you are." Mina thought about the ad she saw on the subway for a McDonald's iced coffee. It had a picture of the drink with the quote, "I'm not falling asleep and ending up in Far Rockaway again."

"I just saw an ad for Far Rockaway."

"You're kidding?"

"It wasn't for Far Rockaway now that I realize how I said that, but it was for McDonalds and funny. I'm guess Far Rockaway isn't a very common destination for people. What would your parents say if they met me?"

"It depends on what you guys were talking about."

"Oh aren't you tricky...What I mean is, how would you introduce me?"

"How do you know I haven't told them about you already?"

"No. Adam I mean it. I'm curious how our meeting would go. How would I be received? As in, how do they feel about non-Jews entering their home?"

"I don't know, that doesn't happen often to be honest, but I am sure that it would be fine. They're not animals, but I thought you said you didn't want to meet them. What's changed your mind?"

"I didn't say I didn't want to meet them. I told you that I didn't want *you* to meet my family. Those are very different things." Mina thought about the other ad she saw that afternoon. It was a penciled drawing of Death, cloak and all, approaching someone as they lie in bed. The person waking to their undertaker asks, 'Are you here to judge me?' Death says, 'No that's not my department, you're thinking of the guy in the white robe.' "But what do Jews think about Catholics, like do they have a consensus in the way Catholics, I mean everyone," she laughed, "...has an opinion on Jews? You know how Italian stereotypes just roll of the tongue for most people. They must have words for this kind of stuff."

"They must?"

"Don't they?" Mina looked away and became distracted by the sights around her. The cab was on 50th and Lexington. "My god! Look at this, where are you taking me? This isn't Queens. Look at them being herded like cattle." Mina commented on the crowds pouring into the street at each curb. "And look at these cops, what a fine job they're doing!" she said with sarcasm.

"Holy shit, she must be freezing!" Adam noticed a Salvation Army bell ringer wearing shorts and a tee shirt. Mina leaned over to look out his window but she missed the woman he mentioned. "Here is good."

"Here! What for?" Adam paid the cabbie and they were soon on foot.

"Mina, this is your special surprise. Try not to ruin it now, okay?"

"My special surprise?" Mina looked up at the tree and was bombarded by people bumping her as they passed. Cherry colored cheeks buzzed to and fro like insects, glancing at their phone in search for their missing parties. It was a madhouse. The tree was sprinkled in its usual colorful bulbs, no tinsel, no ribbon, no bow, and without an angel. It was quite bare and she said something about that to him. But he didn't understand and she waved her hands in the air to say never mind. This was the largest tree he had ever seen, he never had one growing up, and right now he was watching thousands of people gather from around the world to see it. How could he wish for anything more, other than for her to admire it as they were, after all this was her special surprise and only one of the many things he planned for her birthday? He grabbed her hand and she let it stay suspended in hers. It was a fine rhythm they found walking together. He was happy, like a king of the city, walking with his woman admiring the pretty tree that the town had dressed for their pleasure.

"I've been having the strangest dreams," she said as they walked away from Rockefeller Center.

"Anything you wish to confess to me?"

"No. Why are you so vain?" She couldn't help but smile every moment they were together.

"I'm not vain, but my ego is. Oh my God did you see the size of that guy's nostrils?"

"No I missed it." She turned around but saw nothing but long coats. "You know that your nostrils are just the right size for your fingers." He flared his nose as she spoke.

"Why would you start telling me about your dreams if I wasn't in them?"

"Do I only talk to you about things that involve you, Adam?"

"Yes, of course. Why do you think I like spending time with you?"

"I'm still trying to figure that out, but let's not fight."

"You really think you have the upper hand here huh?" Adam asked looking at her out of the corner of his eye.

"I don't even have a hand. You asked me to hang out and mentioned something about a fireplace. I can't say no to a fire. Maybe you know that, maybe you don't."

"I know everything, remember."

"Remember what?"

"Well you used to say that. Sometimes, you used to say I was in your head when I said things right as you were thinking them."

They entered a lounge called Mezcal, not far from where they were. There were only three tapas on the menu that Adam could eat. As much as he was not religious, he was still holding true to the kashrut of no pork.

"Still avoiding the split hooves huh?"

"Yes, my dear. How do you know so much?"

"I learned it from you."

They finished two bottles of red wine. The fireplace was real and a pleasant change-up from those electric hot plates, or worse pretend logs with a gas stove underneath. A mustachioed man with curls at both ends came over three or four times to poke embers, lifting with a pull and pushing to tuck to maintain flame and crackle. Every now and then Adam would put his hand over hers and softly rub the tops of her fingers, circling his fingertip on her nail bed. It was strangely one of the most pleasurable things he had ever done to her. It was so simple. She couldn't believe her cuticles were turning her on, but perhaps this is what happens when you spend enough time without *special attention.*

"You know what I miss sometimes?" Mina just stared into his left eye as he spoke. "Just kissing you," he said licking his lips. "You used to look at me when you kiss me. That's really hard to find in a person." Mina blushed. "You'd look at me like you're looking at me right now."

~ ~ ~

Mina stayed behind while he took Serpico for a walk. She dragged her sock covered toes traipsing around his apartment as if it were the first time. And it felt weird, like maybe she was about to do something for the first time, again. She looked at the bonsai and said out loud, *hello little friend*. It immediately repeated her dreams, this time blending them altogether to one. It was a beautiful painting in her mind's eye. She envisioned ladders hanging from the sky, birds, and even the small fruitless woman pulling at her heart shaped desires from her White Pine.

Chapter 2
Pas de Deux

Song #32 Ma Voix Mon Dieu, Chakra Bird

Mina woke first. Adam was perfectly still with his nose pointed at the ceiling. She turned onto her back so that it was flush against the bed as well. It was snowing, lightly and pleasantly. The apartment was quiet. All she could hear was a steady drip of water beat against the steel railing of his balcony. She turned back to him and this time he was looking at her.

"Hey! You were just sleeping," she said with a full smile on her face.

"Not anymore." Adam rolled on top of her and snuck his arm in the small of her back and hugged her with his whole body.

"I can make coffee if you'd like," he said with his lips resting on her clavicle. She thought about the things they did a few hours ago and it filled her with shivers. "I'll give you your favorite yellow mug," he sang with temptation.

They sat by the bay window sipping a fresh brew watching snow fall on the city in his beautiful downtown facing view.

"I forgot how great this window is," she said.

"Especially when it snows. Look, we may even be able to see your house. He pointed to the ever-reaching sight of the East River.

"Doubt it."

"So Mina, are you excited to be turning 29 in a couple days?"

"I am, and then..." She let her hair fall in front of her face, scratched her scalp and separated curls. They often clung to one another from knotting in sleep. "I'm not even really thinking about it. I have to work this afternoon." She threw her mane back and looked at him without any distractions covering her face. "There's a show at the gallery, I'm sort of hosting. Do you want to come?"

"Tonight?"

"Yea," She found it curious that she had to repeat herself.

"I can't tonight."

"Okay, that's cool." And it was cool, the way he said it, and that he couldn't come, but Mina suddenly felt disconnected and regretted asking him.

She ventured to Brooklyn to meet her parents who were always so glad to see her after a night away. It was as if she walked in moments before they were going to fill out a missing persons report. Marzia was sweet in her sentiments and usually too happy for guilt trips, besides it was Sunday. Mina invited her parents to the gallery knowing they would say no, but did it so they felt, whatever it is that parents feel when their kids include them in their life.

The Gallery looked great, even with shaving cream on the windows, and Lizzy knew enough to wash her hair. The snow had stopped and sunshine battled its way through a suffocating pillow of sky. It was a daytime show: from 2 to 6 pm. Most of the people who came had walked by looking for something like this but there were several members of Simi's social circles present, also. Colton, the only artist present was responsible for the great photographic perspectives of cornfields, and was a fan of the *Just White*.

Mina had taken the initiative of putting out the email book so people could sign their names and add their phone numbers if they liked. Many enjoyed the Chakra Bird painting and the charcoal of the ravens taking off in bunches. Lizzy sat listless and Mina secretly watched her as the hour hand crawled. When Mina needed to move, she walked around collecting empty plastic cups and festive red and gold squared napkins. There was about thirty minutes left to the show and while there was a steady flow of people coming and going, Simi's friends were just getting warmed up. They brought their own vodka and kept replenishing their ice stash with a continuous flow of bodega bags being sent to the back. They were large Italian, Croatian, and Polish men in their forties, passing by Mina each time to get to the fridge to make drinks for the smaller Russian and Polish women chain-smoking in the doorway.

She bent down near Colton to pick up a napkin from the floor and he asked in a whisper,

"Is it too late to get one last refill?"

"This one's on the house," she said filling his glass.

"Thanks darling, I was hopin' to get a buy back." He dropped three dollars into the tip-bowl. The art wasn't so bad, but it wasn't about the art, and she was happy to leave when she did. No one there seemed to be interested in that sort of talk and if they were, they came, saw and left to discuss elsewhere. She couldn't let the word poseurs go, and said it about the many standing in front of the pieces, talking loudly as if they were their own creations but saying nothing of substance. The sun had set and with its disappearance fell the tiniest suggestion of snow. She walked towards Bedford on North 5th with her jacket hood pulled over her head. She reached the corner and zoomed left, but the feet of another walker interrupted her downward gaze. She looked up and saw Phil's familiar face.

"We meet again?" His hands were comfortably bunched in his pockets. His healthy black hair was combed straight back with ends curling behind his ears. He had a clean face with less than discerning features. "You walk like the Nokia snake game."

"What's that like?" She wasn't in the mood.

"With purpose. Going somewhere special this evening?"

"Home."

"You get your computer fixed?"

"No, and I need to."

"Would you mind if I walk with you?" Mina responded by shaking her head no. "Did you back up any of your stuff on your desktop?" Mina laughed at his second question.

"I don't have a desktop. If I had access to another computer, it would be my parent's 1998 desktop." Snowflakes were gaining in size and spotted his hair. "What are you doing now? If you're free you could look at it. I don't have any plans," she said nonchalantly.

"Oh you don't? Good," he said dryly as if their meeting should be out of her convenience. "Well, I told you that I'm around on weekends, so yea I don't see why not. I'm only free for a little bit though," he said glancing at his watch. "You wanna get it and then meet me at my place."

"Yea but we have to pass my house to get to yours, so do you wanna come with me and then we can walk to yours together?" He didn't say anything and neither did his face. He didn't have a reason why her plan didn't make sense, nearly forgot that she lived so close to him, even though waiting outside her house wasn't what he wanted to do. He smiled and nodded. They walked in silence. Mina gauged his age, 36...37... maybe 40 as snow fell between them.

"Where were you coming from anyway?" he asked her.

"Oh I was working this awful art show at The Gallery." Phil laughed.

"Ohhh you're one of Simi's broads?"

"No, please that man is awful. I want no association. I could hardly call what he offers a gallery." Phil continued to laugh.

"But you are associated with him, now." They fortunately rounded Manhattan and Skillman Ave and she was able to spare him what she was thinking about his comments by popping upstairs. As she unlocked the door and hastily collected her things, she realized that he was going to help her and didn't have to. She wanted to offer him something but decided that giving him the few dollars she had was probably more of an insult than anything else. She searched her room for something to offer as a thank you. There was nothing. She felt like a child with no sense of backing her work up and hated to admit to living with her parents. She walked downstairs through the kitchen, and there they were watching television. She greeted her mother and told her no to the questions pertaining to food. She opened the fridge, still searching for something to give him.

"I thought you weren't hungry?" Marzia persisted in the only way she knew how.

"I'm not." To Mina's surprise and forgetfulness, there were two old school coke-a-cola glass bottles waiting to be plucked. These were always in the fridge. Her father loved them and brought them from the pizza shop every week. She tucked two in a black shopping bag beside her laptop already on her side.

She met Phil on his cell-phone. They started walking and he listened to his call more than he talked. When he hung up he didn't speak to Mina immediately. Before they reached Graham they passed an empty alleyway between two deteriorated buildings. The buildings had been decrepit for as long as Mina could remember. Whole pieces of cement and brick were missing in chunks. It looked like someone had kicked them with giant boots or bit them in the way bitten apples are distortedly concave. Corroded metal anchors of a greenish hue were exposed and electrical wires hung between the two buildings. It was the perfect perch for pigeons to debase what was left of the exterior. Two cats chased each other out of the alleyway and crossed Mina and Phil's path before they acknowledged each other.

"Cats are funny. You can't tell if they're male or female." Mina listened closely to the choice words from what she now perceived to be a computer weirdo not geek. "A cat can come up to you, rub against you but not really, just subtly glide against your pant leg or brush your arm, and when you look at it to check it out, you get nothing."

"Do you have cats?" Mina asked him with no idea where this was going.

"No, but the first apartment I had here in Brooklyn was way down by the water in Greenpoint and it had a shared yard with these cats, like six of them. One of them, a black cat with a white nose always came up to me and would rub me just like I told you, and the one thing I wanted to know was if it was male or female."

"You couldn't see if it had balls or not?"

"No. But it could have been fixed, and it doesn't matter that's not the point. Cats are just so effortlessly dismissive. It's the greatest disposition." They passed the dollar store that had been there since Mina was a kid. It brought a memory of a turn-style sticker display that she and Carmella used to twist away from each other. They walked another block and she followed him as he crossed mid-street.

"You know cats aren't dismissive with their own species, right. They know who's who. You ever see a cat in heat? It walks around meowing in desperation, she said catching up with him. "I thought you were into computers?"

"I am. But believe it or not just because this is how I make a living doesn't mean it's the only thing I pay attention to. I make money because people don't speak computer, so I get paid to make sense of something they don't have patience for."

"How profound. I suppose that's all profession is, isn't it?"

"That and knowing your worth, he said ending his sentence with a huff. "And what do you do besides lattés?" He turned to her as he opened the front gate to his house. It was one of the brand new modern apartment buildings that had gone up on this side of Graham, and it stuck out like a sore thumb. She looked up at the monstrosity. It was even with the other three story buildings beside it, but was made from modern gray paneling enclosed by cheap aluminum fencing. "I saw you writing something pretty intently when your computer crashed?" He put a pass-code into the callbox, making sure to cover it so she couldn't see. Mina found him odd and wondered when keys became passé?

"How long have you lived here?" she asked him.

"Coming up on two years." They entered the hallway and Mina traced her gaze up the stairwell, but his apartment was on the first floor. He opened his door and welcomed her into the purest form of minimalism she had ever seen.

"Nice place. Wow you have a lot of art. Look at this stuff." Mina put her bag down and started, one by one, gazing into his collection. "You certainly do well for your *worth*," she said. The front door opened to a galley that had a bar-top and chairs, but his apartment wrapped around the entire first floor. The shape of the place was that of an L with an entrance to his basement in the crook of the letter's shape.

"Well, I've been in Williamsburg for fifteen years, rent wasn't always what it is now. And, I've been lucky. I got involved in a few investments. Do you wanna take out your computer Mina? What do you know about art anyway? You're just a kid." She was a kid, but was much more interested in his collection than defending herself against his smugness.

"Oh I brought you something, for helping me. Here." She handed him the bottles.

"Nice. I haven't had one of these in a while." He was sincerely thankful. "I do love glass bottled cokes. I used to get em all the time at Sal's."

"That's my family's Pizza shop," she said proudly.

"No shit, so you're an old timer then. Who's Sal?"

"Sal was my mom's dad. My dad Joe still works, he's there all the time."

"I know Joe. That guy knows everybody and by name too. He grabbed the cokes and walked into the kitchen. Every appliance was stainless steel and streak less. She placed the computer on the bar-top and plugged it in as he opened their beverages. He came back and clanked her bottle as he handed it to her. "Hopefully, we get this fixed for you." The living room had black leather couch like chairs, four that comfortably sat on a gray area rug with a darker gray border. The art on the walls however were invariably the most colorful part of the apartment. Mina couldn't sit or stand still. She seemed to float from one thing to the next.

Adjacent to the living room and kitchen was a small guest bedroom that had a futon in it and old pictures of New York, including one large print of Times Square, before LCD screens, showing ads by Planter's Peanuts, TWA, and Chevrolet.

"Uh, Mina?" She popped out of the spare room at the sound of her name.

"Sorry I was just admiring your New York room."

"Yea, well I'm extracting what's on your hard drive. I don't know that I will be able to save it all, but it's worth a shot. I'm gonna restore your computer so if it doesn't work, then well you're stuff will be lost and so will this computer, but if it does, then the only hope is that my computer can read the files I've extracted. But any programs that you may have downloaded on your computer will not be saved."

"Okay whatever you need to do." She sat down realizing that she might want to be near him while he did this and not wandering his apartment as if they were friends. "Sorry I'm an artist. I paint a little, haven't in a really long time, but it's just nice to see such a collection. I haven't seen any good stuff lately. I was really disappointed by the last show I went to at PS1, and as you can imagine seeing Simi as a gallery owner, despite that some of the stuff there tonight wasn't half bad."

"All they have at PS1 is garbage," he said with disgust. "Art for the sake of art. You're better off taking a look at five points if you're going over that way."

"Five points? Is that what they call the huge graffiti building?"

"Yes."

"I studied art history. Well, I majored in art history," she laughed.

"And now you work at a coffee shop, so was it worth the 50 grand? And, now you tell me that you are one of the girls that Simi keeps around for his shows. What's your deal Mina?" Phil waited for her to answer.

"I really hate it when people ask *what your deal is*." He turned away from her and ejected a memory stick.

"Sorry?" he said without sincerity. "What do you paint then?"

"I haven't painted in a while. But there is a painting I've been creating in my mind as of late."

"What of?"

"Nothing."

"You're thinking about a painting of nothing? Mina started to sweat. She was uncomfortable. "I can't believe I am going to explain this to you." She was so nervous she was losing sight of what it was she wanted to say. She pushed through her feelings like a train in fog. "I haven't even really put it together in my own head."

"What are you waiting for exactly?"

"Okay, God! It's a little out there. I want to create a sky at dusk with clouds and a hand of some sort, perhaps a really large hand or just the suggestion of fingers made out of clouds, I don't know yet." She stood up for confidence. "And a cliffside along the edge, and below that centered in the composition is a falling woman. The painting catches her mid fall. She's holding onto a rung of a ladder suspended from the clouds." Mina sat back down and closed her eyes as she said the rest. "She has long hair and is wearing a red dress. Her hair is wind blown from the speed of the fall, but perhaps I won't have the ladders there at all and what she holds over her head to reduce the speed of her fall is a single peacock feather. She holds it at both ends bowing it above her like a parachute because she's tiny. I don't know if I said that, but she is very small, like miniature, with a number 5 imprinted on her calf. In the painting, she looks scared, but what she doesn't know is that she is about to be caught by a tree. A sloping Japanese White Pine, with limbs for arms bearing beautiful heart shaped fruits, and its lowest bough stretches over the water just under her."

"Whoa."

"Yea. Whuddya think?" she asked nervously.

"I think it sounds like a lot, but maybe you have a sense of it. Why the peacock feather? And why the number 5 on her leg? What is she falling from?"

"I don't have all the answers. I saw a painting of a peacock today that had something to do with the fifth chakra, and along with the title was a little info that said that ether is the fifth chakra's element. Plus, I had this dream that I had a five on my leg and I was trying to get to the fifth house of the zodiac. It's a lot to explain," she shook her head dismissing her ideas.

"You believe in chakras and astrology? You didn't strike me as the hippie type."

"Well I don't know enough about it."

"TADAH!" Her computer turned on and stayed on. The desktop was completely clean. "Let's see if we can get your files up on my computer now. He sat down on one of the comfortable couch like chairs and pulled out a mouse-pad to control the oversized flat screen, which Mina now realized was an extended monitor for his computer. He pulled them up one by one. Mina stared up at the heading and first pages of some of her college essays and old short stories on his television. He recovered nearly everything and browsed some of her recent poetry while she sipped her coke.

"How unique, you write poetry," he said mocking her.

"I don't write poetry, but it just comes out that way sometimes."

"Are you a writer?" he asked.

"I like writing. You?"

"No, not so much. I'm a reader though. There are readers, and then there are writers."

"That doesn't sound familiar," she laughed.

"Why would it? And why would you being a poet, be unique? Everyone's a goddam poet, or artist in some way." His face said nothing while his words cut right through her.

"I wasn't trying to be unique. I was just writing down some thoughts. Sometimes, it comes out in poetry that's all."

"Well are you a poet slash writer or a painter?"

"I don't know. On the one hand I hear what you *aren't* saying. Like as in I should be able to choose one, but isn't it all connected? Writing is like painting and painting is like writing. You have to add a bit more color or description here and then in other places you might add some water, as in short sentences vs. longer ones and when something needs context, you write in reflection or add retarder to give flexibility to your colors' expression. Composition is composition, no?" She paused for a moment. "They're similar processes I think, just different modes of expression."

"Touché, but maybe it's because you haven't balanced your fifth chakra." He joked but she didn't know how to act. "I should know what the 5th Chakra is about. This Kumbaya-love-is-light- girl I dated surely told me a few times, but I never really gave a shit."

"He opened his web browser and pulled out a wireless keyboard to search Google. The first link that popped up was titled:

"Learn How to Balance your 5th chakra." He began reading in a Richard Simmons voice. *"The symbol for the 5th chakra is in the ethereal circle,* Come on everybody get in the circle! *...Which represents wholeness, as in no independent existence.* He resumed in his normal voice. *"Ether stands for the mind. Those who are balanced in this chakra have given up the illusion of obtaining a separate existence. The chakra's center is located in the throat and represents one's ability to speak and communicate effectively. It is one's true voice. An underactive 5th chakra is the inability to express one's mind, leaving them unfulfilled and often misinterpreted by others. Their relationships will suffer from a lack of transparency regarding their true feelings or intentions. While an overactive 5th chakra is associated with people who have the gift of gab, express themselves to the fullest, and make sure their opinions are known whether they were asked for or not. Often these people are not very good listeners.*

"That makes sense, the peacock had this great light coming from her throat. Can you look up the fifth house of the zodiac for me?" He followed her instruction and read from again the first link that popped up.

"The fifth house is ruled by Leo. That's me, he added. *"It stands for creativity, passion, and pleasure, and enables people to express what's unique about them.*

"Oh look, they even use your word, unique!" Phil rolled his eyes.

"It is what makes them proud. This house shows the manner that one radiates outward, being the house of the Sun. It is the place that the true self creates something that is totally expressive of them. It could be works of art, literature, theatre, fashion, love, or any area that enables playful expression." He looked at Mina and smiled the biggest smile she had seen from him. "See, you should be creating art. All the signs point to it," he concluded and placed his keyboard down. He plugged in a USB stick and began downloading all of her files.

"Well, what do *you* do? Do you express yourself in one contained area Phil?"

"Yes." He took a long slow sip of his coke. "My studio is downstairs, it's the main reason I took this apartment in this awful looking building. Don't think I thought it looked nice from the outside." She laughed and very quickly he flashed a smile. "I saw you looking at it when we arrived. I hate the cheesy aluminum fencing also. Come I will show you."

They walked down a wooden stairway. The building was new, but the basement was unfinished with a cement floor covered in clay dust. In the far right corner was a pottery wheel and shelves of finished clay works. Dead center in front of them was a bunch of scattered charcoal sketches, some with a streak of color. His illustrations were mainly of faces and with the strangest of expressions. Most of them were mad, but that was too reductive of a descriptor. It wasn't just anger or madness. The contorted features were suspicious and foul, full of scorn, ugly, yet mesmerizing. They nearly yelled from their one dimension.

Sometimes one characteristic was larger than the rest and disrupted everything else, like an oversized eyeball or nostril. There were maybe five or six portraits of the same woman with chin length hair. Her hair was always the most negative space on the canvas in all of her portraits, either coming to a blunt edge or spitting out in disarray and she smoked in each piece. She and the other subjects never looked head on and he painted their discomfort on canvas on top of everything else they were expressing.

"You did all of these?" Mina was on bended knee flipping through them with ease.

"Yep."

"They're madness. Really, I didn't know. My apologies."

"That's a new one, madness. Charcoal Madness. I like that a lot. What are you apologizing for?"

"I like how dark they are. Have you always done portraits?"

"No I haven't always done anything. I used to draw with pencil and failed as a painter."

"Who's this?" Mina asked about the smoking woman.

"Trish." Mina looked at him for more information but he said nothing, and she returned to the work.

"My father was a painter."

"What did he paint?"

"Seascapes and portraits."

"Are you from the coast?"

"Yes. Ever hear of Cape Charles?"

"No."

"Oh good. No one has. It's on the southern tip of Virginia."

"Why do you say you failed as a painter?"

"Because my father was very talented. I draw my birds like he used to, but that's all he handed down." She glanced to the other corner of the basement where he had pointed to, and saw a whole collection of birds.

"Oh look at these, a little wildlife? How do you know Simi anyway? You never said," she asked.

"I've known him. I don't remember how we met."

"You ever give him your work?"

"Yea one of those wildlife's in your hand, as you call it. Do you coin everything? He asked me for a big piece so I gave him the biggest one I had."

"Of course you did. I thought those birds looked familiar. You've been at this a while?

"Just a few years, what's with all the questions? I didn't actually want to talk about my work," he laughed at himself and then became serious again. "I just wanted you to see them." He walked over to a small bar that had shelves stocked with crates of records.

"I think your portraits are unique, to use your word," she pursed her lips. "I noticed your wildlife piece today at the show, especially the smaller birds far off in the distance. Why weren't you there?"

"Well, I was gonna stop by." He looked up from flipping through records. Mina was finally looking at him and his immense music collection.

"Whadya got there?"

"Music. I keep all my records down here. I play them while I work."

"You were going to stop by, but? Go on."

"But I saw this hooded woman who couldn't get her computer working." She stood up and walked closer to his record player.

"I need one of these. I just found a bunch of records that I really want to listen to."

"Do you have speakers?" he asked her. "You can't just get a record player, kiddo. You need the whole stereo system."

"I hate that word. Kiddo."

"Sorry, Kiddo..." She browsed through some of the records he had in his crates, and glanced at the grand selection of three unopened Wild Turkey bottles on the bar-shelf.

Song # 33 Primavera, Ludovico Einaudi

He put on a strings piece, and at first it made her think of the song that plays throughout the movie *American Beauty* but then when the tension of the violin heightened, it gave way to a much more beautiful song with crashing sounds that seemed to lift and suddenly fall. Crescendo is all she could think in her head. She wanted to talk about it and express her enjoyment but hesitated feeling that she may not be qualified to have such a conversation with him. She turned to survey more of the basement.

"Who plays with clay? What do you call that anyway?"

"My girlfriend."

"That's not what I meant." Mina laughed.

"I know. I was kidding." Phil didn't smile.

"They're called potters."

"What's your girlfriend's name?"

"Hannah."

"Oh nice. It must be great to be with another artist." Something about him made Mina a talkative nervous. The music distracted her: first with the violin, each note speeding after the one before it. It penetrated her spirit and invigorated her imagination. At the moment, she envisioned white lines speeding on a highway. But then piano strings accompanied the harsh violin and changed the melody. The keys broke her concentration and she was able to resume conversation.

"You would think," he huffed. "Let's talk about your work, ey?" Mina's mind took off again with the music, now on horseback speeding through trees in the woods. "You were telling me about peacocks, the cosmos, a miniature woman, and what else?"

"Oh don't worry about it. This music is powerful. Just some obscure words and a German author, you'll think me a total weirdo if I try to explain it. I've already word vomited my painting. Let me leave on a high note, literally," she slapped her knee making the connection between her metaphor and the music. He cocked his left eyebrow and she felt crazy.

"Okay but I meant specifically about the painting. Do you have a way of starting this project?"

"What do you mean?"

"Don't make conversation so difficult, Mina. Do you have paints for Eve and her cradling tree?"

"It's not the Garden of Eden, stop it."

"Whatever."

"I still have some of my supplies, could probably use more, but I don't know where I would paint. It's too cold to paint outdoors and I have no place in my house. No I guess." She looked at him. It was hard to admit that she had no creative space, but she did it anyway, and she was smiling, because smiling was automatic when she was nervous. She thought about that poor sap, Jerry, from Landmark making meaning from everything and how Adam had described her as completely self-expressed to all those people. If only they could see her now. The music picked up again. It was never ending: fast paced bow-work separated by intervals of soft keys on the piano. "I don't have a place to work," she said adopting his huff making it her own. She felt nearly exhausted, saturated by the music, his effect on her mood, and her own self-doubt.

"Where'd you usually buy your paints?"

"I don't even know it's been so long, I used to go to that place on Canal."

"It's been so long, you kids kill me," he said making fun of her. "What are you 22?"

"29, on Thursday." Mina was doing her best to not get offended.

"Pearl is the name and perfect! I was going to tell you to go there anyway. If I give you a list of things I need, will you get them? In return, you can buy yourself a few things for making the trip."

"What do you mean a few things?"

"They owe me a favor for some work I did for them, and you could put whatever you get on my tab."

"What did you do for Pearl Paints?" Mina interrupted him. "Fix their computers?"

"No I do a lot of things. Anyway, if you pick up my stuff, then you can treat yourself to some supplies so you can start your painting. Deal?"

"Where would I work?" Mina laughed as if he overlooked that very important detail.

"Here!" He was shocked she didn't already understand that. "There's a separate entrance from the building's hallway upstairs that comes out over there. Remember when we first walked in. There are three doors. One's my main entrance, my bike in my bedroom blocks the other, and another one comes down here. You see those steps over there." He pointed to a dark corner behind the stairwell they had descended from.

"You'll let me use your studio?"

"That's what it's for. You're not the first artist to share the space here."

"And your girlfriend?"

"What about my girlfriend? I'm not making a pass at you. You're like 22?"

"I just told you I'm 29!"

"Happy birthday."

"Why do you want to do this?" Mina asked him.

"Because you should paint if you can paint. And I know enough people to get your work out there so you can actually live your life and not work at a fucking coffee shop. Maybe then, you could buy yourself a better computer, so you can write your poetry..." He said poetry in a snobbish voice but softened the blow with a huge smile.

"Why can't you get the stuff yourself?"

"You ask a lot of questions especially about things that don't matter much. I have to go home to take care of a few things, the holidays and such. "Deal?" The strings silenced her. No trotting like Atreiyu in the forest, no speeding on a highway, just falling and spiraling downward with the music to then be calmed by piano and finally the stillness that ended the song.

"Fine," she said.

"Fine?"

"Thank you."

"Let's go back upstairs," he said turning his record player off. She led the way and he closed the door behind them. She stored her computer in her bag.

"Leaving?"

"In a little yea."

"I'm not sure it even matters, but all I wanna know about is 'some word and a German author.' I spend hours, sleepless nights sometimes at the computer reading, up on things that occupy my mind for whatever reason, and I want to see the depths of someone else's curiosity." Mina couldn't believe how kind his face looked.

"Okay. But now with all this buildup I regret you may be disappointed. Do you know what a Zeitgeist is?"

"Yes."

"Okay, do you know who Weltschmerz is?" Mina asked with a smile.

"Who?" He questioned the *who* in her question.

"I don't know I was talking about the Zeitgeist of right now and this guy told me that what I really was talking about was Weltschmerz. I thought because he asked me if I read German Literature that it was an author or philosopher. I've never heard that word before.

"It's not an author. It's a feeling of suffering or discontentment."

"Really?"

"But it's been used in several books, Steinbeck and the Welsh rats, Ralph Ellison, I think Faulkner used it, even... a few albums, I'm sure I have one called Weltschmerzen. You've never heard of it before?"

"Well I've never read Faulkner, or Steinbeck... I guess there *are* readers and writers."

"I thought you didn't know that saying?"

"I don't. I was standing in the middle of some courtyard between buildings on Kent, when I said it. The people that live there share a hallway bathroom, can you imagine that?"

"No. I can't." He typed away on a wireless keyboard. I've seen some of those filthy cubicles they call apartments. But let's see what this says, Sustainability Advocacy Organization." He clicked on a link for SAO that had nothing to do with Zeitgeist in the title, yet it still came up in the search results. "Look, you can join them in their cause Mina. National Zeitgeist Day is March 28th. They have two days, and you can even add your own event and they will publicize it for you." There was a link that brought up a form. He was mocking her but she was very interested and reading the plans. The organization's mission was riddled with buzzwords like: poverty, corruption, homelessness, war, starvation, and this was the theme for all the artwork they were soliciting.

"You should submit your painting? A tree catching a woman, that's holding onto ladders blowing in the wind. If that doesn't scream social sustainability, I don't know what does."

"Does it say where the art is being displayed?"

"It looks like there are a ton of small events but, let's see here," he opened another page. "No, where's the main SAO event? Wait. What's weird is that we're on an extension of the Museum of Natural History's website."

"Really? I wonder if anyone I know is involved in this."

"You know people at the Museum of Natural History?"

"Yea, I used to work there."

"What the hell are you doing at a coffee shop? And Simi? Come on, you can do much better than that, are you kidding me? While you may be intelligent, you are not very smart Mina."

"What do you mean?"

"Doesn't matter. Do you have a good chance at getting involved in this. You used to work there, you may know someone that can help you find out *who* it is you need to talk to." He clicked on a link titled: Submit Art. The deadline's March. 1st. Do you think you can finish it in a few months?"

"I don't know."

"Will you send your charcoal madness to them?"

"If you paint your piece."

"Is this motivation?" Mina asked him with a face full of excitement.

"At its best."

"You know there was this poem with one of the paintings of the corn stalks at Simi's show tonight; did you by any chance see it? Did you even see the set-up before the show?

"No. I gave it to him like a month and half ago," Phil laughed.

"Well, there was this photograph of a cornfield. The perspective was looking out from the center of the field, maybe not the center, but it was looking out to the edge of the field. The artist was there and we got into a conversation about corn stalks. He explained that those in the middle do best from the pollen that drifts inwards from the surrounding stalks. It truly is a collective crop. The person I'm thinking of most that can help me from MNH said something very similar about humans."

"Of course. That's how the world works and maybe why art is so important."

"You're not the first person to say that to me."

"I'm sure a lot of people find art more than important. Try transformative?"

"Not that. To tell me how the world works."

Chapter 3
Shopping Spree

Song # 34 Smoke & Mirrors, RJD2

Mina enjoyed the city's white respite in her walk home from Phil's. There was at least four inches of snow covering the street and because it was Sunday no one was doing a thing about it. She was excited about the idea of painting and having to do it in a timely manner. These were the conditions she remembered painting under anyway, except this was for life not a GPA. Mina was a woman of her word. He offered his space so that she could not only get it done, but also make a difference and that was inspiring. Plus, she really wanted him to submit his foul-mouthed charcoal felons. They may not have screamed sustainability, but were certainly associated with desperation, confusion, solitude, all things Weltschmerz.

She had to talk to Roman soon. It was too bad that she didn't have a way of contacting him and would be forced to try to find him at the museum. She had to let him know what she planned on creating. He didn't even know she was a painter, he didn't know much about her, but she couldn't wait to join whoever it was that blended art and social commentary. Now that she was connected to the Internet, she did more research on chakras, seven tabs open at once, zeitgeist, Faulkner, bonsai's, you name it. She was beginning to understand the meaning behind the symbols of each chakra, and why the artist had used a peacock for that painting. It had little to do with the peacock, but rather the symbolism of a bird. Birds sing and those that had the greatest of balances in this realm were known to have fantastic voices. She also was beginning to get clear on the 7 chakra model, how one's life can benefit from understanding blockages and modes of expression. This wasn't her faith but it provided a meaning for things, in the way religious scriptures did. She saw why people needed something to believe in and how relating to these theories, as the explanation they've been waiting for enhanced their communication. With her bedside lamp on she pulled out a notebook and wrote manually.

There's a hole on my inseam.
My belt has come undone,
so that when I'm standing
in the wind, I'm searching for
things that don't fit.
One large ring
of flapping wings
appear to be moving and contracting
like that hole on my inseam—
together, then separating, but with
patterns fleeting.

Do they fly to let other birds know its time?
In the same way we don't say everything on our mind?
I wish I could tell these birds,
or just one, about my holes.
I know without a word, they'd mend me.
Each black wing capable of nearly anything.

~ ~ ~

Adam and Mina started again like the wind, not a true wind, but the gust brought in by a train entering a tunnel. It hit them in the face with the force of an oversized hand dryer. It felt good, but like that of the underground the attraction was mysterious - even to them- and seemed guided by clandestine impulses of the unconscious. This rush stirred up random garbage. Bags and plastic containers of the material world, playing the parts of their unexamined emotions, catapulted to the surface, but only to fall right back where they came from. Mina showed up for her birthday date with Adam as the sun was setting. She sparkled in a rhinestone dress as she stared out his living room window. He bought her peach roses, and if she had to have roses, these were her favorite. She stared into them while he fixed cocktails. He was hosting and getting ready at the same time. She carried on comfortably in her dress, talking a little to Serpico, browsing through music channels, drawn to *Sounds of the Seasons*: the only tolerable if not enjoyable station his network offered.

Mina, of course, looked for the eyelash curler when she was in the bathroom and to her surprise it was still there. Adam didn't keep his Grammercy Tavern reservations secret and she clung to him tightly as they walked into the restaurant.

"Nothing is what it seems, I've heard such amazing things about this place," he said disappointed.

"I know me too." Mina didn't really care to complain.

"I'm sorry I thought the food was going to be top notch."

"Please, Adam. It's fine. I'm having a great time." She reached across the table to grab his hand, and they looked at each other for a loving moment. "That's what we get for dining in Glammercy," she said pulling her hand away laughing.

"Glammercy? Did you just make that up? I've never heard that before."

"I like the décor a lot though and the gold vests that the wait staff are donned in. These kinds of restaurants are all show though, which sadly reduces their dishes to… props. I think we're just supposed to be happy that we were cast for tonight's performance." She was smiling but he knew she meant it.

"Ya know, you're the best kind of snob."

Their conversation shifted from dinner to his latest real estate details. She cheered his efforts saying it was a good fit for his personality and shared her newest project. She described the painting to him in as much detail as she could without confusing him. Speaking visually is not second nature to everyone and as Mina considered this truth, she was curious how people started using that phrase. Can someone have a second nature? In the middle of adoring him, she noticed a thin white line resting above his jacket's chest pocket. She didn't keep handkerchief wearing men in her company often but knew the cloth should have some shape to it, maybe come to a point like the top of a triangle or puffed out like whipped cream. She stared at it even when she didn't want to. After dinner, they shared champagne and strawberries at a place called Flute. They were still in *Glammercy* and decided to act the part since their casting conversation. They arrived to a booth already reserved in his name. He handed the little card with a scripted Adam Roehmann to her.

"You keep that." She removed the pillow sitting between them so he could move closer. He did and she brought her lips to his cheek.

"Can I do something to you?" She asked him seductively blowing breath down his neck. "Something nasty…" She held onto the 'S' sound, letting air slowly seep from her mouth. He could only nod in response. She licked her lips pulling back from his face to glance at him. "Are you sure?" With one hand around his neck, she leaned in and snatched his handkerchief. "I want to puff your pocket square."

"You're such a shit!" She unraveled the material on her knees while looking at him from the corner of her eye. He distracted himself by refilling their glasses with Dom Perignon Rosè. She pressed her body against his to neatly return the handkerchief. A waitress brought over two *birthday cake* shots and an empty rocks glass holding a bursting sparkler. This was the glammercy way: no song, no clapping, a little smoke filled air and vanilla bubblegum flavored liquor. They walked to 3rd before catching a cab uptown.

"You're such a little shit, ya know that? Only you would do something like fix my handkerchief. Why does the straight fold bother you so much?" They waited for the light to change so they could cross Park. He was serious and his volume was close to yelling. Mina didn't answer him until they started walking.

"Why would my playing with your handkerchief bother you? Are you mad that I didn't think it was already perfect? She didn't wait for an answer. "You know what I read in this article a long time ago, one of those nights when I was at home pining for you."

"What does pining mean?" Adam resumed his normal volume.

"Me sitting at home waiting for you to call me, crying, sometimes drunk by myself, depressed, trying to make sense of what happened between us, anyway that's not the point. The article was written by an Orthodox man, that's right I educated myself on your religion as much as I could." She was drunk, nothing mattered other than the point she was about to make. "I thought religion was going to bring me closer to you, pahhh," she laughed loudly, slapping her knee as she did when she was in hysterics. Her laugh sounded just like her father's when she was really worked up. Adam waited for the rest of the story. A cab pulled up and they fell into it. "The guy who wrote the article was drawing similarities between Christians and Orthodox Jews. Basically saying that with the way things were going, he was finding that his moral alignment was getting closer and closer to Christians, well Catholics, to be specific."

"What!" Adam shouted. "I don't believe you!"

"I know! You can imagine why I read on. Anyway his grounds for agreeing with Catholics were based on their struggle to live a moral life in an amoral world. But what I thought was so interesting, that I guess I always knew but never examined closely, is that the inherent difference in Christianity and Judaism is the question of the Savior or Messiah," she laughed. "...as you call him."

"Right..."

"Christians, all Christians, New age, Protestant, Baptist, Roman, whatever...they all have a Savior, albeit a short life, but still they have one. Meanwhile, Jews are still waiting. She hung her head chuckling waiting for him to catch up, and then shouted, "Isn't that so telling Adam! She whacked him on the chest with the back of her hand. "You're always saying that all Jewish girls do is complain, and I'm sure you've heard the general stereotype about Jews being... well... an unhappy people," she put her hands up, as if it had nothing to do with her. "This is what they say, Adam. But I get it now. Now... I get it. I really got it! How could they be happy? Everyone, literally everybody else got a Savior but them! Or maybe, to get back to your handkerchief, perhaps... their predisposed state of unhappiness is what stops them from seeing the good in anything, like how bad is it to have my fashion sense for a moment? Huh? You know what I think? Perhaps Adam, they wouldn't even recognize the Messiah if he showed up!" Mina just stared at him. He bit the insides of his cheek. He didn't have the energy to argue. No resistance was stronger than her when she was like this.

"A very profound and interesting concept, my dear. One that we may never figure out." He was done with the conversation. "Right up here, you can pull in the front lobby area," he instructed the cab. He grabbed her arm and pulled her out his side of the car, aggressively sliding her rhinestones against the folds of the backseat. He narrowed her walking space and pushed her towards the brick wall side of the fountain. Her arm and shoulder brushed against the bushes.

"What's the big idea?" she asked with a half smile protecting her arm from scratches. "Quit pushing me, bully."

"The idea is you in the bushes." He tried to lift her without letting her know what body part he was going for but she was too aware even in her drunken state. The two of them were soon locked with hands clasped above their heads and equal force coming from both sides. The more time they spent grappling, the funnier each of them found it, and as they edged the side of the fountain Mina noticed the water.

"You wanna go for a little bird bath Mina," he grabbed her around the waist and lifted her over the spouting stream. "Where's your Savior now?" He held her right over it with excitement in his face. She trembled in his arms, sure that he was going to drop her. He let out a laugh, one that mocked her laughing at her own jokes at his expense. At the last second, he returned her to his chest and with mutual uncertainty and excitement they kissed out of breath.

Chapter 4
Sixteen Dollars

Mina was spinning like those treasured molecules she often thought about. She was working like an insane person, arriving at Atlas by five am to brew the usual self-serve drip varieties. She played classical music at a loud volume and customers mentioned it too, that they liked it, that it was the best part of their day, better than Christmas music, they would say. They tipped her well sometimes up to 100 bucks for five or six hour shifts. They were all the same folks too, getting their coffee fix before the L carried them underwater and into Manhattan. Phil stopped by around the second week of December to give her a folder with a list of items he needed and the value that he and Pearl agreed on. He wished her a happy holiday, as he'd be gone and told her that no canvas was going to paint itself, urging her to bring her records over to listen while she worked.

"Are you house-sitting now?" Beth asked as she peeked over Mina's shoulder to look into the folder.

"No, she's feeding my cat." Phil answered Beth directly even though her question wasn't directed to him.

"Getting close with the computer geek are you?" Beth didn't buy Mina's story that they kept walking into one another and called him an undercover stalker.

Her trip to Pearl Paints was like a time warp. It brought her back to the hours she used to spend sifting through art supplies. She even went into a bodega to buy some water but to her surprise they were still carrying Mystic, even the boysenberry flavor she used to love. She was smart enough to use Phil's tab as a way to buy Christmas gifts in addition to supplies. She bought Sophia a bunch of beaded jewelry, drawing pads and nearly fifty sticker strips.

She found a peacock feather in the aisle with the inks and brushed it against her cheek as she continued to browse through acrylic paint. Most of Phil's list was to be expected, but there was also a bunch of other miscellaneous stuff that just didn't seem to fit him or his work. He was so precise too, with the item number written right next to the item name. She found some arts and crafts stuff for Carmella and a wedding photo book for G, even a Yankee box with little collectibles for her dad, and a huge photo album for both her parents. Mina felt good, getting gifts for her family and helping Phil like some glorified personal assistant. She also felt like she was being fully realized and how lucky it was that she and Adam were going through similar experiences, him with real estate and her with art. She called Francine, why at that precise moment as a Christmas shopper- slash artist- slash personal assistant, she didn't know. She talked on her phone as she sorted through her own list of colors: cerulean, chromium, and cobalt in 32 oz tubs, of course.

She asked Francine about her plans for the holiday and as Mina expected, it was nothing out of the ordinary. Francine just got out of a relationship, wasn't completely devastated, but it was just so typical. There had been several times when they reconnected after a stint of silence only to find that they had been living parallel lives without knowing it. Francine mentioned Mina's birthday and suggested they get together to celebrate. Mina eased into a simpler time the more she listened to Francine's voice and laughter. She threw violet, aqua and turquoise into her cart. She saw the peacock parachute she planned to paint perfectly in her mind now. Francine was loud and fun and as she filled Mina in on some of the successes and failures of the people they knew as kids, she was brought back to high school and even some early college for a moment. She picked up raw sienna, gold, and magenta for the cliffside if that was still part of her painting. Mina browsed through neutral colors for her lady in red's skin tone, and some grays for clouds in smaller 8 oz and 4oz tubes. Francine was effortlessly happy and tended to make a scene so that others could join in her laughter if they wanted to. She didn't need drinks or anything highbrow but people didn't know how to handle her. Those that did were her biggest fans, but most people couldn't tolerate the attention that followed her. This was part of the reason their friendship had been so difficult to maintain, that and sometime in sophomore year, Mina felt she outgrew her.

Greens and browns for the bonsai were tossed into her cart as she did her best to catch Francine up on everything to date. This was difficult to do in one conversation. Their excitement began to dwindle, and Mina's neck tired from holding the phone. They made tentative plans for the near future, 'before the New Year' they said at the same time. These kinds of promises were what they habitually made to one another. Neither Mina nor Adam had solidified plans for the years end. She wasn't even thinking about it, yet as she ended the call she realized this Christmas might have Adam in it. Sure, she had her family, and they would have the usual Christmas Eve dinner, but it's not like he had plans, and he was so into Christmas now that she felt bad not inviting him.

When she was done checking out, mounds of Pearl Paint shopping bags closed in on her. Her persona went from celebrity personal assistant to what some people call, a bitch. She called Gio and asked him for a ride. He had just woken up from ending 24-hour shift and reluctantly agreed to come get her. She told him that she had bought him a present and that she was sorry she often called when she needed something. Despite the scoring of a brand new easel, and a 4 ft by 5ft canvas, she now knew why Phil needed her help, this was going to be some job getting everything back to Brooklyn.

Afternoons began to look very different. She returned from work around noon, quickly walked Rags, and went to Phil's to paint. She did her best to avoid bullshitting about the wedding, the dress, the cake, the menu, the flowers, all choreographed around lilac and very expensive. Marzia asked as many times as she could about Mina's date, and the *Jewish boy*. Mina was skilled at redirecting Marzia's attention by asking about the accumulating pile of "Toys R' Us" clippings. First there was one or two under a Christmas photo magnet of Sophia and Michael, but then more showed up curling from of the memo box also magnetized to the side of the fridge. As the days went on more newspapers arrived with more Christmas inserts, and more toy pictures were being saved. Soon though, the presents themselves were going to take up the whole corner of the living room.

Mina typically stopped by Sal's to grab a Stromboli and seltzer before working in Phil's basement. She was smoking regularly now too. She bought a pack of cigarettes at the deli once a week and smoked and sang as she danced her way through her painting. It wasn't easy at first and she didn't know where to start. In fact, the first few times she was in the basement all she did was look at Phil's music collection and check clay pieces for initials. She knew that she wanted to start with the sky but couldn't bring herself to begin. An unrecognizable apprehension filled her with dread. It had been so long since she did as much as hold a brush. Mina, the singer, sang songs appropriately about love, begging Mina to examine her intentions for the painting more closely. The image hadn't started out with sustainability in mind. It was directly related to her feelings of confusion, a period of limbo, the good and bad of playing small, the wanting or waiting for her insides to match her outsides. Each of the painting's elements had been crafted by her subconscious and the woman's fall was a journey of symbols and metaphors pertaining to the human condition: the absurd fine line between liberation and free fall: a quest for meaning, connection, and love.

She was really good at finding ways to distract herself from starting, like looking up everything there was to know about peacocks and their meaning across cultures, reading more information on Weltschmerz and the context many great thinkers before her had attributed to it. She needed to flush out her ideas by drawing something. She started with pencil and then used some of Phil's charcoal for shading and dimension. She sketched clouds and hung faint ladders from each of them. The ladders were tiny ropes with slit like rungs that fluttered way off in the distance.

It wasn't paint on canvas yet, and she hadn't even started to make the shape of her falling beauty, but it was something. She was still contemplating how to illustrate the woman's body, which limbs were going to be extended and in what direction, and questioning if the woman should look up at the ladders as if she dropped from them before her fall, or longingly as if to be reaching for them. She studied her sketch, the outline and shading of the clouds, cliffside, and her rough stab at a bonsai in the bottom corner. Her images were barely on paper but enough so that she could mentally rearrange them, and although it might have been procrastination, she decided to go see Roman.

~ ~ ~

She got reacquainted with the massiveness of the museum's fossilized guards. The front desk of course did not have a way of finding Roman. She paid her suggestive price, which was now $10, instead of $8, and walked her way to the Hall of Earth. It was the ultimate serendipitous moment to see him coming towards her, from the far end of the hallway out of that same elevator she met him in, the elevator that seemed to start this entire journey of understanding. She hugged him and just stayed there for a while. Mina handed him the starry pouch and stone she bought for him with a smile that split her face in two.

"Its scientific name is Chalcopyrite but most of these chakra intuitives, or hippies..." she said with a smile, "call it Peacock Ore. Consider it a Chanukah gift. The energy inside it is said to bring about universal information, to you and to others *by* you, and I thought it was fitting since the Universe is where we met.

"Thank you Mina, but I hardly deserve such a thoughtful present. You're very sweet to bring me this gift. And you? You look much, much better. Things have picked up I take it."

"I'm better, yes, and have been very productive."

"Good to hear it. With what may I ask?" He rolled the stone to his fingertips then back to his palm, letting the iridescent purplish blue properties catch every bit of light.

"I started painting, again. Well, this is why I came here actually. I came across the Zeitgeist Event that the Museum dedicated some space for in March."

"I don't know this event."

"You don't. It's affiliated with the Sustainability Advocacy Organization."

"Oh yes, SAO. I don't know this event or the organization really."

"I wanted to know more about it, and submit art if possible."

"I didn't know you were an artist Mina."

"I know. It was something I dabbled in and then maybe left behind but have been bringing back and I just want to know what the chances are of submitting a piece.

"I wouldn't know. SAO was co-founded by someone on the board. Did you already submit your paintings?"

"No, and its just one. But it's great and has everything to do with the message."

"Good! But, I am going to have to get back to you about the people involved. He walked towards his office, opened it and sat at his desk. He took out a small piece of paper and asked Mina for her email.

"Tell me a little about your work?"

"Well it's a larger piece, and there's a woman in free fall that's about to be caught by a Japanese white pine. Above her, a huge sky with big pillow-like clouds hanging tiny drop down ladders that sway in the wind, I think. It's not complete yet."

"Lovely. Stairways in the wind. Sounds Good. I'll be in touch." He shoved the paper in his chest pocket and rushed off after they said their goodbyes. Taking the stairs down reminded her of the fateful lay off just a few months ago. She walked through the park and created some of those fantasies she was so good at, about her success as a painter, others of a Christmas Eve with Adam and the potential conversations that would come up between him and her parents. Part of her hoped that no one else was coming over now that he was invited. She made faces to herself wondering what would become of the meat sauce sprinkled with cheese on his plate, but she was driving herself mad, he ate meat with cheese now, it was only shellfish and pork that he avoided. She never, in all of her depressed delusion living in that miserable 35th street apartment thought that Christmas Eve with him and her family was possible.

Mina and Adam's time together was partitioned by her subway commute to and from his place. The peek-a-boo of advertisements and innuendos were commercial breaks for the spin art of Mina's internal palette. She was pursuing the only thing that mattered more *not* to have than it did to question. She saw him when it fit her schedule, but quite frequently due to her need to be physical with him. They continued their playful accents and made up characters and in this go around, she initiated more than him. She used the faces she saw in and out of the subway as inspiration for who she was going to be. She made it a game, and was more enigmatic each time they were together. Sometimes she called him with accents, British, Russian, ghetto. He followed her lead for the most part and tried his best to keep up. It was easy for him to accept her invitation on Christmas Eve. He was so excited to have an authentic Italian meal, just like she used to tell him about. He even asked about the browned meatball, and made jokes that maybe her mother would offer it to him instead of her father.

Marzia was more aggressive in greeting Adam with her questions than she was charming. Joe's standoffish self had created an awkward arrival. Mina did her best to keep glasses filled, but she wasn't used to having company in her parent's house. There were things that she wanted to do but didn't out of respect. Wine soon warmed everyone's spirits and by dinner there was full conversation. Marzia served her husband first followed by Adam. Adam thought about dinners at his house and his mother rarely, if ever, served his dad. He looked into Joe's plate and felt like he had done this before, like he was included in the joke and belonged exactly where he was, until he saw pepperoni swimming with Joe's meatballs.

"There's pork in the sauce?" Adam asked.

"No, just ground beef, beef on the bone for flavor and some pepperoni," Marzia answered.

"Pepperoni is pork though Ma. I forgot," Mina said sincerely hiding her face with her palm. "Adam doesn't eat pig," she told the table.

"What do you mean you forgot? I don't make my sauce any other way you know that, Mina?"

"I know. I didn't think about it. Sorry." Mina apologized to her mother and then to Adam.

"It's fine don't worry about it. I will have some spaghetti and a little butter and cheese. I'm sure it's delicious."

"I'm so sorry Adam," Marzia felt bad that he wasn't going to have any of her sauce.

"Is it a religious thing?" Joe asked. He was dying to get to this conversation.

"Please it's fine. Yes it is," Adam answered Joe. "But it's no big deal, really. I'm okay."

"Oh you know what?" Marzia removed her napkin from her lap as she stood to finish her sentence. "I have a few meatballs cooked that I didn't throw in the sauce. I keep a few out because I always make extra. How about I heat up one of the plain meatballs for you. No pork, just beef."

"That would be great. I've heard so much about your meatballs."

"Mina talks about my cooking?" Marzia asked Adam while looking at Mina.

"Of course she does." Adam and Marzia stood in the kitchen fixing his special plate. He loved that Marzia was catering to him. He glanced at Mina with a blushing smile to make sure she knew he loved the attention. Mina just rolled her eyes.

"Don't wait dad, they'll be back in a second. Please just enjoy. Merry Christmas." She put up her fork and cheers'd his. It was something they had done since she was a little girl. Adam and Marzia joined within a couple of minutes and once again everything was back to normal.

Joe asked Adam what he did for work, but before Adam could answer, Joe completed his thought.

"I feel a little out of the loop because you knew Mina for some time now, but we don't know much about you." It was a man's subtle way of taking a stand and saying something important without saying it at all. Adam explained how he was in finance but that he had hit a bit of a rough patch, right about the time that Mina moved back home and with that, he tactfully took the blame for not being able to meet sooner.

"Rough patch? What happened?" Marzia asked.

"I made some deals that were less than fruitful and it blew up in my face. I lost a lot of money and clients, and well, just got a bad taste from the whole thing. It's a strange game. It's all about timing, and like anything else: you don't know what you don't know."

"You were in stocks?"

"Investment planning, but some stocks too. I've made a switch though. I'm in real estate now."

"That's great money! Start selling the apartments here in Williamsburg. We need someone to put a little fire under these contractors' behinds. I've never seen anything like this. They start one building and before they can finish what they've started they leave it for another. No one wants to work anymore, or maybe they want to work but they don't care about doing a good job," Joe said.

"I'm working in both rentals and sales in Five Towns, Long Island, and maybe Manhattan also," he crossed his fingers, but I heard you guys have a family pizzeria?" he asked looking at both Marzia and Joe.

"It was my father's but Joe's taken over now. Have you been?" Marzia was happy to talk about this. It had been a while since she told the story of her father's dynasty.

"No. Mina hasn't invited me." Mina smiled, shaking her head at his ridiculous talk, and Marzia looked at both of them trying to sniff out the truth.

"You should come by. I'll let you throw a pizza." Joe started laughing, at first a little to the side of the table, and then within a few seconds, perhaps at something he saw in his mind that no one else was privy to, he couldn't stop laughing. "I'll let you throw a pizza!" he repeated, laughing that wild open-mouthed cackle that Adam knew from Mina so well. Adam started laughing too. It was contagious and soon Mina and Marzia joined them. Joe put his arm around Adam's back and patted it.

"That's good," he said wiping a tear from his eye. "So tell me about your folks, what do they do?" Adam looked at Mina before talking and then spoke directly to Joe.

"My parents grew up in the city and moved to Long Island, to a community called Five Towns near Far Rockaway. My father is a florist, has been for twenty years, and my mother was a teacher for a while. She's stopped and started many times but is retired now. Mina listened intently as she didn't know any of this information. She thought the art of floristry was a weird profession for a Jewish man.

"Do Jews even have flowers at their funerals? I don't know how I know this, but I thought that they didn't send or receive flowers when someone passes," Mina asked.

"She's so smart. Isn't she?" Adam asked no one specifically. Marzia and Joe silently agreed. "It's true that we don't have flowers at our funeral services, but that doesn't mean we don't send flowers to the bereaved of other communities."

"He does well, your father?" Joe asked.

"No one sends flowers?" Marzia asked.

"Yea, its recession proof, as many people say." Adam repeated what seemed to be his automatic response to this question.

"That and he probably doesn't have to worry about giving discounts to his own people." Mina raised an eyebrow. She thought about Adam's bonsai and wondered if that green thumb of his was an inherited one.

"How could no one send flowers?" Marzia hadn't moved on.

"We just don't."

"Different strokes for different folks, I guess. Tell me do you have brothers and sisters?" Marzia changed the subject.

"I do. I have two sisters, and a brother."

"Wow! You have a big family. What does your family say about you spending time with Mina?" Joe got straight to the point.

"My family loves Mina." Mina looked like she had been punched in the stomach. "They know a little bit about her and how great she is with my dog."

"Oh! Mina didn't say that she met your family," Marzia said giving Mina a look of betrayal. Mina blinked in disbelief keeping eye contact below the table.

"Excuse me," Mina whispered as she left the table.

"What kind of dog do you have?" Joe asked.

"A boxer named Serpico. He's great with Rags too."

"Serpico! So, you have a thing for Italians, eh."

Mina splashed water on her face in the bathroom. She pressed her eyeballs into her skull and made circular motions on her temples. She looked in the mirror with her mouth permanently open. She was smiling, but didn't know why. This wasn't funny. It was awful that he could lie about such a thing, so effortlessly, and on Christmas Eve! Even though she wanted to, she couldn't call him out on it. The last thing she wanted was to have her parents see him as a liar. That would have been more to deal with than him actually being a liar. Mina came back to the table and returned her napkin to her lap as she sat down.

"Mina, your mother bought something special for you," Joe said welcoming her back all too aware of what was going on.

"What'd you buy?" Mina asked.

"Oh it's gonna be so good," Marzia rubbed her hands together.

"What did you buy?" Mina repeated her question playfully. She was relieved she didn't have to explain how she knew Adam's family.

"You'll see. Help me clean the table."

"Adam, you want coffee?" Mina made her coffee rounds from the kitchen.

"Yes, please."

"Dad?"

"What do you think Mina?" Of course, Joe wanted coffee, but he was a little upset that she lied about meeting Adam's parents. He was proud of her independence as he had always been, and he liked Adam, but it killed him to know that she wasn't interested in an Italian man. Mina made coffee, and talked angrily to herself. The special surprise of cannoli cake was soon brought out of the fridge.

"Holy Cannoli," Adam said with the first bite of cake in his mouth.

"I knew you were going to say that," Mina snapped at him.

"No you didn't."

"You gotta be sharp. Never let them see you comin'. If they see you comin', they don't want to look at you," Joe said reaching for the sugar at the center of the table.

"My God, this is delicious." Mina closed her eyes as she chewed.

"You know what I want to play," Joe said to the table.

"What?" Mina asked.

"Do you remember when we used to play monopoly as a family?"

"And Gio used to cheat as banker? Yes. How could I forget?" Mina turned to finish the story for Adam's benefit. The dessert had temporarily lifted her spirits. "My cousin Gio used to keep all the 500's in his hand, obviously right there where everyone could see. He wasn't even slick enough to leave a little in the bank."

"I think the game is in the upstairs closet. I saw it when I was getting all the Christmas Tablecloth for your mother. That's what made me think of it. You play Adam?" Joe asked.

"Of course. Why Not? I'm in real estate now, it only makes sense," Adam finished his last bite and rubbed his belly. Mina walked upstairs to find the game.

"I wanted to tell you but didn't want Mina to make fun of me. Your tree is really beautiful Marzia. I took Mina to the tree at Rockefeller Center and she said something about how bare it looked. At the time, I had no idea how she could say that, but it's true. Your tree is ten times the tree we saw. Marzia loved gold and draped a thick beige ribbon with golden edges around her tree. Most of her ornaments were of angels and little putti, in addition to a few white and gold balls. "I've probably never seen an angel on top of a tree in person, only in movies. I've been looking at it the whole night. It's just beautiful."

"Thank you Adam, that's a very nice thing to say. I love my tree."

"But she doesn't like putting it away, right?" Joe said with a smile.

Adam's tactic in Monopoly was to buy everything he landed on, and somehow the board knew that and didn't land him on many properties. One of his first purchases was New York Ave from the orange block and it seemed like every throw of the dice had someone land there. Like clockwork, he would look up at the player without any expression and say: Sixteen dollars. Depending on how he was doing, he might have added a please after the amount, but most of the time he just put his hand out and stated the price. But when Joe landed on it, after having just paid him last time he rounded that corner, he spoke before Adam could.

"I know, I know, 16 dollars," he said in a whine. He handed him the fake money. "Just like the Jew to keep asking for money," he laughed comfortably by himself and just like before, Mina, Adam, and Marzia followed with chuckling of their own.

"Oh you think I'm funny, Adam said playing on Joe Pesci's character from Goodfellas. "I amuse you. You think I'm a clown," he waved his hands adding flare to his impersonation. His next roll took him to the community chest.

"Marriage services! 25 dollars! He handed Mina the colorful bills. He showed the card to Mina who was also banker. On it was the *yikes* face of a groom holding a bride next to him and reaching into his pocket for $25.

"Will you be joining us at the wedding in New Rochelle?" Mina was instantly furious with her mother for asking that question. She crushed her molars against each other in a silent and painful pulse. Mina didn't forget to mention it to Adam, the liar. She wasn't sure if she should invite him.

"No I don't think so, Mina didn't tell me about a wedding."

"That's right, I didn't. Your roll Dad."

"You should come. It'll be fun. Good family, good times." Joe still hadn't picked up the dice leaving the game in a standstill as he added his own invitation.

"Are we playing?" Mina asked her father.

"Of course. What's the matter Mina?" Marzia asked.

"Nothing."

"It's okay if you don't want to invite me," Adam said to Mina. "I just think it's nice that your family wants me there."

"Of course you do," Mina huffed. Joe rolled and the game continued. Actual tension was replaced with fake hardships of owning hotels and falling into bankruptcy. Joe won the game and Mina reprimand her mother in the kitchen.

"What would make you think that was a good question to ask?"

"Every time I ask you about him, you say nothing, but your face tells me something else," Marzia wasn't skilled at whisper yelling forcing Mina to pat down the air between them telling her to lower her volume.

"What does my face tell you Ma?"

"That you like this boy?"

"So you thought you'd invite him for me?"

"The wedding is in May, why wouldn't you ask him?"

"Exactly Ma, May is five months away. Do I really need a date right now? I don't know if I'm going to be seeing him in five months. Now what am I going to do, disinvite him?

Joe, big monopoly winner, sat next to Adam in the living room and told of his adventures in real estate here in Brooklyn before he met Marzia. Mina made her parents open her gifts and promise to put the photos from the basement in the albums so that they could last for years to come. Mina left with Adam shortly after that and even though it was nice to see her parents kiss the liar goodbye, she was still mad. She couldn't even walk close to him on the sidewalk as they made their way to the subway. He could feel her tension and asked if everything was all right.

"Adam what the hell is wrong with you? Why would you say that? Why would you make them think I lied to them about meeting your parents when you're the real liar?"

"When did you tell them you didn't meet my parents?"

"What does it matter? I didn't lie to them and tell that I did. That's for sure."

"I'm sorry. I didn't know what else to say."

"What does meeting your parents have to do with anything? Are you not confident in who you are, that you think me meeting your family makes you more likeable? How ridiculous! The way you spell it in all of your text messages, reeeeediculous. And what was that shit about your fucking dog? Why on earth would you mention the *one* detail that your parents appreciate *so much* about me was how good I am with your dog? What a useless lie!"

"I did tell my parents how good you are with Serpie, and that you call him that," he said like a small child.

"Okay.. so.. That still doesn't mean I met them!"

"I know, but back when I used to go home for Shabbos after spending a few days with you, I'd think of you the whole night. I would be locked up with my family, with little to distract me, and I would smell you everywhere on me that I just found a way to talk about you.

"Telling them that I'm good with Serpico is talking about me?"

"Yes, well," he laughed a little to himself. "My sister or one of her kids would be playing with Serpico and he would do something that maybe you commented on before, and I don't know I told them... that... you were my dog walker."

"You what!"

"I know. It's ridiculous."

"Great. So not only do I have to make up a story about meeting your parents, I am meeting them as your dog walker. Perfect! I don't even know your mother's first name. I don't know what she looks like, what she sounds like, or..."

"She looks exactly like me except with a wig on," he interrupted her.

"Are you kidding me?"

"No."

"That's awful."

"I know but its true, we have the same exact face, and I am her favorite, wonder why? Also, her name is Carol, as in Christmas. Don't you just love that?"

"How fucking appropriate." Mina looked at him without an expression. She lit a cigarette and exhaled smoke in the space between them. He reached for it, but she didn't share.

"Mina, when you were reading up on my religion, did you ever come across the Hebrew word *chait*?"

"Nope."

"We Jews don't have a concept of sin. We don't believe in a handed down original sin, and we don't seek forgiveness through faith or prayer."

"So?"

"All Jews have is chait, which means: to miss the mark or to make a mistake. I'm human. I make mistakes."

"My stomach hurts."

"From this?"

"Maybe, but the wine, the food, cake, dog-walking."

"I'm full too. It was delicious though and totally worth it. Thank you for inviting me. I had a wonderful time. I hope I didn't ruin it for you." Mina looked at Adam and felt like something was missing. She wondered where her anger went, why it went, and couldn't believe how lucky he was that she wasn't going to make a big deal out of this.

"I'm not so mad, it's just that now I have to deal with telling my parents that I wasn't completely honest before, and make up a lie to cover up yours."

"I realize that." She scanned his face. Something was definitely different. She tried to talk herself out of it, as surely he was the same. She imagined going home with him and their usual routine but wasn't exactly excited. She envisioned him with a wig on, a caramel colored old lady wig and it made her laugh. He smiled back. He grabbed her hand and rocked it until her whole body swayed at his control. She joined him into the city despite her reservations.

Chapter 5
Sex Drive

Song # 35 Voice on Tape, Jenny Owen Youngs

Christmas came and went as it usually does. The week that hangs between then and New Years was an illusory state. People were celebrating and gift-giving with the ones they loved and had spent the whole past year with and yet at the same time were contemplating all the ways they were going to be different in the year to come. Corporate folks were off practically the whole month of December. Guests and those visiting from overseas stayed to the end of 2006, making Atlas the busiest Mina ever saw. And even though the streets were packed with unfamiliar faces, she was rather unscathed by people rushing to and from buying and returning gifts. She remained dedicated to her deadline, and kept a tight schedule doing it too: waking up at the crack of dawn taking Rags out if she got up, but by this time Rags wasn't sleeping with her neck across Mina's. She knew better and waited it out until Marzia woke. Mina then wasted some of her midday hours at Atlas. It was like a stand-up routine. She made jokes and small talk that didn't take a lot of effort while her muscles repeated memorized motions of foaming, pouring, stirring and counting change.

She blended her sky. It was a great first coating and even darkened the areas for the Cliffside and tree, which she decided were definitely in. She rectified the situation with her parents by telling them a makeshift story about running into Adam with his parents on the street while walking Rags, but kept true to the fact that she had never entered their home. Beth started seeing a man she met on a dating site that she couldn't shut up about. He was a strange white kid that only wore black, at least on the profile pics Mina saw. Beth was borderline obscene with the details she shared of her sex life and Mina barely paid attention. Her sky, bonsai leaves, and free falling beauty were what she focused on, and although it wasn't done, everyday she took notes from the Earth. She was pleased with her grayish- blue dawn and carefully layered sparks of color poking through the ether of her canvas.

"Here's another one, look. He sends me this shit." Beth showed Mina pictures her new beau had taken of the scratches she left on his back. "He likes it," she said dropping her phone in her apron.

"You should try to come to his New Year's party, what do you and your ex have going on?"

"Would you stop calling him my ex? You know his name." Mina was laughing as Beth begged for correction every time they spoke about Adam.

"I know, but he's still your ex, whatever. Do you guys have anything planned?" Seth's place is really nice with a huge balcony. It's not like the bullshit here in Williamsburg.

Mina's time with Adam was becoming somewhat scheduled spontaneity. She painted for several hours then caught a train to his apartment for the night and this happened anywhere from 1 to 3 times a week. She'd spend the rest of her nights in Phil's basement working the texture of her cliffs. The browns, greens, and reds were laid on thick with the palette knife's edging. She was perfectly fine sleeping alone and yet she couldn't deny that sometimes she longed to let go of everything and just feel Adam's weight on top of her. She offered the suggestion of the SoHo party and he was open to it, but Adam really wanted to bring in the New Year at a club called One. Meatpacking wasn't Mina's first choice, but she was being easy for a change. Her days blended into one, and before she knew it, the night was behind them. She remembered starting that Eve early. They mixed some Maker's and ginger ale at his house, he renegotiated with a vodka cranberry, and she put away a quarter of the bottle by herself. One, the overpriced club, was expectedly pretentious designed in palm trees and other summery decor. The drinks were astronomical and Mina didn't go into her wallet for one sip, but continued on her golden-liquored path to delirium. Adam knew the bouncers when they got there and together they skipped the line arm in arm.

Mina was drunk, thankfully; otherwise she would not have been able to stand Adam's dancing. They were up and down from this little booth they had scored, moving to songs that they both liked and could sing along to. Next to them were a bunch of expert dancing metro men. They weren't professionals but skinny guys who loved to move and looked great doing it. Mina had been talking and laughing with them for the majority of the night. They even stole her for a few songs while Adam watched. They were a party of eight, two dressed in drag, with big hair and overdone make-up, but beautiful and called themselves the diesel divas, as in retail associates from Diesel the store. Mina loved this and the more she talked with them, the more Adam shook his head saying, 'Only you Mina, Only you.'

Song # 36 Is it all over my face, Loose Joints- Arthur Russel (Larry Levan Remix)

They left the hot crowded club with the dancing queens. Adam was okay with the change of plans. Mina had her leg on top of him in the cab and pulled her dress up to tease him, carelessly sitting next to and making jokes with some of the divas they shared the ride with. They pulled up to the Archive, a massive building that had bull nosed edges to its triangular shape, sitting between Christopher St. and Greenwich Ave. She remembered walking through the arches of the lobby, passing the done up tree and empty cardboard boxes tightly wrapped with bows that she just had to pick up and shake, and then holding onto the railing as they made their way down less fancy stairs to a basement. The party was packed like an underground club with a serve-yourself bar, more drags, strippers, and headdresses all moving to house music under black lights. Adam was dancing well even though their drinks spilled a little when they came too close to one another. All of a sudden in the middle of the craziness, a large shirtless man wearing a tiny bow tie started to countdown from ten. Sparklers were lit and so many of them. It was as if people were dancing with these kiddie fireworks in their back pocket the whole time. Those that weren't already wearing 2007 glasses had put them on, and the whole sea of sparkling light shimmering off skin looked like a beautifully exaggerated night sky.

A chick wearing glasses with a martini for the number seven handed Mina a sparkler. She held it high in the air and Adam kissed her as the party screamed Happy New Year. They made out for a while with noses pressed against each other's while someone unseen played the traditional end of year song, except that in this basement party, confetti didn't glitter the air. Without the sounding of a fire alarm, the haze from the handheld fireworks set off the sprinkler system and left people laughing, screaming even, as they scattered away from spouts but still getting drenched.

"Where do you want to go now?" he said smearing the sides of his head to get water off. Adam had pulled Mina up the stairs they came from and the lot of the party was now outside. The streets were packed with people trying to look good as they found it difficult to walk.

"The bathroom," she said laughing. "I probably look like a hot mess. Do I have mascara on my face?"

"No, not too bad."

"Not too bad! "She rang her hair out over her shoulder.

"Where's your friend's party, didn't you say it was in SoHo?" Adam asked her but she had walked towards a parked car to look in the mirror. "We're not too far, you could just call her instead of checking yourself out."

"You wanna get on me about being vain, please wouldn't that be a little like calling the kettle black?" Mina cleaned her eyes.

The rest of the night came to her in strange pieces. They left SoHo talking for a while, making phone calls to people, wishing them well and trying to find out where to go next. It didn't help that New Years in the city was fucked for getting through to someone on the first dial. They both made half-assed attempts at wrestling in vestibules between phone calls, but didn't have it in them. She called Francine and Beth while he made his own phone calls in Hebrew. Mina had to try Francine's phone three times, and in between the first two tries and the third, she called Beth. Beth didn't answer either. Mina and Adam talked to each other like they hadn't in a while about future visions of themselves and what was wrong with the world.

Francine called back. She was surprisingly in the city, leaving some uptown bar but didn't know where she was going. Beth texted the address of the party, but they didn't end up going after Mina answered Adam's only question about her.

"What do you mean what does she look like?" Mina finished another water bottle.

"How does she look? What type of girl is she?" Adam repeated.

"She's kind of pale, slightly Goth, pretty fun. Huge knockers" Mina laughed as she said the truth. Adam didn't say anything about not wanting to go, but he made a face and a grunting sound of disgust. It was the exact face and sounds he made whenever he looked at pork or talked about it. Mina wondered how she had missed such an ugly part of his personality. They met Francine at Lex Bar on 38th by his apartment; their usual last stop before they called it a night. Ray, one of Adam's friends from the Corinthian was there, sporting three girls that hung on him like an animated boa. They were the kinds of women that used men for everything they had and he had a lot. Mina attempted to fix her make-up in the bathroom, but the mirror kept moving on her, until Francine told her to close one eye. The girls dance-hugged and told disconnected half-stories of their youth to those that weren't listening. Ray seemed to know someone or maybe he just had it like that, but after Francine left the bar with her friends, they moved the party to the Corinthian hot tub. At first, it was just feet and legs that Mina dangled in but with a joke pull that underestimated his strength, Adam held Mina in the warm water dress and all.

She snuggled into his comforter, the bubbly sips from a Pellegrino and the chill from walking soaking wet in the hallway sobered her nicely. He laid her down in his bed and she felt like she sunk deep into the center of it. Late nights weren't as fun with her morning schedule but his persistence energized her. He was as close to her as space would allow, and just as their night was paced, he performed in intervals and it was sublime. His timing and skill were like music and Mina coasted in every layer he poured over her. She saw colors and moved in his suggestion. The breeze that came through the window cooled their sweat and water sprinkled flesh. She was his subject and he painted her, and despite how unfamiliar he was at the art she was splendidly colored. He drew from his imagination and together they shared love, humming to a victory piece that celebrated the chaos of their night.

Chapter 6
Without a Hitch

It was a new year and her painting was way ahead of schedule. It had been 8 weeks since she started, but old pressures of school taught her how to produce quickly and efficiently. Phil was pleased with her talents and said so in his usual backhanded way.

"It's not that I didn't believe you, but its really coming along. I like the work you've done with the sides of the cliff and all the layers in the stone. You even put a little burgundy in there. It's very life like and done well. I know you have more to go, but it's so much more concrete than when you explained it to me. I think you have a good chance at doing this for life, kid. It all depends on your lady in red."

"Her and her peacock parachute." Mina reminded herself that she still had a ways to go.

"Oh right you're giving her have a peacock feather over her head. I forgot."

"Yep, and its going to be difficult, not the colors or patterns, just the perspective. I always struggle with perspective," she admitted.

"Perspective! Why I failed as a painter! Charcoaling a face is just a face. It's easy."

"Maybe for you. I see you've been producing since you came back." Mina pointed at his growing collection with her paintbrush.

"Yea I thought a lot about what you call them, my charcoal madness," he laughed. "It made me think of having a show with that title, besides a deal's a deal. I told you I would submit my work. I'm one-upping the agreement. I won't submit to that event, but I will put something together."

"You're putting on a show? Since when? Where?"

"Galapagos." This was another abandoned industrial space now used as a theatre and well known for art installations and improvisational performances."

"Really? I didn't know they did private shows."

"I know the owner. He's all about it. But, I want you to help me with the layout. And, since I'm calling it Charcoal Madness, you have to be involved. I gave you full credit already.

"Credit? For what?"

"For the title and the show. Besides there will be a bunch of people there that can help you with your work and maybe a budding community that you can become an integral part of. You should take advantage of the things you know, guide them and be guided."

"Are you serious? What people?"

"Do you love serving coffee that much? And living with your parents? Is that something else you love doing?"

"No. What are you saying crazy!" Mina scratched the space behind her ear with the top of her paintbrush. "She drifted for a second into an imaginary world where she was a Warhol of her own time: this generation's driving force and platform by which they would get known. "But what people, and am I even qualified to do this sort of thing?"

"Mina, I'm gonna be 43. I've been involved with art my whole life and you inspired me. I know a lot of people, friends, and family, just people. They all do something different but they all support art. You can get a salary from a space if you consistently put up good shows, maybe using Galapagos and Simi as a place to start. Simi is definitely a start. We both know him. Why not use his space?"

"And what do I even call it? An art agent?"

"Call yourself whatever you want. You'll be helping artists and working for a cause that you really care about, and the best part is, you'll continue to make time to paint."

"You make it sound so easy." Mina stepped back from her canvas and put down her brush. "I like how much thought you put into this, but I don't know it might be a bit ambitious right now. Tell me about your trip? We've been like ships in the night. Did you see all of the stuff you had me buy?

"Yea. Thanks. I've noticed you're quite the smoker as well."

"Um, is that cool?" She thought about how many cigarettes she burned in that basement without his permission.

"It's fine. Surprisingly, it doesn't go upstairs. Hannah smokes sometimes."

"Oh how is she, did you see her for the holiday?"

"Yea it was good. I saw her whole family in Chicago."

"How was that?"

"Unbearable. Her dad's dying. She's gonna stay there for him."

"Oh I'm sorry. How's that gonna work out?"

"It's not."

"Oh."

"It's fine. It happens. No one is guaranteed forever Mina. She wants me to live there, and there's no way I'm leaving the city. Anyway, I saw some of your records. I love this Mina, what a voice she has." He turned towards the record player and put on one of her English albums, starting with the standard *Someday*. It began with a big band and applause, and then her beautiful singing:
Song #37 Someday, Mina

"I know that someday, you'll want me to want you...when I'm in love... with somebody new..."

Mina went back to her painting and the two of them worked side-by-side moving their heads to jazz horns. She was just about done with the cliff. At least for now, it seemed like the right time to move on.

"You expect me to be true... and go right on loving you..."

It was hard to say bye to any one element once she started working on it, but she knew it was best to move around the canvas. She hated having an image fall behind while others came close to completion. She searched for where to paint next. The woman's dress blew in the wind reflecting sunlight and shadow in different hues of red, but Mina still hadn't painted her arms or legs in focus.

"Although I'll be feeling pretty blue...I know that I will try to forget about you...."

Mina fought with herself about how the feather should look or the hand and fingers clutching it. This was proving to be the greatest challenge in the painting. The most important element: her subject's salvation or demise in one single feather. Just the thought of finely tuning her free-falling beauty made her pull out greens for layering the Bonsai instead.

Adam wasn't very much involved in Mina's art or her dedication to her work. When she thought about it, he didn't know anything about her time at all, not even who Phil was. He once asked where she painted and she told him a friend's studio and when he asked whose, he was satisfied with the name Phil. They spoke about her art sometimes, but he preferred entertaining her with stories about his work, how much time he spent on the phone, and the crazy personalities he had to deal with. There were perks to his realtor status, one being access to some of the most incredible apartments. He would often say he had the keys to the city and he did turning some of their nights into midday rendezvous. She met him on North Moore for their very first lunch-in. That was the first apartment of the many empty spaces they baptized before he would show it to a prospective buyer. Sometimes her phone would ring and he would just start talking as if they were already in the middle of a conversation.

"Okay so I'll meet you there in an hour."

"Where?" The secrecy excited her. She imagined he did this to be discreet but role-playing had been one of the more constant ways they related to one another.

"The Clock Tower apartment we talked about yesterday, you're husband said he was very interested. I'll meet you in the space you just tell the front desk that you are there to meet Adam, the realtor."

"The one in Dumbo?" Mina's eyes lit up at the thought of it.

"Yep, just became available for viewing. 12 sharp."

He loved that she played along, but these naked lunches only served as mere breaks. As penance, her lady in red was the only thing she worked on upon returning. Sometimes staying at Phil's till midnight to make sure she put the time in. If she saw Adam in the day, she didn't think of meeting him in the evening, and he never called to tell her otherwise. If Phil was home, he'd join her in the basement, make a drink for the both of them and just sit and talk. He enjoyed her focus and sometimes they worked together, but mostly they just conversation.

Adam and Jacob started attending conferences more frequently, visiting places like Miami and Vegas to learn from big names in life coaching, sales, and real estate. She told Adam that elbow rubbing didn't guarantee success but her opinion didn't matter. She watched Serpico when she could, turning his dog walker story into reality. In her stay, she noticed a growing collection of books by a man named Anthony Robbins. Mina hated the sight of this goliath and turned over everything he was on, even removing magnets from Adam's fridge. By Valentines Day, her lady in red and peacock parachute were completed. A dark cavernous eye made from an uneven blending of blue, black and eggplant swirled above her. Her only salvation was nestled in the center of the feather. This dark vortex of paint seemed to display her entrance into the world yet present in her grip was stark desperation. She hung suspended, bending time and flashing humanity: the precipitous nature of depression in the quest for meaning, the fragility of life and the duality of reaching great heights as compared to the inevitable freedom of letting go.

Mina just stared at her creation and watched her drop. The tree's catch was purposefully painted without certainty. She saw it as it was in her dream, how it had changed, and how refreshing it seemed on canvas as something she had completed. There for all to see were the symbols of her inner world. The paradox and vulnerability shared by all: fear, hope, stasis, apathy, and inability to comprehend one's power. As she continued to stare, Mina realized that art is a collection of interpretations, a scrapbook of everything one sees, reads or notices in what seems at the time of observation as an inconsequential moment. She heard Roman's wisdom in her head and was reminded how everything one needs is right under their feet. She looked deep into the negative space of her creation, the background of her sky and the title, *'Elevate Her,'* surfaced.

Chapter 7
Left Unsaid

Spring started so quickly, like the time it would take for her lady in red to actually fall straight through prickly pine and be swallowed by Earth's purest form. Some days the sun greeted the land with a blaze that demanded walkers to hold their coats. It was trickery too because it didn't consistently show up. People were happy to know that winter was over, to be done with shoveling, hats, boots, and gloves. New York's best season had begun. She was able to meet Roman twice, just to catch up because Stephen Krauss, the Art director loved Mina's work and took her under his wing. The acceptance by the SAO's Zeitgiest show had made Mina's voice and vision part of the spirit of her times. She even contributed to the copy on the pamphlet as part of her work with Stephen.

Adam was away during the SAO exhibit, which was disappointing but then again he was traveling extensively now and not just to and from conference centers around the US, but he had a new set of wheels. His recent closings were the last three needed to convince Jacob to lease a vehicle for him. The Manhattan office he worked so hard to get into cut one of his favorite ties in praise. Someone took a picture of it and that was all that mattered. Referrals were already rolling in and in a short while he wouldn't have to work so hard.

There was of course an element of his success that turned her on, but he was the kind of person that could do anything well. He surprised her with the car at Atlas two days before her show. The two sank their teeth into delicious gelato before taking a joy ride. They passed a popular framing shop and amongst the family and pet photos he glanced at a couple smiling on their wedding day.

"I'm going to miss you so much when I get married?"

"You're an idiot." Mina said. It was an automatic response. Coconut and hazelnut complemented each other so nicely in her mouth and she was thinking about taking trips to the beach and Coney Island in the sexy black on black BMW convertible. He was leaving the next day and in two days she was making history. There was nothing that could bring her down, and she had such little time to get into what that comment of his actually meant. This evening, she had yet another dinner with Stephen and friends at a new restaurant she didn't know. Her nervousness always subsided after a glass of rosé, but handshakes and chitchats still took a lot out of her. She always thought about her conversations with Phil to gain confidence when her palms started to sweat. If she could survive some of those incredibly awkward moments with him when she first entered his apartment, she could get through anything.

When she finally showed Adam her painting and pictures from the event he snatched the phone and stared in amazement.

"You did this? It's incredible!"

"Yes. I know. It was so much fun. I wish you were there." They were finishing a late lunch. This was the first time they were seeing each other in two weeks. Now that her big day was over she gave Gio and Jessica's wedding her full attention. She had already tried on her bridesmaid dress and the fitting process was underway, but if she was going to ask him, tonight was going to be the night. She was eager to sit, drink, and look beautiful in lilac next to Adam as they celebrated love, yet she went back and forth about asking him. She didn't have anyone else in mind, and she could have gone alone but didn't have reason to. It was a busy time for the two of them, even then as they were sitting waiting for the bill, he scrolled through emails and texts.

"Oy Vey! This guy. He wants the house," Adam said. "I know he wants the house. I saw it when his wife came to see the property, but they ask me such ridiculous questions." Adam began impersonating his client, '*Uh sir, will there be enough space to pull our beds apart during Niddah?*' "I, of course, tell them there's more than enough room, but its like, come on, get your shit together. If you want the house, then buy the house. End of story."

"What's a Niddah?" Mina asked innocently.

"A woman's period."

"Men don't sleep next to their wives when they have their period?" She was nearly heartbroken at the thought of this happening to her.

"No. Beds are pulled apart and couples sleeps on opposite sides of the room."

"Are you kidding me? She couldn't believe what he was saying and how he was saying it."

"It has something to do with the fact that they'll be too tempted and menstruation is impure therefore the woman is impure. I am not a hundred percent on the details, but it's in the Even HaEzer." This was the name of a religious text they conveniently never discussed. "I know they can't touch during and seven days after. She can't make the bed. They can't see each other naked. They can't even hold the same object during this time."

"You aren't sure of all the rules that pertain to you and your future wife? But how is this possible? What makes you hazy on this particular detail? You seem to be so well versed in everything else?" Adam didn't have anything to say, he scrolled through his phone in the same way he watched television. She wondered how a couple could share a bed without a middle to cuddle in. It crossed her mind to ask him how he felt about giving up his king size mattress for a full, or worse a twin, but it was useless. He was aggravated and she didn't want to get into a religious discussion with him. But how could Orthodox women stand to be alienated by their own husbands for something they had no control over? They reached the car and she put her hand on the door but didn't open it. It was a heavy door, something about the way it sealed to the convertible top made it harder to open than ordinary beamers plus she felt weak, subdued, and disgusted by how his people treated their women. He was already sitting in the driver seat and had turned the car on. He rolled down the passenger window to speak with her.

"What are you doing my dear?"

"Thinking..."

"Oh yea. About what?"

"I have my period. I don't know if it's a good idea I come over."

"Oh stop. Don't be a maniac. Get in the car." Mina scrunched her nose, got in and sunk into the leather seat. They did their normal routine of a hot shower and comfortable sprawl on his bed. He started to bite her all over and it tickled. She had forgotten about the Niddah conversation until, "You don't have your period, you liar."

"I think it's sad that your people do that to their women."

"It's not sad. It's just how it is. There are things that your family does that no one questions. It's the same thing."

"What do you think about my family?" Mina pulled her face away from his a little and sat up to hear his response.

"Why are you asking me that?"

"Because now that you met them they ask about you. That's what Italians do. Even if they don't like you, they'll still ask about you."

"I think they're great."

"Of course, but I mean we've never even talked about them after our Christmas Eve monopoly game, where they basically invited you to the wedding."

"No. I knew you'd ask me."

"But, I haven't asked you."

"I can't go." She noticed a change in his face. He looked like he had bad news to say.

"What do you mean you can't go? Why can't you go?"

"Because it's Un-Orthodox. I can't go into another house of worship."

"What!" It would have mattered less to her if he just didn't want to go, maybe nonsense, but better than using religion as an excuse. "This is bullshit! I'm leaving." Mina stared at him in shock, wondering how they got this far. She pushed her weight off of the mattress, grabbed her clothes from the drawer he designated for her. She looked at herself in the mirror and recalled bad dreams, they were always short, and in them he had said strange things in passing like: It's time for a man to do what he wants. She shoved her foot into one of her pants legs and reached for her bra on the floor. She felt faint. She put her shirt on and saw his calm expression in the mirror. She walked into the living room to find her shoes and bag. He followed her wearing his robe.

"This is unbelievable Adam. I think you've been working in Five Towns too long. Maybe those little hats have gotten to your head. Hi! I am a non Jew!" Mina yelled and slammed her pointer finger into her chest. "Remember, I'm Italian, with Italian blood, a Catholic schooling and family! Whom you've met! We have sex nearly every time we're together! You use everything you're not supposed to, and on Shabbos you break every law. You drink. You smoke. You're a total fucking hypocrite." Mina hyper extended each finger listing the ways he was wrong before slamming his door.

Chapter 8
At Any Rate
Song #38 Touch, Daughter

A lightning flash reveals the organized usually hidden under clouds but it all happens so quickly, almost as if it was unveiled by mistake. It is a familiar pattern, like vessels stretched across an eyeball, leaf markings and root systems. Things designed to absorb, create, and sustain life. What is seen above encasing this world is actually mirroring the inner workings of a single body. The storm infected her with stillness and reflection. She sat quietly on a gray train seat. The other day out of nowhere, Adam asked her how many people she slept with. Mina thought it was weird when he asked, even considered him guilty of having sex with someone else or many loose women that would have him postulate such a question but nothing came from it. It just dissolved like brush strokes of white paint on a white wall. She didn't have to see it if she didn't want to. She tried to remember when that happened but her faculties failed her and she could only stare at the frenetic specks of color on the train's car floor.

As she got above ground, she stomped all of her weight on a large puddle to watch it splash. After thunder has run from what its done, everything remaining seems purposeless. Regardless of their specificity, these items—strange memories and awkward moments foolishly brushed aside in the name of love—were now in plain sight and demanded attention. An umbrella blown inside out and a half-eaten ice cream, and a few steps down a white bucket and black boots, suddenly there looking back and interrupting the normal flow of things.

~ ~ ~

Mina arrived at Charcoal Madness to find Phil sitting by himself. Lucky for him, there were two bars and the other one had all the action.

"Hey what are you doing over here all alone? This is your time to shine."

"I'm going for full-blown celebrity, what about you?"

"Oh me too," Mina brought her dainty pinky-raised hand to her chest as royalty would. "I'm riding your coattails. Remember?" Mina batted her eyes.

"There's a price for that kind of ride, ya know."

"You celebrities are all the same," Mina turned her body to look at the crowd. Phil's menacing images threatened each other from across the room and told everyone there to fuck off.

"What's your love life like anyway Mina? You've never shared so much. There's got to be someone."

"We haven't really seen each other in the way we used to," she paused. There's been so much to do..." She opened her arms to the space in front of her suggesting that Charcoal Madness had been a bigger priority.

"What's, *like you used to*? You *used* to see him frequently, or you used to see him in a particular way and now you don't."

"I've stopped counting the differences between us, besides I'm not very good at math, more of a reading-writing-painting person."

"I'm very good at math," he said. "But these decisions aren't made in the way you think they are. They just happen."

"What decisions?"

"If you like math or not?"

"Oh boy." Mina sunk her chin to her chest. "How about a little wild turkey for old times' sake?" She ordered two shots from the bartender. "We are going to sit here," she pushed his shoulder to rotate his seat, "And watch people admire your work, and we're going to pretend like we aren't even noticing. So make me laugh loudly, because that's what full-blown celebrities do." They grabbed the shots and drank together. She made a sour face as warm bourbon never got easier.

"More of a reading-writing-painting kind of person huh? Why haven't you seen your boyfriend?" She laughed loudly at his persistence and disheveled hair.

"Okay I can see that this conversation is all about what you want? To be honest, I don't know what he is, but I wouldn't call him a boyfriend."

"You don't know what he is, because you might have broken up without knowing."

"Maybe. What's with all the questions?"

"I'm tired of the questions too Mina," he shouted. "Why do you think I am making someone else talk? That's what." She was seeing him drunk for the first time. "I was at the bar minding my business. You joined me, so now you answer my questions."

"I did though Phil... things between us just aren't the same as they were before, satisfied?"

"When did they change?"

"I can't remember. We're just very different."

"Did you guys have a fight?"

"No. We don't really fight. He has zero tolerance for drama, but when I say different, it isn't in the typical sense you're thinking, like he likes football and I like philosophy. He's an Orthodox Jew, but only to some people, to me or you he would act like just another guy." she laughed at herself... "It's a very unique situation."

"Shiza! How did you get mixed in with that and I have to ask, did you guys use a sheet?"

"No." Mina laughed at him. We didn't actually break up either." Mina thought several times that she should just call Adam and properly end it, but it seemed like too much energy to have yet another sit-down about the same old thing, when they could just as easily not speak for a while, and have good times here and there. Thinking of him as she did before was easier than working through who he was becoming to her. Minus the Bonsai, he still had Al Pacino on more than one wall of his apartment and a mass-produced cityscape. She still wasn't a fan of champagne or brightly colored martinis. He tried too hard and to be extravagant for the sake of it, like naked women habitually posting photographs and videos for attention. He ran around like a big shot but was too scared to eat pork and be with a woman who may have had partners before him. It was unimaginable that their sex had become a reason for interrogation and sudden insecurity.

"This isn't the first time I would have to remove him from my life, and we're hardly connected as it is."

"You guys split once already?"

"Kind of."

"Mina, people break up for a reason. You should know better, well you will now. But you're learning. This is what I was talking about! We rarely make these kinds of decisions as most people think we do."

"I'm gonna need another shot before you drown me in your allusions." They drank without clanking and silently endured the burn.

"You ready?"

"As I'll ever be." She wiped her mouth.

"You don't decide what you're gonna to go to school for, what job you're gonna have, who you marry, or how many kids you have, where you live, even the person you become. These things just happen. People don't make decisions, despite the time they spend debating with themselves in their head."

"How did you come to this root of all decision epiphany?"

"I didn't. It came to me."

Song # 39 Stars Burn Out, Lacunae

~ ~ ~

Mina woke the next morning to the impressive song of birds coming through her window. She watched them dip their beaks into a puddle of water nearly scraping their faces on cement to drink what they could get. It was early April, a few weeks after Phil's show. Mina and Adam were experiencing about a month of awkward swing and a miss communication. He wrote her one long email insisting that he was an asshole and still working through some things but that he wanted to see her. She hadn't responded and ignored a few texts, but took his call when he made it. He told her that he would come get her and they could spend the day in the park having a picnic.

"No I don't want to."

"Okay, what would you like to do?"

"Maybe go to a Yankee game this weekend? The season just opened," she suggested.

"I'll tell you what, I'll even invite my brother and we'll make a day of it."

"Okay but then he or I will be like a third wheel, how about I invite one of my friends as well?" Francine and Mina had been seeing bits of each other since the New Year. They were able to keep true to bi-weekly manicures and pedicures. It was usually during these couple of hours that they caught up on most of each other's going on. Mina was in the habit of describing the artists she worked with and the events she attended events, but today's conversation was mostly a prepping for the game as they took the train to meet the boys at the stadium.

Dov, Adam's brother, was a skinny dejected man. There was a tenuous feeling of sincerity left by his smile but with so little to say, he was just odd. It seemed to Mina, from the pictures she had seen, that at one point he might have been attractive, but nerves got the better of him. He didn't seem as hypocritical as Adam, but to even be there was duplicitous, so impressions didn't mean much. This was how men from their community existed, sowing their wild oats until it was time to get married and then the poor woman, who hadn't yet touched a man, marries and has kids with someone she only knows half truths about. When the four met up, Dov's bony anxious face undressed Mina and Francine starting with their feet. The four carefully descended to their seats sipping the head of their Stellas.

Mina watched Adam gawk at two young blondes taking selfies with the stadium behind them. But before she could be offended, Metallica's Enter the Sandman sounded and awakened Francine's inner head banger. She stopped mid head rush to make Scooby doo squigglies. Somehow inner city education found its way into conversation as Adam had asked about the origin of the Mina and Francine's friendship. Mina let them discuss as she tried to hold and eat a mustard striped pretzel. The announcer interrupted their banter, 'The Annual Grand Giveaway.' A bingo ball appeared on the Jumbotron. The animation of a canyon shot a ball with $1000 written on it onto some empty seat in the stadium. Section 326, Row 11 Seat 17 flashed on the screen.

"Wait a minute! That's my seat! I can't believe it! I won!" Francine shouted bouncing up and down.

"Did you really?" Mina asked.

"No you didn't," Adam said.

"No," said Francine." Look that's our section, we're in Row 11 and I'm in seat 17." Adam put his beer down and pulled out his ticket. He read the seat number behind him. "But my dear," he paused. "That's not your seat..." he smiled fluttering his eyes. He was full of filthy implication.

"What are'ya tawkin about?" Francine asked in her Brooklyn accent. "It is too my seat, look." She pointed to her chair and leaned forward so he could read the numbers behind her.

"Yea but who bought the tickets?"

"Holy shit!" Mina shouted. "How much is the win?"

"It's the annual *grand* giveaway." Dov added. It annoyed Mina so much that he was there: a mere token glorifying Adam and his half-assed attempts at sharing her with his family.

"That's unbelievable! Congratulations," said Mina.

"Ahem, don't forget who invited you here," Adam said.

"I won't. You's are good luck!" Francine twinkled with happiness.

Song# 40 Running up that Hill, Chromatics

Mina was getting the start of a stress headache. It might have been the sugar water this stadium served for beer, or the yellow #5 heavily added to her mustard, or what was happening. There was so much she couldn't believe and so much she didn't understand. Like Rodin's Thinker, her brows came together and the pressure in her skull roasted her insides. It was completely unexpected yet inevitable, of course the Jew, the real Met fan and ticket purveyor would ask for the prize. She didn't blame him for wanting the money, and she didn't even blame him for being rude to Francine. It was her idea to come here and Francine was her invite, and she wasn't going to lie, this whole thing was her way of making the most of a bad situation. She thought back to the first game they attended together. It was last year at Shea Stadium along the 1st base line and the whole game he talked about how little he could align himself with people who wore jerseys. It was one of his usual, *There Are Two Kinds of People in the World*, conversations. She rarely paid attention to this rant, but maybe there were two types of people: those who wanted to catch a ball wearing their favorite player's jersey, and those that went to games because it was something other people did.

Just another example of how he tried too hard, but she was getting the sense this condition of his was much worse than she even imagined. She saw it like masters enjoying fast paced Othello, each square had been occupied, the score was in, and all that was white had now turned black. He drank champagne like the young girl who doesn't know what else to order, because like her he longs for the status associated with bottles of bubbly. He didn't *get* the passion that fired fans up to wear a jersey with their favorite player's name on it, but that didn't stop him from wanting to be around it. And then it became clear, he pursued that which caused a divide for him. He didn't want to accept what he was or wasn't and as a result tried *on* everything around him. Of course he was going to ask for a share of the $1,000 that Francine won. He was lost and the only person Mina could be mad at was herself. Deep inside of him was the budding maturity of a 16 yr old girl riding around in her brand new beamer.

"Mina come with me to claim my reward," Francine said snapping Mina out of her windfall. Adam pulled Mina down into him as she tried to pass making her way to the aisle.

"Tell her that she should share her winnings with us. She didn't come here alone."

"What's the matter with you?" She shook her head at Adam and caught up with Francine.

"Let's get another beer too," Francine talked fast and speed walked to the next beer vendor.

"You tell me, Meen, I don't know what to do. He's your friend." Mina didn't respond and walked with her eyes on the people in front of her. "Mina are you even listening to me, you look so spaced out?"

"No way! Don't give him anything. I don't like the way he's acting."

"I don't want to make things weird between you two just because of a stupid reward. Maybe he has a point. He can have it, if he really wants it, or I can do the better thing and give it up to all four of us, even though his brother is so weird. What the fuck is that name about? Seriously Jewish or not, who names their son Dove?"

"Do what you want Francine. If I were you I would keep the money."

The girls came back and sat next to each other. Francine decided on her own to give Adam, $500 dollars, all of which he did not accept. Francine left the trio for the train as they walked to collect the precious BMW. Mina sat in the back at her own request on the drive to Dov's place in Queens.

"Are you mad?" He asked now with just the two of them driving. They were already over the Queensborough Bridge and would be at Adam's place in no time. Mina had been silent since her goodbyes to Dov and still, even to his last question.

"I paid for her ticket, ya know?"

"So!" She shook her head at disapproval that his position was the same even after Francine offered him money.

"So?" he asked.

"You offered to pay for it! No one twisted your arm. The tickets weren't hard to get or expensive, so stop!"

"I'm kidding. I'm just fucking with you, I love fucking with you. You know that right?"

"Are you?"

"Of course! So it was her seat, it doesn't matter who paid for it, or that she housed a sausage. It's fine. I'm just fucking with you. *Charguhhhh.*" He made fun of the way Francine screamed charge at the game, just a little over an hour ago. She had a prolonged *Uhhh* after most things she said. It was how some people put emotion in their speech, as in *Stoppuh, Pleaaaasuhh. Whyyyuh,* and *Noooouhh.* It's half-whine and half-yell, but not enough of either. It was just the way Francine talked.

"I could just see you two wearing your catholic school skirts sporting little Italian horns around your neck?"

"I never wore an Italian horn around my neck, you lunatic."

"Are you sure? Its okay if you did."

"I didn't!"

"Okay but my people strap themselves with a leather box to pray, so it's okay if you did. We're in a judgment-free car baby."

"Shutup! Just shut the fuck up. You think that you can just slip in and out of all of these characters and use them to make jokes and be amusing. Those are real people, with real lives. Those nuances you emulate work so well because they truly exist, not because you're funny! And just because you like to carry on for a moment with real details doesn't make you real. You know what your problem is? You're blank! You're an empty shell. That's all. Judgment free my ass! It's easy for you to take on the affects of others but you're not celebrating them. You think you're better than them but you aren't, and for all the decisions you don't make regarding the important things in your life, namely how you live, you're nothing."

"And what about you? Are you everything, Mina?"

"No. Not everything, just something." He pulled the car over.

She uncoiled her legs and turned away from him. She scanned over his black and tan dashboard, how perfectly moisturized the leather was and the patterns in the faux wood paneling around the radio and buttons. She looked up at his little tree air freshener. Some loves are actualized and others destroyed, and this was a turning point for them. Maybe it was timing. Maybe their love was like that of a ripe mango, to be quickly devoured and subsequently washed off the skin. He told her to walk away nearly a year ago and for what? To run up behind her, ask her to stay, but only to see if she would. He may have confronted his parents about his faith, but it was all out of convenience, not choice.

"You're a coward. You do what's easiest." She opened the passenger door.

"Mina, wait." She gave him one last look from outside the car. The top was still down, and she looked into his eyes, but there wasn't the ocean view she loved so much. No stars burning in his nighttime eyes. Adam got an empty feeling in his stomach and thought something terrible, but worse than the feeling in his belly was the realization that this thought, as devastating as it was, wasn't new. And despite his efforts, it was being retold like some hurtful joke. Laughter sounded in his ear, and there in an empty room of his mind, was an older version of himself laughing at his expense. The voice knew better about Mina, tried to warn Adam about the choices he was making, told him what would happen a hundred times, but now with it all played out, could only laugh.

Song #41 You Can't Resist It, Lyle Lovett

Made in the USA
Columbia, SC
01 September 2022

66410069R00126